DIRTY LAUNDRY

A ROBYN KELLY MYSTERY

DIRTY LAUNDRY

LIZ OSBORNE

FIVE STAR
A part of Gale, Cengage Learning

Detroit • New York • San Francisco • New Haven, Conn • Waterville, Maine • London

GALE
CENGAGE Learning™

Set in 11 pt. Plantin.
Printed on permanent paper.

LIBRARY OF CONGRESS CATALOGING-IN-PUBLICATION DATA

Osborne, Liz.
  Dirty laundry : a Robyn Kelly mystery / Liz Osborne. — 1st ed.
    p. cm.
  ISBN-13: 978-1-59414-857-6 (alk. paper)
  ISBN-10: 1-59414-857-0 (alk. paper)
  1. Hospitals—Employees—Fiction. I. Title.
PS3611.R34D57 2010
813'.6—dc22   2009050631

First Edition. First Printing: April 2010.
Published in 2010 in conjunction with Tekno Books and Ed Gorman.

Printed in the United States of America
1 2 3 4 5 6 7 14 13 12 11 10

To my girls, Colleen Mallon, Alexis Hulett, Cyndi Osborne, and Janielee Osborne. You are all strong, vibrant women and I love you very much.

ACKNOWLEDGMENTS

My sincere thanks to all who helped me write this book: Members of my two critique groups, Megan Chance, Elizabeth DeMatteo, Linda Lee, Jena MacPherson, Melinda McRae, Karen Muir, Joanne Otness, and Sharon Thomas. Thanks for your suggestions, patience, and friendship. I'd like to thank Dr. Richard Atwater, MD and Dr. Steven Burrows, MD for their help with the clinical aspects of the story. Any mistakes are mine. I'd also like to thank Alan Christensen from the King County Fingerprint Lab, and Barb Mallon for her area of expertise.

CHAPTER 1

It was Friday afternoon.

Friday the 13th.

To make matters worse, tonight was a full moon.

I was not having a good day.

My name is Robyn Kelly. I manage the Patient Relations Department at the Madrona Bay Hospital and Medical Center, which means when someone isn't happy, I hear about it. Madrona Bay is a picturesque suburb of Seattle on the east side of Lake Washington. Last fall, I turned forty, and after a near brush with death, I decided that being forty was better than not being at all. I don't need glasses yet, but I do keep a spare box of hair color to disguise the silver creeping into my black hair.

It was early afternoon on this ominous day when I took a momentary break between phone calls. I stared in dismay at the precarious stacks of paperwork on my desk that were supposed to be dwindling, not growing.

"Rob!" It was Connie Wagner, my assistant. Her desk is positioned in the front office to shield me from anyone who walks in the door. Her voice had that harried edge to it. She hadn't been with me long enough to experience the rare double-whammy Friday. I hoped today didn't scare her off.

"Yes, Connie?" Yelling between offices was our modified primal scream for bad days. We'd used it a lot today.

"I'm transferring a call from Susan Wong. I don't have a good feeling about this. Can I go home now?"

I smiled at the plaintiveness in her young voice. Connie liked to think she had psychic abilities. "No. If I have to stay, you have to stay."

"Yeah, but you get paid big bucks to put up with all this insanity," she grumbled.

I didn't bother to ask what big bucks.

The phone on my desk rang. I took a deep breath before answering. "Hi, Susan. How's it going?"

"I've had it, Rob," she snapped. As the nurse manager for the 3-West unit, Susan was usually unflappable, so this must be something out of the ordinary even for a hospital.

"Haven't you discharged most of your patients for the weekend?"

"Yes, but I'd take a whole unit full rather than put up with this one's crap."

"Uh-oh. What's going on?" I reached for my latté and took a sip.

"I have this jerk who's flashing my nurses. The pervert," she snarled.

I choked. "He's what?" How full-moon-Friday-the-13th could we get?

Susan sighed. "Well, not exactly flashing. But he lets his sheet slip when they come into the room."

"And you think he's doing it on purpose?"

"If I thought it was an accident, that'd be one thing. Like if he was on meds or something. But this guy's a real punk, Rob. He leers at my nurses, daring them to say something. I've talked to him, but he denies it. Says it's their wishful thinking." She snorted. "My nurses would never be that desperate. So I thought maybe if someone from administration . . . someone with authority—"

I leaned back in my chair and rolled my eyes. "And you want me?"

"On a day like today, I'll take whoever I can get."

"I'm not sure if I should feel complimented or maligned," I said with a laugh. "But I know what you're saying. I'll be over in a few minutes."

"The patient's name is Jason Hilliard. He's in room 312. Thanks, Rob. I owe you."

"Again," I finished for her as I hung up the phone. I stood and shrugged into my red linen blazer. If I had to play the role of administrative heavy, then I needed to look the part.

I rolled my chair aside and had taken two steps toward the door when Connie appeared. A petite blonde who wears her hair in a ponytail, Connie is usually full of spunk. She wasn't spunky now. Her eyes were wide with fear.

"Connie?" I reached for her. What could have scared her so?

She shook her head and said in a hushed voice, "There's someone here to see you."

A shadow fell across her shoulders, blocking out the overhead light.

. . . the shadows loomed out of the dark alley. Malevolent. I turned to run, terrified the man would catch me before I reached the busy street . . .

I shook off the memory and looked up to see the tallest black man I'd ever seen off an NBA basketball court. I swallowed hard. His gaze darted around my office. Then he pushed past Connie, bumping her into me, and slumped into the chair next to my small conference table.

His tattered clothes were filthy, and my stomach lurched at the powerful smell that quickly overpowered my small office. His gnarled hands clenched and unclenched in agitation. He could have been sixty. Or thirty. Or any age in between. It was impossible to tell. What did he want here?

I grabbed Connie's shoulders and turned her toward the outer office. Pasting a smile on my face, I said, "Thank you,

Connie. I'll take it from here. Oh, and would you pull the yellow file for me?" That was our secret code to call Security.

I turned back to the man seated before me, shoving down the fear from that time in New York City, a time I'd forgotten. Until now. His head swiveled from side to side, his gaze taking in the room.

I shoved down my panic, then said, "My name is Robyn Kelly. How can I help you?" I didn't want to sit down yet, and I didn't want to move any farther from the door. Just in case.

"Miz Robyn. Nice ta meetcha." He reached up as if to doff his hat, then seemed surprised that it wasn't there.

For a moment, his gaze landed on my framed Doors of Dublin poster, then it took off again, ricocheting around the room, bouncing across the window, the jammed full bookshelves, the stacks of papers on my desk and the credenza. My breath held. One swipe of his long arm would destroy any semblance of order.

"And you are?" I prompted.

"William, ma'am. William Jones."

His manners eased my apprehension. He might have some problems, but I didn't sense any immediate danger. Still wary, I turned my chair from the desk to face the conference table and gingerly sank into it, reassured that I was still between him and the door. "How can I help you, Mr. Jones?"

"I needs help, ma'am."

"That's what I'm here for," I said. "What seems to be the problem?"

"I needs lotsa help," he whispered. His hands started working the remaining button on his coat. Buttoning and unbuttoning. Buttoning and unbuttoning.

My anxiety inched up. I pushed it down again. I was safe. "Where do you live, Mr. Jones?"

"In the park, ma'am."

This was going to take patience. With the number of city, county, and state parks within a fifty mile radius, that didn't exactly narrow it down. "Which one?"

"Central, ma'am."

That stopped me. "Central Park?"

"Yes, ma'am."

"But that's in New York City."

"Yes, ma'am. That it is."

I studied my visitor. "Mr. Jones, do you know where you are now?"

Startled, he looked at me just long enough for me to see the fear in his eyes before he glanced away again.

"You're in Washington State. Near Seattle," I said gently. I waited to see if that registered with him. He frowned, as if it was too much information to process.

I had to admit, I was baffled too. I mean, how did a homeless person get from New York City to Seattle? He didn't look as if he'd flown direct from JFK, and how could he have negotiated the trains?

And even if he'd managed to find his way to Seattle, how in the world had he ended up in my third floor office of a suburban hospital in a community with lousy rapid transit connections? It boggled my mind.

"How did you get here, Mr. Jones?"

He frowned again. "Ah don't rightly know, ma'am," he mumbled.

The threads holding the button finally surrendered and the button popped to the floor. William Jones followed it, falling to his knees and grabbing for it as it rolled along the wall.

One pant leg hiked up above his boot, and I saw something that made me gasp.

William jumped up. "What's wrong?" His eyes were wide

with fear. He towered over me, but by this time I was no longer afraid.

I reached out my hand, stopping short of touching his arm. "It's . . . it's okay, Mr. Jones. Please, sit down."

He followed my direction, still fidgeting with the button in his hand.

"Mr. Jones?"

"Yes, ma'am?" His gaze resumed its darting survey of my office.

"Mr. Jones, may I look at the back of your leg?" I asked, keeping my voice slow and even.

"My . . . why'd you wanna do that, Miz Robyn?"

"Please, William?" I had to act calm and reassuring if I didn't want him jumping up and knocking things over. Or something worse. I quickly squelched that thought.

He stood again, wary, nervous, but he turned and let me lift the pant leg. I gagged at what I saw. A deep open wound full of writhing maggots. I dropped the fabric.

Swallowing to keep the bile from my stomach from rising, I stood up and went to the door. "William, I'd like you to come with me, please."

"Where we goin', Miz Robyn?"

"I'm taking you to see a doctor—"

"No! No doctors!" William raised his arms as if to ward off an attack.

"What's going on in here?" Tom Geralding, the barrel-chested, retired marine who was head of hospital security, stood in the doorway. Despite his commanding presence, Tom was one of the gentlest men I knew.

I glanced at Tom, then back to William. "Everything's fine, Tom," I said, making eye contact with William. Then, I smiled. "This is William Jones. He's visiting here from New York City, and somehow he found his way to my office. We were just talking about a sore on the back of his leg that I think needs to be looked at."

"No, Miz Robyn. Don't take me to no doctors."

"But—"

"Please, Miz Robyn. Them doctors, they hurt me something awful." He clutched his head and rocked back and forth, his eyes closed.

Alarmed by his reaction, I touched his arm. "William?" He flinched, then opened his eyes, so glazed with fear that I didn't want to do anything to traumatize him more.

I looked at Tom. He raised his eyebrows and moved toward Connie's desk; it was my call. "Would you see the doctor for me?" I asked William again. "Just to let him look at your leg? If you don't want him to do anything more than that, he won't. Okay?"

William glanced at me, then around the room before settling back on me. He nodded, once, very slowly, and took a step toward me. Leaving Connie and Tom behind in the office, I led William out the door and around the corner to the elevators.

Fortunately, the elevator was empty, and we took a short, silent ride. When we stepped off, I pushed the buttons for every floor, hoping the opening and closing would reduce the potent *parfum de la rue*.

The ER was located on the first floor of the north wing, with the reception desk and ambulance entrance at the far end where patients would arrive from the parking lot. I led William down a hall, past empty exam rooms on our right. A creative designer had chosen white—paint, floor tiles, cupboards, sheets and privacy curtains—with stainless steel accents. I guessed the sterile look was supposed to make patients feel confident, but definitely not comfortable.

I kept up a steady monologue, occasionally asking a question that William answered with hesitation. In some respects, he was

15

like a child, and I felt the weight of his trust.

When we reached the ER reception desk, I checked out the lobby. A few small clusters of people sat on taupe chairs that blended into the mauve walls with framed prints in similar tones. Frowning, I studied the people for a moment. I couldn't tell if they were waiting to be seen or waiting for someone who was being seen; they all had that anesthetized look of people on hold. They glanced up from their books and magazines and recoiled at the sight of William and started whispering to each other. A few pointed at him. But, hadn't I done the same thing? Hadn't I been repelled and fearful of someone so different from me? For now, I brushed away the guilty twinge of my conscience.

"Robyn, what brings you here?" Jamie Rice, the triage nurse, emerged through the swinging doors that led to the other side of the ER. In her early thirties and full of fun, her white lab coat scarcely covered the shocking pink turtleneck that set off her tanning bed tan. No one in Seattle could have that good a tan naturally, especially in April. Her gaze landed on William, and she took a step back before turning an intent stare at me.

"Hi, Jamie." I rested my hand on William's arm and looked up at him. "This is William Jones. I'd like someone to examine him."

Jamie's mouth tightened as she glanced at the people in the lobby. Then she said, "Sure. Bring him on back here. We'll deal with the paperwork later."

I tugged on William's sleeve and gave him an encouraging smile as we followed Jamie through the swinging doors. Jamie stopped in front of a private exam room rather than one that had several beds with curtains around them for the illusion of privacy.

"How's this?" she asked.

"This'll be fine, won't it, William?"

"Yes'm," he mumbled, staring at the floor. His gaze started

flying around the room again, his frown deepening.

"William?" I tugged on his arm to draw his attention to me. "I wouldn't do anything to hurt you. I only want to help you."

"Yes'm."

"And Jamie here," I said pointing to the nurse, "wants to help you too. Right, Jamie?"

"That's right. I'd like to take your blood pressure, Mr. Jones, and your temperature. Would that be all right with you?"

William nodded as if resigned to the inevitable. I motioned for Jamie to join me in the hallway.

"Besides the obvious, what's his problem?" Jamie asked with a concerned frown.

"He's got an awful sore on his right leg," I said in a low voice, smiling over Jamie's shoulder at William to reassure him. "And it's got maggots."

Jamie's doe-brown eyes widened. "You're kidding. That's Seattle ER stuff."

"Wish I was." Holding my smile in place for William's benefit, I said, "He seems like a nice man. Rather confused, but polite. He says he lives in New York City's Central Park, but he has no idea how he got to Seattle, let alone Madrona Bay. Or my office. I suspect there's a history of mental illness."

"No, duh." Jamie laughed softly.

"Or maybe some developmental disabilities? And probably no insurance," I added with a sigh. Glancing at the wall clock, I groaned. "Oh, Jamie, I'm supposed to be on 3-West talking to a patient for Susan Wong. Can I leave William with you? I'll be back in fifteen minutes. Twenty at the most."

"Go. He'll be here when you get back."

"William?" I stepped to the door of his exam room. "I have to leave for a few minutes. Jamie's going to take good care of you, okay?"

His brow furrowed as he struggled to understand. After a

moment, he nodded his head very slowly. "Okay, Miz Robyn. I waits here for you."

"Good. I'll be back."

I hurried down the hall to the elevators and punched the "up" button. I wasn't looking forward to confronting Jason Hilliard and his slipping sheet. We met all kinds in the hospital, and we tried to make allowances for people being stressed out when they were sick. But there were limits to what the nurses had to tolerate; this was definitely on the wrong side of those limits.

In a few moments, I stepped out of the elevator and strode across the vestibule that led to the 3-West wing of the hospital. I'd told Susan I'd be right there, and that was at least twenty minutes ago. She was going to kill me.

She didn't kill me, but she glared at me when I found her at the nurses' station. Glancing at the wall clock, she pursed her lips. "Be right over, huh?"

I shook my head and gave her a placating smile. "Susan, if I told you what happened you'd never believe me."

She lifted her chin. "Try me."

"A homeless man from New York—"

"All right, all right." She laughed and threw up her hands. "I give up. Didn't know you had a flair for fiction."

"That was the truth," I insisted.

"Uh-huh. Whatever."

"I'll talk to Mr. Hilliard right now. Room 312?"

"Too late." Susan shook her head. "He's gone to respiratory therapy for testing."

"Really? What's he in for?"

Craning her neck, Susan looked around, then silently motioned for me to follow her to her office. She was a sinewy bundle of energy, and I had to walk double time to keep up with her. After she'd shut the door, she leaned against it and crossed her arms over her chest. "He's a young guy, twenty-six—"

"Twenty-six? I expected someone older," I said.

Susan shook her head. "No, a young pervert with a recurring staph infection. From what I've been able to piece together, the guy's father is a doc so he knows a lot about medicine. We've been giving Hilliard antibiotics to treat himself at home, but he keeps getting reinfected."

"Really? Any idea how?"

She shook her head. "Dr. Transel suspected it was coming from the PIC line," she said, referring to the peripherally inserted catheter, usually placed in a patient's upper arm so they can inject meds themselves.

"How odd." I didn't have any formal clinical training, but I'd learned enough over the years to know this was very unusual. "Any idea how it's happening?"

Susan grimaced. "That's the weird part. This guy's been in and out of here over the last year. Comes in with a roaring infection. We treat him, get his white blood cell count way down, and send him home with antibiotics to be sure the infection doesn't pop up again. Then, he's back in here a couple of months later with a full-blown infection. Exactly the same strain."

"The same strain?" I frowned, not sure what she was alluding to, but it didn't sound good the way she'd said it.

She hesitated, then said, "We think he's self-infecting. This time, we swabbed the PIC when he came in and the culture practically overflowed the petri dish, it was so concentrated with bacteria. He's got to have a supply of staph, and he's injecting that through the line instead of the antibiotics."

I gasped. "Good Lord. He's doing it to himself?"

She nodded. "Might be Munchausen syndrome."

I thought about it. "That's the only thing that makes sense, isn't it?"

She nodded again. "Deliberately making himself sick just to get attention is bad enough." She shrugged. "But this guy'll wait too long one of these times, and we aren't going to be able to stop the infection. Then he'll be a goner."

"Munchausen's and a twenty-something pervert," I said wearily.

"Yeah. What a combination." Rolling her eyes, Susan pulled away from the door and opened it. Over her shoulder she said, "I'll call you later when he's back from respiratory therapy."

"Oh, goody. I can't wait to meet this guy."

After we reaffirmed that life was never dull in a hospital, I left Susan and headed toward the elevator. I couldn't believe it. I'd heard other reps talk at conferences about these patients who injured themselves deliberately or made themselves sick just to get attention. I remembered one story I'd heard about a man who'd developed his biofeedback skills to the point that he could mimic the symptoms of a heart attack. Some people never ceased to amaze me.

I pondered the motivation for doing something like that as I returned to the ER. The hall was empty, and I went straight to the room where I'd left William. He wasn't there. I stopped. That was strange. Thinking that perhaps I'd remembered wrong, I checked a couple of nearby rooms as I made my way to the reception desk but found no one.

I pushed through the double doors leading to the reception area. A young man with peroxided hair, wearing a black rock music t-shirt under a light blue lab coat, was sitting behind the front desk for the evening shift. He looked at me with disdain.

"You aren't supposed to be back there," he snapped.

Surprised, I cocked an eyebrow. "I'm not?"

"No. You have to check in with me, and I'll tell you when you can see the doctor," he said with an imperious toss of his head.

"Oh, really." I turned to face him directly so he could clearly see my name tag.

He glanced at it, not long enough to see who I was, but long enough that he should have recognized me as an employee. It didn't make any difference in his attitude. "Your name?"

"Robyn Kelly. Call Jamie for me, please." I turned and walked away from the counter before I said something more.

"I need your patient number."

Incredulous, I turned to look at him. Did he honestly think I was here as a patient? I considered how I would tell Charley Anderson, the ER manager, my opinion on his choice of employees. Where did he find these people? "Oh, forget it. I'll find her myself."

I pushed back through the swinging doors and heard "I'm calling Security" as the door swung shut. Good. I'd like to see Tom's face when he found out who had invaded the ER.

Like the other patient wings, the ER was an elongated "u" shape, with a string of supply, staff, and special treatment rooms down the middle. Halls on either side connected them to the exam rooms that lined the outside walls.

I'd come down one hall looking for William on my way to the reception desk, and now I started up the other side. I found Jamie in the nurses' lounge.

Jerking my thumb toward the reception area, I said, "Jamie, who's the kid working the front desk? He's awful."

She wouldn't meet my gaze. "I don't know. Hal something, I think. He started last week."

"Well, I'm going to have to talk to Charley. Hal Something has the customer service skills of the Gestapo."

Jamie should have laughed. Instead, she picked up a clipboard and started out the other door.

"Jamie? Where's William?"

"Hmmm?" She seemed extremely intent on the empty form on her clipboard.

"William Jones," I said, suddenly very uneasy. "The man I brought down here less than thirty minutes ago."

"Oh. Him. Well, you see—"

"Where is he, Jamie?"

"It wasn't me, Robyn, honest." She paled under her dark tan. "It was Dr. Park."

I threw up my hands. "What was Dr. Park? Where is William?"

"He's not here."

That stopped me. "You've already admitted him? That fast?"

"No," she whispered.

Bewildered, I stepped toward her. "He had a terrible sore on his leg. You couldn't possibly have treated and released him already."

The nurse's hands shook as she inched her way toward the door. "It wasn't me. I didn't know until it was too late."

Alarmed, I gripped her arm. "Jamie, what did you do with William Jones?"

Chapter 2

"Jamie," I repeated with growing agitation. "Where is William?"

I heard the distinctive clink-clink of a collapsing gurney, then the thwump-thwump of double doors closing outside. From the alarm that crossed Jamie's face as she glanced over my shoulder, I knew. I whirled around and frantically flung open the doors to the ambulance bay. A uniformed young man was climbing into the driver's seat.

"Wait!" I hurried toward him. "Where are you going?"

He eyed me with suspicion. "Why do you care?"

With that kind of response, I figured action was better than words. I sprang to the rear of the ambulance and wrenched the doors open.

"Hey!" the driver yelled. "What the hell you think you're doing?"

"William?" Despite my panic, I spoke softly to the solitary person shrouded in the darkness of the ambulance.

"Yes, Miz Robyn?"

"You can come out now."

"I'd like that." He unsnapped his seatbelt and scrambled out.

"Hey, lady." The driver swaggered toward me. "I don't know who the hell you think you are, but you can't take this guy. We've got doctor's orders to take him to Harborview."

My hand on William's arm, I turned to face the driver, struggling to control my rapidly growing anger. "I am taking this man back inside. And if you ever want to transport this hospital's patients again, you'll leave now. Got it?"

My threat would be hard to carry out, but I had to take the chance. I was aware of the other ambulance attendant coming up behind William and me, but I didn't look away from the driver.

He broke the stare first, then shrugged. "No skin off my nose," he said as he stomped to the front of the ambulance, then returned with a multi-copy form. He shoved it and a pen at me. "Sign this."

I scanned the form, a release of liability, and signed, adding my title and office phone number, then handed it back to him.

I waited until both attendants climbed inside the ambulance and drove away before I released my grip on William's sleeve and turned to look at him. "Are you okay, William?"

"Yes, Miz Robyn." He frowned, his gaze bouncing off the building and parking lot. "You promised you'd be right back. Those men were taking me away."

"I'm sorry, William. There was a mix-up. It won't happen again."

"I'm obliged to you."

"Yes, well. Let's go back inside and see what's going on." I calmly led the way and found another empty exam room for William to wait in while I got to the bottom of this.

I strode down the hall to the physicians' lounge and looked through the glass inset before opening the door.

I shut the door behind me. "Dr. Park?"

A dark-haired man jabbed the computer keyboard and turned toward me. Behind wire-rimmed glasses, dark brown eyes scrutinized me. He was so lean that he reminded me of a whippet. "And you are?" he asked.

I had always wondered how a seated person could look up at someone and still make them feel they were being looked down upon. Dr. Park had perfected the technique.

I could play the game too. I leaned negligently against the door jamb and crossed my arms. "I'm Robyn Kelly, Patient Relations."

"That's nice. If you'll excuse me, I'm quite busy right now." He turned back to the computer and started typing.

I chose to ignore the not-so-subtle hint that I was to leave the busy doctor alone. When the door didn't close behind me after a suitable length of time, Dr. Park turned around to face me.

"What do you want?" he snapped.

"I want to know why William Jones went from the exam room to an ambulance bound for another hospital."

Dr. Park gave a long suffering sigh. "We can't treat him here."

"Why not?"

"I can't discuss it. Patient's right to confidentiality." He had the audacity to look as if I should know better than to ask such a question.

"I see." In a slow, quiet voice that belied my outrage, I said, "Dr. Park, I brought Mr. Jones to the ER. I know what's wrong with him. I also know that we're fully capable of treating him here."

"Now, look—"

"No, Dr. Park, you look," I said evenly, the anger now creeping into my voice. "I don't know what the policies are at the other hospitals where you work, but we don't do wallet biopsies at Madrona Bay."

"I never—"

"We both know what wallet biopsies are, Dr. Park. A patient is brought to the ER, and before checking vital signs, the doctor checks to see if the patient has insurance or can pay the bill. If he does, come on in. If not, then ship him to the public hospital. The taxpayers can pay for it."

"You don't know what you're talking about."

I approached the seated man and looked down, way down, at

him. "I'll bet my job that if I searched this whole department," I said with a sweeping gesture, "I wouldn't find a single piece of paper with Mr. Jones's name on it. He doesn't exist, does he, Dr. Park?"

Dr. Park had turned a bit gray, confirming my suspicions. Then he glared at me and said, "Who are you, Pollyanna? This is the real world, Ms. Kelly."

"We don't turn anyone away from this hospital," I said firmly. "I'm sure Dr. Bridgeway would be very upset to hear about this." Larry was the chief of staff for the hospital. In addition to being an excellent physician, he was a good man.

"Go ahead," Dr. Park said, gesturing toward the door. He lifted his chin. "It won't matter. My physician group has a contract to cover your ER, and it doesn't say anything about not triaging patients to other hospitals."

I shrugged. "Maybe it doesn't, but I'm sure it says something about abiding by this hospital's policies. And treating every patient who comes in the door is one of those polices." I looked at him speculatively. "Do the other physicians in your group know you're putting their contract at risk by doing this?"

Ignoring his glare, I turned on my heel and left the physicians' lounge. I was so mad I could hardly see straight, but the first thing I had to do was find someone else to treat William. I wasn't about to leave him in the same room with Dr. Park, let alone be treated by him. I'd let Larry Bridgeway deal with Dr. Park and his ER physician group later.

I spent the next half hour fast-talking my way past a beleaguered medical receptionist at the clinic down the hill from the hospital. She absolutely, positively, did not want a late-Friday afternoon drop-in patient. After wearing down every barrier she threw at me, I escorted William to the clinic myself. The Family Practice doc took one look at William's open sore and promptly admitted him to the hospital.

By the time I had William settled in a private room on 3-West and returned to my office, it was long past quitting time. Connie had left. I made a note to myself to call Larry first thing Monday morning, then started to gather up a few files to work on over the weekend.

Then I stopped. I had survived a full moon Friday the 13th, and that called for a reward.

"No!" I declared to the empty office. "Not this weekend." I plopped the files back on my desk.

I was halfway home before I remembered that I hadn't talked to Jason Hilliard about his slipping sheet.

A day off, I thought, as I sipped my coffee and looked outside the kitchen window, anticipating a free weekend. I grinned at the thought of spending the whole day working in the garden. How wonderful that would be. Seattle in the spring is vibrant and colorful, exactly what I needed after two weeks of non-stop rain.

After dressing in yard work clothes, I called my father for our weekly Saturday chat. In his mid-sixties, he still lived and actively worked his cattle ranch in Colorado. After my mother passed away, I'd worried about him living alone, but the widows in town kept him well fed and entertained, especially Lois, and the ranch hands were close by if he needed anything. Still, I was concerned about him; he was getting older despite protests that he felt as good as when he was twenty-five.

When the answering machine picked up the call, I wasn't surprised. He was probably out riding and checking on the herd. Lately, though, I knew he sometimes didn't answer out of sheer stubbornness because I couldn't help asking how he was eating and sleeping, which was guaranteed to annoy him.

After leaving a brief message, I drove to the nursery for bedding plants and bark. When I returned home, I spent an hour dispatching some early weeds from my flower beds before planting the colorful annuals I'd bought.

Finishing a big section, I leaned back on my heels and stretched my back, breathing deeply. The brisk breeze carried the scent of the neighbor's freshly cut grass and filled me with the joy of a beautiful day to spend as I wished. Splashes of color were everywhere. The fluorescent pinks and reds and yellows of tulips, azaleas, and rhododendrons brought a smile to my face. This was why I lived in the Pacific Northwest.

A tan sedan turned the corner and made its way toward my house. The sight made me grin. Only police detectives would drive such a nondescript tan car, and only one police detective ever bothered to enter this cul-de-sac. As the car stopped next to my driveway, I stood and tugged off my leather gardening gloves.

"Morning, Detective," I said cheerily.

"Hi, Rob." Wearing well-worn jeans and a flannel shirt, Matthew Pierce lumbered across the lawn. He was a detective for the Madrona Bay Police Department. About ten years older than me, he and I became acquainted when a hospital patient had been murdered last year. Since then, we'd grown to be good friends.

Pierce stood about six feet tall and was in reasonably good shape, although I couldn't picture him chasing suspects down alleys or scaling chain link fences anymore. His dark hair had more than a touch of gray, and his once firm jaw was softened by age. At times, his brown eyes had the weariness of having seen too much.

"How come you're driving the company car on a Saturday?"

Pierce snorted. "The captain thinks the other detective, Dick Nash, and I are stupid."

I raised an eyebrow. "Oh?"

"Yeah. He tells us he's going to let us take the cars home

28

with us. Like it's a big benefit. What it really means is he thinks he won't have to fill two vacant detective positions because he can call us any time."

Incredulous, I asked, "Can he get away with that?"

Pierce shrugged.

"Doesn't he have to pay you for being on-call?"

"The union's dealing with it. But I don't want the extra money. I want my days off to be my days off," he said with a long-suffering sigh.

I nodded. "I'm sympathetic with that."

Pierce's eyes widened as if I'd announced the earth was flat, then he laughed.

"What's so funny?"

"You," he said, still chuckling. "When was the last time you came home without bringing work?"

"I may bring it home," I said with an indignant toss of my head, "but I don't always work on it. And, I'll have you know, I deliberately did not bring anything home this weekend."

"Really?" he said skeptically, but the grin on his face said he was still amused. "So you're not tempted to work inside today?"

"On a beautiful day like this?" I spread my arms wide. "How could anyone resist?"

Pierce approached the upside-down garbage can lid I'd been using to collect the weeds. Hands on his hips, he nudged the pile with his boot. "Waging war on the wee sprouts, are you?"

"Those wee sprouts have already flowered and were about to go to seed," I responded with righteous indignation. "Then I'd be fighting them for another ten years. It's obvious you live in an apartment—"

"Condo."

"Residential unit." I sniffed. "Clearly, you don't understand the joys of home ownership."

He shook his head. "The lawn that always needs mowing, the

watering, the bugs, the pruning, every weekend spent in the yard and hobbling to work on Monday with a sore back and aching arms. Yup, I sure don't understand those joys at all."

I decided to ignore his sarcasm. "So, what brings you here?"

"I thought you might like to try that new place in town for lunch. If you can tear yourself away from all this fun."

"The restaurant that took over from the dance club?"

He barked a laugh. "You mean the drug club."

"Really? I had no idea. But then, I don't know anyone who's ever been there."

He nodded. "Smartest thing the city council did was revoke that place's license. It was a nightmare."

"I'd love to go to lunch, but I'm waiting for Josh and one of his buddies." Josh was my son, a sophomore at the University of Washington, majoring in mechanical engineering.

"When do you expect them?"

"Any time now. I went to the nursery first thing this morning and bought some bags of potting soil and bark. The boys promised to unload them for me."

Pierce gave me a look that said he'd scored a point on the condo versus homeowner debate. "When do you expect them?" he asked again. This was a focused man who wanted specifics.

"What time is it now?"

Pierce glanced at his watch. "It's eleven-twenty."

I sighed. "They were supposed to be here an hour ago."

"I'll unload the car. Then we can go eat."

"Oh, I don't know." I hesitated. "Those bags are awfully heavy."

He glowered at me. "Are you saying I'm not strong enough?"

"No, of course not," I said quickly

"You think I'm too old?"

Evidently, I'd offended his masculine pride. But I really didn't want him lifting all those bags. "They're really heavy. They were

30

sitting outside and the bark and dirt got soaked during last week's rain."

"I think I can handle a few bags—"

"Twenty."

"Whatever. Where do you want them?"

Since there was no dissuading him, I walked to my Ford Explorer and raised the rear door. Pierce's gaze followed my finger as I pointed to each of the flower beds. "I want five bags of bark for each of those. The potting mix goes in back."

"Not a problem." Pierce hefted one bag of bark over his shoulder and tucked another one under his arm.

I wanted to say "be careful," but I couldn't think of a way to do it and not insult his manly pride. I hadn't lifted the bags myself because I'd hurt my own back a couple of years earlier and now tried to respect my physical limits. So I stood quietly, smiled supportively, and considered what I would say to Josh for being late.

A few minutes later, Pierce picked up the last bag of potting soil. "This is it. I'll set it on the deck and then we can go."

Grateful he'd made it with no problems, I beamed. "Thanks."

He disappeared around the corner of the house. I tossed the weeds into the yard waste barrel, put my tools and gloves away in the garage, washed my hands while I was there, and waited.

And waited.

With growing concern, I hurried to the backyard and spotted him, lying on his side next to the deck.

"Matt!" I shrieked. I rushed to him. His eyes were closed, and he wasn't moving. I gave him a gentle shake to see if he was conscious.

"Don't touch me!" he snarled.

"What's wrong?" I cried. "Talk to me."

"Just don't touch me," he said again, this time through gritted teeth.

31

I stopped. If he was talking, he was breathing. If he was breathing, he didn't need CPR. "Tell me what's wrong!"

His only answer was a groan that broke my heart.

"I'll call 9-1-1."

I scrambled across the deck toward the sliding door and opened it enough to let myself in, but not enough for Taffy, my golden retriever, to sneak out. Whatever Pierce's problem, he didn't need eighty pounds of ditzy dog bouncing on him.

I grabbed the phone, punched in 9-1-1, and gave the dispatcher my address and told her to have the paramedics come to the backyard. I grabbed a bottle of aspirin from the cupboard and filled a glass with water. Then I returned to Pierce.

"The medics are coming." I knelt next to him and took his hand. "Is it your heart? I've got an aspirin and some water."

"It's not in my heart," he whispered. "It's my back. But I'll take that aspirin. It hurts like hell."

I placed the aspirin on his tongue and lifted his head just enough to help him swallow some water. "Everything was going so well. What happened?"

"When I dropped that last bag, something twanged." His voice was filled with agony.

I winced. "Twanged."

"Uh-huh. Oh, geez, it hurts." Pierce closed his eyes and breathed raggedly.

I gently patted his shoulder. "The paramedics'll be here in a minute."

From a distance, I heard a siren. The sound grew louder until it rent the air. Then it cut off.

"I'll be right back." I left Pierce and hurried around the house to flag the paramedics. A man and a woman, both in uniform, emerged from the aid car and pulled out their metal emergency cases.

"What happened?" asked the woman. Her name tag said "Benoit."

I guided them to the backyard and pointed out Pierce's prone body. "My friend's injured."

Her partner, whose name tag said "Wischer," dropped a silvery case on the deck and bent down to open it.

"I think it's his back," I said.

"It *is* my back," snapped Pierce.

"Well, hello, Detective," said Benoit jovially. "What've you done to yourself?"

"Marcia." Pierce lifted his hand in greeting, but the movement brought a sharp intake of air.

"Pretty bad, huh?" said Wischer. He sounded more sympathetic than his partner.

"You could say that," Pierce said in a painful whisper.

"What happened?" Benoit gently wrapped a blood pressure cuff around Pierce's arm.

"He was carrying bags of bark and potting mix from my car," I explained.

Nodding, Wischer removed Pierce's shoes and socks and ran his finger up Pierce's instep. "How many?"

Relieved to see Pierce's foot jerk, I said, "Twenty bags. Fifteen bark for out front and five potting mix for the back. And they were wet from last night's rain." I felt a twinge of guilt that I'd expected Josh to carry these same heavy bags.

Benoit nodded toward the pile of bags on the deck. "Those the ones?"

"Those are the ones," I responded with a regretful sigh.

She went to the pile and hefted one. "Yup. That'll do it. What's that make it this week, Ken, six garden backs?"

Wischer thought for a moment before continuing with his assessment of Pierce's condition. "That sounds about right. You're in good company, Detective. We've scraped a number of Madrona Bay's dignitaries off their backsides the last couple of days."

Pierce grunted. I very much doubted that he felt complimented to be included in that group.

After the paramedics completed their examination, Pierce asked, "How bad is it?"

"Don't know for sure," Benoit said. "There's no obvious nerve damage. We'll stabilize you and bring you to Emergency. The docs will know more after they take some x-rays."

"Terrific," Pierce snarled.

I stepped aside and watched as the paramedics eased Pierce onto a back board and strapped him in. Then they maneuvered him onto a collapsible gurney and raised it to roll him to their aid car.

"Are you taking him to Madrona Bay?" I asked.

Wischer nodded. "The city has its medical contract there."

"This wasn't on the job," Pierce said.

"Sorry, Detective. Our orders are to take anyone with police or fire to Madrona Bay."

I followed the paramedics to their van. After they slid Pierce inside, Benoit climbed in with him and Wischer slammed the doors shut.

"I'll lock up here and meet you at the ER," I said.

"Take your time." Wischer's blue eyes were full of understanding. "He'll be there awhile."

"That's what I'm afraid of," I said with a heavy sigh. "He was only trying to help."

Wischer patted my shoulder. "Don't blame yourself," he said in a low voice. "When these guys decide they're invincible, you can't stop them."

"If you say so." Still, I felt guilty. I should have done something to stop Pierce from lifting all those heavy bags.

After I watched the truck disappear from sight, I turned to

see Pierce's car, the nondescript, department-issue tan sedan, parked in front of my house. We'd have to figure out a way to get it to his place.

But, right now, I had to leave a note for Josh and get to the hospital. The note was succinct:

> *Pierce hurt his back carrying the bark and potting soil;*
> *I'm at the hospital;*
> *start spreading the bark around the flower beds;*
> *I'll be back in a couple of hours;*
> *I expect you to be home.*

Josh wouldn't need body language to interpret my mood.

Not knowing whom I might run into, even on a weekend, I took a few extra minutes to clean the dirt out from under my fingernails, put on some make-up, and change into a business-casual outfit of tan slacks, a red collarless top and a navy linen jacket with three-quarter length sleeves. I decided that adding earrings and a necklace would be too much for ultra-casual Saturday.

When I drove into the hospital's employee lot a short time later, I spotted the aid car in the ER's ambulance entrance. I parked and trotted across the lot to enter the ER through the ambulance entrance, triggering the buzzer that let staff know an ambulance had arrived. I spotted Benoit and Wischer talking to Charley Anderson, the ER manager. He responded to the buzzer by glancing over the medics' shoulders to see who had come in, then returned his full attention to them when he saw it was me.

I held back while they talked. A quick peek through the glass-paned doors to the ER waiting area told me that Charley had a full house.

Charley finished with the paramedics and approached. "You're looking for Detective Pierce." It was a statement, not a question.

"How'd you know?"

"Where they picked him up. I recognized your address."

I grinned. "There are no secrets, are there?"

He grinned back. "Not around here."

"Who's on today?"

"Mike Skinner. He sent Pierce straight to Radiology for back and neck films. When he gets the results, I'm guessing he'll contact the orthopedist who's on call this weekend."

"Sounds good. Should I wait here?" I asked, even though I knew the answer. Connie would be impressed with my ability to predict Charley's answer since she's the one who claims to be psychic.

Charley shook his head. "It's going to be a while, Rob. This is the first really nice weekend this spring, and we have a torrent of walking wounded. Broken bones, bee stings, you name it."

If he hadn't been so busy, I would have talked to him about his new receptionist, Hal, and the incident with Dr. Park. "Okay. I'll be in my office, then. Call me when Pierce comes back from Radiology?"

"You got it."

"Don't forget," I admonished, waving my finger at him as I started down the hall.

Charley clutched his chest. "What, and have you file a complaint against me?" he said with a laugh. He waved his clipboard and disappeared through the swinging doors to the waiting room.

My stomach growled, loud and rumbly. Fortunately, I was the only one who heard it. I checked my watch. It didn't take a genius to know Pierce wasn't going to take me out to lunch, or to dinner, for that matter. I decided to pop down to the cafeteria before going to my office.

The eating area was mostly empty. I recognized a few uniformed employees taking a break at one table and waved a greeting. Here and there sat patients' relatives, grim-faced and holding serious discussions. I entered the serving area and considered the possibilities—soup, salad, or sandwich.

"Robyn!"

I turned to see Cherie Duncan, the dietary services manager, standing behind the serving tables. "Hi, Cherie."

"What are you doing here?" About my age, she had short, frosted hair that gave her heart-shaped face a pixie look. Definitely a soup-and-salad girl who worked out regularly. I'd have to ask her how she managed it while working the hours she did. She wore the standard white lab coat over her street clothes, although they looked more casual than during the week.

"A friend of mine is in the ER. Why are you here on a Saturday?"

She gave me a hard look. "Are you in a hurry?"

I shook my head. "Not really. I'm waiting for him to get back from Radiology."

"Good. You're just the person I need. Come around to my office." She disappeared through the swinging door into the kitchen.

This sounded suspiciously like work for me. I exited the serving area and went down the hall to her office. When I got there, Cherie was with one of her employees, a young woman I guessed to be in her early twenties with frizzy blond hair, make-up that verged on gothic, and a sultry pout.

"Rob, this is Tina Wilson," Cherie said.

Tina crossed her arms over her ample bosom and acknowledged the introduction by glaring in my direction. "I don't care what she says," Tina said to Cherie. "I'm not, you know, going back there."

"What's the problem?" I asked.

Cherie pursed her lips. "Tina's assigned to deliver meals, but she's refusing to take the dinner trays to her floor."

On the surface, this sounded like an employee relations issue, not patient relations. "Can she trade with someone else?"

"That's part of the problem," Cherie said, shaking her head. "Brad called in sick today—case of sunshine flu, I'm sure—and I need Tina to deliver all the dinners tonight."

"I'm not going up there," Tina said heatedly. "I told you. You know. I'm not, like, putting up with his crap again."

"Whose crap?" My sixth sense told me the answer before I even asked the question. Connie would be impressed again.

"That scum-sucking slime in Room 312."

My eyebrows went up, and Cherie rolled her eyes. So much for a positive customer service attitude. I wanted to laugh at Tina's graphic description, but this definitely wasn't the time or place to drop my official role. "What did this scum-sucking slime do?" I knew what she'd say, but needed to hear it in her own words.

"He come on to me, you know. Like, that's what he did," Tina said. "He, like, says he don't want his dinner from the kitchen. He, like, you know, wants to eat me." She turned bright red, from embarrassment or anger, I wasn't sure which, but either was understandable.

"I see. Who is this patient?"

"Jason Hilliard," Cherie said. "Regular diet."

"Tina, let me say first of all that he has no right to treat you that way." Tina's shoulders dropped about three notches along with some of her hostility. "I know we talk about giving good customer service even if patients are difficult—"

"But—"

I held up my hand to stop her. "Even if patients are difficult. But, there is a line between what we will tolerate and what is unacceptable, and Mr. Hilliard crossed it. I'll have a chat with him." I looked from Tina to Cherie. They both nodded. "Okay.

I'll run up there now, then come back to let you know what happened."

"Thanks, Rob. Is that okay with you, Tina?" Cherie asked.

"Yeah," Tina mumbled. She still looked wary.

"I mean it," I said to her. "We don't expect you to take that."

"Sure," Tina said, but she didn't sound convinced.

"I'll be back in a few minutes."

I would have loved to pass this task off to a male administrator, or even a male janitor. But this fell into the flip side of my job—dealing with inappropriate patients. They had rights, but they also had responsibilities, and one of them was to not give the staff a bad time.

After leaving Cherie's office, I was still hungry, but only gave the cafeteria a longing look as I passed it and took the elevator to the third floor. Ignoring my growing hunger pangs, I prepared myself mentally to be tough with this pervert. Then I wondered: Susan had said this wasn't Hilliard's first hospital stay, but it *was* the first time I'd heard complaints about him. Had he always been such a pervert, or was his behavior during this visit something new? And if so, why?

I made a brief side trip to my office to get my nametag. I wasn't as official looking as I had been yesterday, but I was glad I'd taken the time to change out of my jeans and clean under my fingernails before coming in.

Backtracking, I crossed the large lobby-like area in front of the elevators and headed toward the patient rooms. 3-West was quiet this afternoon. I stood inside the swinging double doors and looked down the long corridor to the room at the end and shuddered involuntarily. Even after all this time, I couldn't see that room without remembering the murder that had taken place there last fall. Talk about a nightmare.

I was here to see Hilliard, but, of course, like most people, I procrastinated when it came to unpleasant tasks. I decided to take a quick detour and check on William first.

3-West's layout was the same as the ER's. The patient rooms were along the outside walls for the window views, with the center core filled with a variety of small rooms and closets, most with doors opening to both hallways. The nurses' station was halfway down the hall. William's room was across from Hilliard's, with a family meeting room in the core blocking them from each other.

I knocked on the open door before poking my head inside. "William?"

"Who're you?"

Oh, dear, he didn't remember me. He squinted at me, as if mentally rewinding his memory tapes.

The homeless man's face gradually lit up with a shy smile. "Miz Robyn? You come to see ol' William?"

"I sure did. How're you feeling?" As I pulled a chair close to his bed and sat down, I noticed several flower arrangements on the windowsill. Probably left behind by other patients. The nurses must have brought them in here.

"Okay, Miz Robyn." He frowned, then brightened. "The food's good."

That was something I didn't hear every day. I grinned. "I'm glad to hear that. How's your leg?"

His eyes widened. "The people's nice here. But sometimes they does things that hurt real bad." His gaze started bouncing around the room the way it had when he'd first come to my office. "I was scared, Miz Robyn, real scared. I thought they was gonna cut it off. But the nurse, she said they'd fix it so's it'd be okay."

"I'm really pleased for you, William. Have you seen anyone else?" I knew the admitting doc had ordered a psych consult.

William thought long and hard before nodding. "Yes, Miz Robyn. This real nice man came and talked to me for a long time. He was real gentle like. Didn't try to touch me or look at my leg. Just talked."

Relieved, I released the breath I hadn't realized I'd been holding. William had a long way to go, but he looked so much better. Even his mental status was better, coherent and aware of his surroundings. Dr. Baker, the psychiatrist, must have figured out which drugs would help the most.

"The other man came too," William whispered. He looked at me, frowning fearfully. "About the money."

It was my turn to frown. "The money?"

"He wanted the money."

It must have been someone from the Business Office wanting to know if William had the means to pay his bill. "Don't worry about that, William."

I patted his hand to reassure him and was pleased he didn't flinch away. Apparently he was no longer afraid of me, as I was no longer afraid of him. "The money's all taken care of."

That seemed to puzzle him, but he finally nodded.

"Is there anything I can get for you?"

William's brow furrowed in deep concentration as he considered my question. "No, Miz Robyn. I's doing okay."

"Good." I stood up. "I have another patient I have to see, William. But I'll be back, okay?"

"That's fine, Miz Robyn."

The short-cut to Hilliard's room was through the door to the family meeting room that stood between William's room and Jason Hilliard's room. But the door was closed. Rather than knock and possibly interrupt a family, I went the long way around.

As I came up the other hallway and approached the half-open door, I saw Hilliard lying in his bed. I knocked on the door and stepped in. "Hello, Mr. Hill—"

My stomach dropped. His eyes were wide open and staring off into space. The IV tubing tied in a fancy knot around his neck twisted it in an awkward angle.

I didn't need to go any closer to know that Jason Hilliard was dead.

CHAPTER 3

When asked later, I couldn't explain why I reacted the way I did. It was a gut response.

I bolted for the nurses' station. A woman I didn't recognize was sitting in front of a computer inputting the afternoon medications list for the patients. She was older, chunky, with fly-away gray hair and totally focused on her task.

"We need to call the police," I told her.

She tilted her head toward me, but her gaze and attention remained on the monitor. "Not now," she said in a distracted voice. "I'm busy."

I circled the counter until I could read her name tag. "Amanda," I said sharply.

"What?" She scowled as she finally looked at me.

"Call the police."

"Why?" She squinted at my nametag as she stood up.

"Jason Hilliard is dead."

"Don't be ridiculous," she scoffed. "I checked on that obnoxious young man not half an hour ago."

"Well, that obnoxious young man is dead now," I said.

She picked up the phone and hit 0. After a pause, she said, "This is 3-West. Code—"

"No! Don't call a code. Call the police." I moved as if to lunge over the counter to fight her for the phone. That's not my style, but if I had to, I supposed I would. I remembered how the last crime scene had been inadvertently destroyed by the staff trying to revive the murder victim.

Her unflinching scrutiny on me, she said into the phone, "Never mind. Cancel the code." She slammed down the receiver and came around from behind her desk. "You better be right about this."

I followed her down the hall. "Don't touch anything," I warned as she entered Hilliard's room. I stood in the doorway and watched in amazement as she checked for a pulse, and when she found none, she reached for the tubing tied in such an unusual knot around Hilliard's neck.

"Don't touch that!"

Her hands stopped in mid-air, and she glared at me. "What is it with you?"

"Don't touch anything! Can't you see? He's been murdered. This is a crime scene."

She started for the tubing again.

"Don't touch it! There might be fingerprints. Don't touch anything until the police get here!"

She looked at me, and then at the tubing. "Humph. You're right. He's dead." She sailed past me, no emotion, very professional, and yet, I sensed the words "and good riddance" float through the air behind her.

Stunned by her reaction, I stood frozen to the spot, but I quickly recovered. I stepped closer to look at the knot but didn't recognize it. Catching up with Amanda, I said, "Now we'll call the police."

"The doctor on-call should be notified first," she said firmly, never slowing.

I couldn't believe it. What part of this wasn't she understanding? I was having a hard time too, but at least I acknowledged what was really going on. We'd had a . . . I sighed. We'd had another murder. And I'd found the victim. Again.

"No. We call the police first," I insisted. "Look, everyone

knows Jason Hilliard was obnoxious. After seeing him with that tubing around his neck, even you have to admit he died under very suspicious circumstances. And, according to what you said earlier, you may well have been the last person to see him alive."

"Fine." She stopped so quickly I ran into her. "I'll call the police. *Then* I'm calling the doctor. And the AOC," she said, referring to the administrator on-call, the highest ranking nurse manager in the building on evenings and weekends.

"Fine."

From the nurses' station, she punched a 9 for an outside line, then 9-1-1. "This is Amanda Whitcomb, Madrona Bay Hospital. We need to see a police officer about a dead patient. 3-West. Absolutely no sirens."

She paged for the on-call physician and for the AOC to come directly to the unit, hung up the phone, and eyed me with annoyance. "I didn't think you management types worked weekends." She sounded as if I'd deliberately plotted to disrupt her work.

"I'm not usually here on Saturdays," I replied. The whole situation was surreal. I'd found a dead patient, and here I was chatting as if everything was normal with one of the most annoying nurses I'd ever met. "I brought a friend to the ER."

"I see." She grimaced. "Why aren't you down there?"

"I had other things to do while he was being tested. One of them was to check on Mr. Hilliard. Susan Wong, the nurse manager for this unit, asked me to."

"Probably could have saved yourself the trouble. He wouldn't have listened. The punk." Amanda sniffed. "He'd have maneuvered his sheet to give you a show, then said it was an accident."

I opened my mouth to say something when I heard the staccato click of heels coming down the hall.

A woman about my age wearing an unbuttoned white lab coat over a stunning cream silk blouse and black linen slacks came into view. I silently groaned and wished, again, that I was anywhere but here. Of all the people in the hospital, why did this weekend's AOC have to be Paula Rodriguez?

Every once in a while, you meet someone who sets your teeth on edge. They have attitudes and express opinions that make a normally calm, civilized person want to strangle them.

I'm sure she was very nice, and other people really liked her. But Paula was the person who brought out my evil twin, and I seemed to have the same effect on her. She was one of the hospital's nursing administrators, and she was tall and willowy, with a flawless olive complexion and hazel eyes. She always looked chic with beautiful clothes, silky hair with every strand in place, and weekly manicures. I may have wished I had her looks, but it was her personality I didn't like.

Paula scowled at me. "What's going on?" She directed her question to Amanda.

Clearly pleased to pass the whole situation over to someone else, Amanda nodded toward me. "She went to a patient's room and found him dead."

"I didn't hear a code called. No one beeped me." Paula checked the beeper in her pocket to confirm she hadn't been paged.

Now it begins, I thought with a silent sigh, and jumped in with both feet. "I told her not to call a code because he was already dead. Not just dead, but murdered."

"And when did you get your M.E. license?" Paula snapped, referring to medical examiners who determine the cause of death.

"Anyone who isn't blind could tell this guy was past reviving," I snapped back.

Paula glanced at Amanda, who shrugged and nodded confirmation to my statement. "Regardless," Paula said, "this hospital has policies to protect patients—"

"—and the hospital." I couldn't stop myself from throwing that in because that was what this discussion was really about. That and the fact Paula thought she finally had something on me. She'd always felt my department was nothing more than internal spies, always looking for someone doing something wrong. Fortunately, her opinion was shared by only a few other people in the hospital.

"Policies to protect patients," Paula restated. "Has the on-call doc been called?"

"Yes," Amanda answered as she began to walk away. Then with a sly glance at me, she added over her shoulder, "And the police."

"The police!" Paula whirled to face me as Amanda disappeared around the corner. "You called the police because someone died in a hospital? Like that never happens?

"I should have known," she continued, hands on her hips. "You can't leave things alone, can you, Robyn? You were involved in one murder, and now you miss all the attention so you try to stir up trouble again." She started down the hall toward Hilliard's room.

"Now wait a minute," I said, hurrying to keep up with her. "I don't look for trouble. But he doesn't look like someone who'd died peacefully in his sleep. He *was* murdered. It was the—"

"And you've seen so many you can tell the difference?" Paula scoffed. "Leave medicine to the experts and mysteries to the writers, Robyn. You should have enough to do around here without interfering with us."

When we reached Hilliard's room, I stepped in front of Paula, blocking her at the doorway. "But there's—"

The tubing was gone.

Hilliard still looked quite dead, but the tubing I'd seen knotted around his neck was missing. My heart sank. I was really in for it now.

"It's gone," I knew I sounded lame. But I had to keep up a valiant defense of my actions. "There was IV tubing tied around his neck when I found him."

My fast-talking excuse was cut off by the distinctive squeak of leather and the clink of metal as a police officer came down the hall. I looked in that direction with relief. Maybe now I wouldn't have to fight to keep everyone out of the room to protect any evidence. "Officer Tomlin!"

"Ms. Kelly," the officer greeted. He was an affable young man, dark-haired and with the requisite macho mustache. "Haven't seen you for a while."

We stood in the hall as I quickly introduced Paula, who just as quickly apologized to Officer Tomlin for the inconvenience, for what she was sure was a big mistake. A mistake, she repeated, that was all the result of my overactive imagination.

"Look, there was IV tubing tied around his neck when I found him," I insisted. "That's how I knew he didn't die of natural causes."

"What tubing?" Paula pointed at Hilliard through the open doorway. "There's no tubing. I'll be sure to send you a copy of the Incident Report," she said in a nasty tone.

"Ah, ladies, before you go any farther." Officer Tomlin held up his hand to keep us from entering the room. Then he carefully approached Hilliard's bed. "There may not be any tubing now, but from the redness and bruising I can see where something was tied around his neck. And from his eyes, I'm pretty sure he died of strangulation. You could be right, Ms. Kelly. This definitely warrants more investigation."

He backed us farther away from the doorway and contacted his dispatcher to call for a crime scene team and a detective. Then he roped the area off with yellow "crime scene" tape. Paula was furious, and I think it was mostly because she didn't have something to hold over me like she'd first thought. And hoped.

The next hour was a bit of a blur. Officer Tomlin questioned me and finally tracked down the missing Amanda, who claimed she'd gone outside for a cigarette break, of all things. At least she confirmed that IV tubing had been knotted around Hilliard's neck when she saw him.

All the while, I couldn't believe a patient had been murdered. *Another* patient, I amended.

Another patient *I* had discovered. That was the sobering thought.

Of course, it wouldn't be confirmed that he died from strangulation until the autopsy was complete, but even I could tell he hadn't died of natural causes. Annoying Amanda still insisted to anyone who would listen that he was alive and well when she last checked on him. But given her obliviousness when I'd first taken her to his room, I had to wonder about her powers of observation.

In the meantime, I found a quiet spot where I could watch and listen, yet still be out of the way—in the doorway to William's room. While the police were distracted with their investigative procedures, I stealthily crossed the hall and entered the family meeting room and opened the door that faced Hilliard's room. Then I returned to my post. It wasn't a perfect view, but it was the best I could manage under the circumstances. I worried about how Pierce was doing, but there was no way I could leave 3-West until I had been questioned by the investigators.

The on-call physician arrived and after seeing the crime scene tape and talking to Paula, announced we should call if we needed him. Lucky man.

From halfway down the hall, I could hear Paula on the phone calling other administrators and insisting they come in. I grudgingly agreed she was right to pass this problem off as soon as possible to someone with more authority than either of us had.

Surprisingly quickly for someone off on weekends, Howard Knowles, the hospital administrator, arrived. This was the first time I'd seen him in casual clothes: faded jeans and a long sleeved brown plaid shirt. It was jarringly out of character for my favorite "bean counter." He nodded to me in acknowledgement, then Paula immediately redirected his attention toward her. That was fine. I could wait to explain my side of the story. I sighed heavily. What a mess.

Amanda complained loudly and vehemently from the nurses' station when the police wouldn't let her take another smoke break, and again when they wouldn't let her go home at shift change. Everyone on the unit, patients, staff, and investigators, knew the union was going to hear from her on Monday.

I also thought my observation post was a good place to keep William from getting too agitated. The sights and sounds of all those uniformed officers and investigators disturbed William almost as much as my suggestion the previous day that he see a doctor. I sought to calm him, but I wasn't having much impact.

"It's the money," he mumbled. "Always the money."

"Don't worry about the money, William."

"Is the man still out there, Miz Robyn?"

"The police are still here, William." I cast a brief look over my shoulder at him and tried to smile reassuringly. "You're fine. No one's going to bother you."

My words had no effect. He worried the edges of his sheet from one corner to the other, then back again. "I don' wanna go to jail," he whimpered.

"You're not going to jail." I tried to keep the edge from creeping into my voice. It was, after all, at least the twentieth time I'd told him that. "You haven't done anything wrong."

"It's the money. Always the money," he repeated. His gaze

darted around the room.

There was no convincing him that he wouldn't go to jail for not paying his hospital bill. Watching William for more than ten seconds made me dizzy, so I returned to watching the police.

The crime scene unit had arrived quickly, but it took a while for a detective to show up. An irritable bear of a man whom I heard the others call Captain Roberts commandeered the nurses' station for preliminary questioning.

When it was my turn to be interviewed, I paused a moment to study him before I approached. He was a big man, well over six feet tall and with a bulky build. He reminded me of a bull ox. His jowly face and bulbous nose indicated he enjoyed his food and drink. His bushy gray-brown eyebrows matched the shrubs growing from his ears and nose.

"Captain—"

"You are?" he snapped. He barely glanced at me as he flipped to a new page in his pocket-sized spiral bound notepad.

Intimidated by his size and manner, I wanted to step back. But I held my ground. "Robyn Kelly. I—"

"Someone said you work here."

"Yes, I manage the Patient Relations department."

"What're you doing here on a Saturday?"

After what Pierce had told me earlier about Captain Roberts, an inner voice warned me not to mention that Pierce was here. "I came to check on a patient admitted yesterday."

"Who was this patient?" He still hadn't looked at me.

"William Jones. He's—"

"Why'd you go to the victim's room?"

"I was asked to speak to him. Several employees had complained about him. He—"

"Was he dead when you found him?"

"Yes. He had tubing tied—"

"Did you call the police?"

"As soon as I could. The nurse on duty insisted on seeing him first."

"Why?" He looked at me then, his eyes narrowed. "You got a reputation for lying?"

"No! Certainly not."

"What did you touch in the room?"

"Nothing. The nurse started to untie the tubing but—"

Captain Roberts snapped his little notepad shut. "I think that'll do it for now. Don't make any travel plans for a while." He brushed past me and started to leave the nurses' station.

"Don't you want to know about the knot?" I called after him. But he'd already pulled out his cell phone and speed dialed.

I leaned against the counter, stunned by his brusque questioning. He was obviously in too much of a hurry to care about this case. I couldn't believe he was so disinterested that he didn't even take any notes. Was his memory so good that he didn't need to? But then, why open the notepad? His interviewing methods didn't bode well for solving the crime quickly or correctly.

A short time later, back at my vantage point in William's doorway, I learned why he was glossing over the surface on this initial round of questioning.

"Where's Pierce?" Captain Roberts roared at Officer Tomlin as they stood inside Hilliard's room.

"I wouldn't know, sir."

"He's not answering his beeper. Nash is on vacation this week, so Pierce is on-call."

Pierce had said the real reason he'd been given a car was to be on call twenty-four/seven. From Captain Roberts's attitude, he'd probably expect Pierce to get out of his bed in the ER and conduct the investigation. If he could find Pierce.

Pierce! I needed to check on him, but after all this time, I had no idea where he was or what was happening to him.

I waited until Captain Roberts left Hilliard's room, then I caught Officer Tomlin's attention through the open doors of the family meeting room. I nodded toward the elevators. He returned my nod, and we met outside the unit.

"You been standing there long?" Officer Tomlin asked me.

"Long enough to know what's going on."

"Yeah, well, I guess the captain doesn't like his weekends disturbed." A smile tugged at the corners of his mouth.

"Neither does Detective Pierce," I said with a sigh.

Tomlin shook his head. "He's going to catch it when Captain Roberts finds him."

"I'll let you in on a little secret." I proceeded to tell him about Pierce's injury.

Tomlin whistled softly. "The captain'll love this. Nash on vacation and Pierce laid up."

"I wouldn't count on Detective Pierce being much help the next couple of days."

"That means the captain is doing the twenty-four/seven for a while. This is going to be a very long week. I wonder if I can request a temporary transfer to another division," Tomlin said wistfully.

"I'll make a deal with you. You let me slip away from here for a while and when I come back, I'll let you know how long that transfer needs to be for."

"Has Captain Roberts interviewed you yet?" When I nodded, Tomlin craned his neck to check police activity on the unit. "I don't think you'll be missed. If anyone asks, I'll cover for you."

"Thanks. I'll be back."

I slipped into the stairwell and eased the door shut so it didn't slam. No point in calling attention to my departure.

As I sneaked down the stairs, I thought about—what else— the murder. Hilliard may have been a scum-sucking slime, as Tina so succinctly put it, but that alone wouldn't justify murder.

Other than that, why would someone want to kill him?

I certainly didn't know the answer, but I couldn't stop myself from speculating. The list of suspects might not be very long; this was the weekend and the hospital was relatively quiet. Not like last fall when we'd been swamped with patients, staff, and reporters after a major pile-up on I-90. The memories of that time still gave me the willies.

I stopped. Wait a minute. What was I thinking? I couldn't get involved with this. I *wouldn't* get involved. I learned my lesson the last time. This was not my problem. I had enough to do without meddling in a suspicious death, I told myself, and I affirmed my resolve to keep away from all murder investigations.

My first stop was the cafeteria. I figured the chances that Cherie had not heard about Jason Hilliard's untimely demise were slim to none, but it wouldn't hurt to close the loop. Passing on information wasn't violating my vow to stay out of the investigation.

The grapevine wasn't as swift on weekends. Cherie hadn't heard yet. She was stunned, to say the least, and left the cafeteria in a daze to find Tina and tell her she didn't need to worry about being harassed when she delivered tonight's dinner trays.

That task completed, I picked up a tall latté at the espresso stand and headed to the ER.

CHAPTER 4

My next stop was the physicians' lounge located in the middle of the ER's row of exam rooms, the same room where I'd confronted Dr. Park the day before. I found Mike Skinner, a family practice doc, entering some chart notes into the computer. On weekends, one side of the ER served as an urgent care service for the walking wounded. It was less expensive for us, and less expensive for the patients who didn't need full-blown trauma services. That left the really serious stuff for the contract emergency physicians. Like Dr. Park. I sure was glad Pierce hadn't had to see that jerk.

"Mike?"

"Oh, hi, Robyn," he said.

"Have you finished with Matthew Pierce?"

He shook his head. "You really messed him up."

"Oh, no." My stomach flip-flopped. "What's wrong?"

He looked at me over the top of his half-moon glasses.

It took a moment for me to get the silent message. "Oh, right. Right. Patient confidentiality. So where is he?"

"I sent him down the hall to wait for . . . Ron Downing is coming in to see him."

I cringed. Ron was an orthopedist. "He needs surgery?"

Mike shook his head.

"Oh, all right." I threw up my hands in defeat. "I'll go see him and find out for myself. Give you guys one in-service on confidentiality and you don't forget a thing."

Mike chuckled. "You're the one who beat it into our heads not to say nothing to no one."

"Yeah, yeah. See you." I left him laughing. Figuring that Pierce might think more kindly of me if I brought a peace offering, I returned to the cafeteria and found an apple fritter. Lots of sugar and grease. Just the thing. My latté was almost gone, so I picked up another, decaf this time, and one full-strength mocha for Pierce. Juggling the goodies, I returned to the elevator and used my elbow to punch the button back to the first floor.

Mike hadn't specified which exam room, so I continued checking rooms until I found the one I wanted. Pierce was lying on the bed, his eyes closed.

"Hi, there," I said quietly.

A grunt was all I got back.

"How're you doing?"

"Just fine." Pierce sighed. From the dreamy quality of his voice, he'd had a pain shot and the medication had kicked in. Pierce didn't look like he was in any condition to find the door, let alone investigate a murder. Captain Roberts was going to be very, very disappointed with his detective's mental acuity.

"I brought you something." I held up the coffee and napkin-wrapped fritter.

Pierce opened his eyes and looked in my direction, but I wasn't sure how well he was focusing. "That's nice."

Relieved that he wasn't going to snap my head off, at least not right now, I approached the bed. "You probably shouldn't eat while you're lying down. I'll put it on your tray for later." I looked at the fritter, then said, "Want a sniff?"

"Mmm-hmmm."

I waved it slowly under his nose.

"Mmmm. That's good."

"Do you want to smell the coffee too? I brought you a mocha."

Pierce sighed, more of a resigned sound than the earlier relaxed sigh. "If that's the best we can do."

He took a deep breath, then another one before signaling that he'd had enough of smelling the coffee. "Thanks, Rob."

"I'm so sorry," I blurted.

"It's not your fault." Pierce's hand patted the bed absently where he thought my hand should be. "I should have known better." His words trailed off until he was whispering. "That's what I get for showing off." He didn't look at me, just kept staring at the ceiling through half-mast eyes.

"Hopefully it's not too bad." It was sweet that he'd actually tried to impress me, which of course made me feel even more guilty.

"Hello, hello," came from the doorway.

I turned to see Ron Downing, and I grinned. "Is this what the well-dressed orthopod wears on the weekend?"

"This is what an orthopod wears while doing his own room addition on the weekend," he said. Despite the long white coat covering his clothes, what I could see of his jeans and athletic shoes were covered with paint splatters. I'd always thought that orthopedists were carpenters at heart, and Ron was living proof.

"Is the baby's room going to be sky blue?" I asked.

"How'd you know?" With a puzzled frown, he flapped the coat open for a better view.

"It's in your hair."

Chagrined, he ran his fingers through his dark brown hair. "I thought I got it all out before I drove in, but I'm not surprised. So, what have we got here?"

"You tell me, Doc," Pierce said.

Surprised at how normal he sounded, I turned to study Pierce more carefully. His eyes were open, staring hard at Ron, but I suspected it was taking everything inside Pierce to pull himself out of his medication haze. Somehow I didn't think he'd be trying so hard to be in control if Ron had looked closer to sixty than twenty years old.

I made quick introductions, then explained to Ron what had happened.

"That's what I thought after looking at the x-rays and reading Mike's notes. Would you excuse us, Robyn?"

I left and paced the hall while Ron examined Pierce. In a few minutes, Ron called me back in.

"Are you sure you want me here?" I asked Pierce.

He nodded, then faced Ron. "How bad is it?"

Ron had turned serious, the consummate professional as he explained to Pierce the damage he'd done to his back. "I think what we're dealing with here is a severe lumbar strain. You stretched those lower back muscles way beyond where they were prepared to go, Detective."

"So what's the bottom line?" Pierce asked with a nervous catch in his voice.

"At this point, I doubt you need surgery. In the old days, I would have kept you here for a few days. But that was before insurance companies decided they knew how to practice medicine better than physicians. Now we have to send you home with muscle relaxants, pain pills, rest, and a referral to physical therapy. You'll need to stay off your feet for at least five days, except for doing your exercises. And no driving with the meds I'm prescribing. You may even have trouble operating the remote," he added with a grin.

Pierce didn't seem amused. "I guess that's okay. As long as you don't do surgery. I don't want anyone cutting on me."

"Good. I'll order the meds. Rob can pick them up at the pharmacy and take you home."

Before he could log onto the computer and enter the treatment plan, I said, "Ah, Ron, can I talk to you for a minute outside?"

With a puzzled frown, Ron glanced from me to Pierce, then back again. He shrugged and said, "Sure."

Ignoring Pierce's glare, I led Ron out of the room and down the hall until we were out of Pierce's earshot, no matter how hard he tried to listen.

"What's up, Robyn?" Ron faced me, arms crossed, more puzzled than annoyed, but the annoyance was there, something I always worked very hard to avoid in my working relationships with the docs.

"You know I don't meddle in how you guys practice medicine."

"True, although you do make sure we're fully aware of the patient's perspective from time to time." He gave me a narrowed-eye stare. "Is that about to change?"

"Well, let's just say that circumstances are a bit different this time and—"

"Look, Robyn, I know you're feeling guilty because this guy hurt his back at your house—"

"No, no, that's not it at all." Were there no secrets around this place? "No, it involves his job. You see, there's been . . . there's been a murder on 3-West—"

"Another murder?" His annoyance at being dragged away from Pierce's room was gone, replaced by amazement.

"Well, yes. But that's not all." I quickly explained about Detective Nash being on vacation, the two detective vacancies, and Pierce being on-call day and night. "So from what I've seen of Pierce's boss, there'll be no bed rest or pain pills or muscle relaxants because the captain will have Pierce back on the street investigating this murder."

"That's not good, but there's nothing I can do."

"Yes, there is. You can admit him."

"Robyn—"

"What will happen if Pierce goes home this afternoon and by tonight has to start investigating the murder? He'll be in agony, right?"

Ron's head bobbled from side to side in reluctant agreement.

"And there's the risk that he'll injure his back even more?"

Ron barely nodded.

"And it could cause permanent problems?"

"Well—"

"And require surgery?"

"All right, all right!" Ron raised his hands in surrender. "I'll admit him!"

When I grinned, he added, "But you owe me." His eyes had narrowed again.

"No, Ron, I'm trying to help you provide the best possible care to your patient."

He smirked. "Yeah, that patient perspective thing again." After I smiled sweetly at him, he said, "Well, we'll go back to the old standard of treatment then. I'll have him admitted to 2-West and we'll go from there."

"Thanks, Ron. I know Pierce will appreciate it."

"Don't count on it," Ron said with a laugh. "Wait until you see what's involved."

We returned to Pierce's room to find him in high dudgeon. "Have you come to an agreement?" he snapped.

Ron glanced at me, then turned to face Pierce. "I've changed my mind about your treatment. I think you'd be best served by staying here."

He logged onto the computer. As he typed, he said, "I'm admitting you to 2-West."

Pierce inhaled sharply "Why?" Then he glared at me.

Ron looked up from the monitor and looked Pierce straight in the eye. "Because it guarantees you'll recover more quickly without any complications."

"What did you say to him?" Pierce asked me.

"Mr. Pierce, Robyn does not tell me how to treat my patients." Ron's tone left no room for further argument. "How's the pain?"

"It's okay."

Ron nodded. "I'll leave orders for another shot if you get uncomfortable later. If it gets too bad, we can put you on IV medication."

He logged off the computer. "Okay, a gurney will be here to take you to 2-West. I'll see you up there shortly." With a nod to me, he left the room.

Pierce frowned at me. "What's going on?" He gestured for me to hand him the apple fritter.

I shrugged. I didn't want to tell him about the events on 3-West for fear he'd get out of bed before the gurney arrived. Hopefully, Ron had plans that would keep Pierce confined to his bed.

Pierce swallowed a bite of the fritter and licked sugar off his fingers. "He looks awfully young."

"They all look young these days. Ron's good, though. Graduated from the UW, did his residency back east and is Board certified in orthopedics. He's been here six months, and his patients love him."

"Well, you would know."

Pierce finished off the fritter, followed by a few sips of his mocha, then I got a damp paper towel to wipe the sticky frosting off his hands and face. I didn't know what to say; I certainly wasn't going to entertain him with my big plans for the garden.

For his own unknown reasons, he wasn't pressuring me about why he was being admitted instead of going home. Maybe he knew Captain Roberts would have him up and about as soon as he tracked him down, even without the murder to investigate.

"How long do you think I'll be here?" Pierce handed me the washcloth.

"I don't know. Ron didn't say."

"Hope it's not more than a day or two. I have a stack of actives on my desk."

I didn't want to tell him that he was probably going to be here at least a week.

An orderly entered the room with a gurney. I'd never met him, but we'd seen each other around. We nodded in greeting.

"Mr. Pierce? Let's get you on this gurney, and then I'm going to take you to 2-West."

It took less than fifteen minutes for Pierce to be gingerly eased onto the gurney for a ride in the elevator, and then be settled in his room. I watched his face, but he only grimaced in pain a couple of times. Hopefully Ron would continue to keep him that comfortable.

"Here we go." Ron breezed into the room, followed by two nurses.

Pierce took one look at the ropes and pulleys they carried and swore under his breath.

That was my cue to leave. With mumbled apologies and excuses, I edged out of the room.

Besides, I'd been gone from 3-West for two hours, far longer than I'd expected, and it was time to return before Officer Tomlin was in deep trouble for allowing me to escape.

I needn't have worried. The unit was still in a state of confusion. Paula Rodriguez was gone, but Howard Knowles, the administrator, was talking to Captain Roberts. From their expressions, the discussion was not going well. I reminded myself that finding Jason Hilliard's body did not make this my problem. I was justifiably curious, but that was as far as it went.

"Rob." The deep voice came from behind me.

"Hey, Tom." It made sense that the head of Security would

come in. "Did Paula call you in from home?"

"Are you kidding? I'm the last person she'd call. No, one of my guys saw the patrol car and figured I better be here. I'm glad I am."

"Didn't want to miss any of the police action, huh?"

Tom's expression turned serious. "It's a bit more complicated than that. After checking with the nurse—?"

"Amanda?"

"Yeah. She's a piece of work." Tom snorted. "Helpful? I've never had so much trouble with a nurse before. All I wanted to know was if she'd notified Hilliard's emergency contact. That's a pretty reasonable question under the circumstances, don't you think?"

I nodded my agreement.

"But she wouldn't tell me, and not only wouldn't she tell me, she wouldn't let me get the contact's name and phone number from his chart so I could make the call. She said she was talking only to the police."

"So what'd you do?"

"I figured they had enough going on, so I told the officer, the one we met last time, that I'd give them a hand. He didn't think the captain had even thought about notifying next of kin, but he agreed that nurse is a pain in the—. So I swung by the office and got the info off the admit records." Tom took a moment to smile smugly for out-foxing Amanda.

I grinned with him. "We can be resourceful when we have to."

"That's right. So I call, and guess what?"

I shook my head. "What?"

"The number's wrong. People there never heard of Jason Hilliard."

"That's weird."

Tom snorted again. "I haven't even gotten to the weird part

yet. I tried everything. Had the admitting rep do an Internet search for the contact. Called the phone company. Nothing."

"Is that the weird part?"

He shook his head. "Nope."

He looked around, then took my arm and guided me to a quiet corner where we wouldn't be overheard. By this time, I was really curious.

"What's going on?" I whispered.

"When we couldn't find the contact person," Tom said in a low voice, "we started looking for Hilliard, calling the home number he gave and so forth. Nobody's ever heard of him."

He paused, so I said, "Really?"

"Address is in the middle of Lake Washington."

"You're kidding?"

"Place of employment never heard of him. Nothing on the Internet or directory assistance."

I slowly shook my head and frowned. "So what are you telling me?"

Tom crossed his arms over his barrel chest. "Jason Hilliard doesn't exist."

CHAPTER 5

"What do you mean, he doesn't exist?" Exasperated, I clutched Tom's arm. "The man exists, I know he does. I've received complaints about him. I saw him. He might be dead, but he exists."

The security manager's eyes narrowed. "Whoever you saw was *not* Jason Hilliard. There is no such animal."

I stared at him with disbelief, then I asked, "So, if he wasn't Jason Hilliard, who was he?"

Tom shrugged. "Beats the hell out of me."

I nodded toward the police still investigating the scene. "Do they know?"

Tom shook his head. "Not yet. They'll find out soon enough, I'm sure."

I thought about what this meant for finding the murderer. "According to Susan, this guy's been admitted here a bunch of times. How come we didn't know about this identity thing before?"

"He was private pay," Tom replied. "Wrote a check for his bill when he was discharged."

I took it to the next step. "So no insurance company was involved."

"That's right. If insurance was billed and the guy turned out to be a fake, we'd have been looking at fraud before now."

"Tom, he *was* a fake!" I said.

"You know what I meant," Tom responded.

"I know, but I couldn't resist. Heaven knows we could use something to lighten the mood."

"Well, if you'd stop finding dead bodies, it'd be a lot easier." His lips curved with a hint of a smile.

"Okay, okay." I raised my hands in surrender. "So back to our mystery victim. What about a Social Security number? We ask for that even if insurance isn't involved."

"If we didn't bill insurance, we'd have no reason to verify his number. Now, we can't check until Monday morning when the government offices open, but I'd bet it's false too."

"Did he have any other ID?"

"Don't know that either, but my guess is that everything's a fake."

I frowned as I tried to come up with other possible explanations for this puzzle. "Was it identity theft?"

"Not sure yet. He could have just made it all up."

"Really? But, why?"

Tom shrugged again. At that moment, I spotted Howard and Captain Roberts leaving 3-West. I turned to Tom. "Do you want to tell them?"

He followed my line of vision and sighed heavily. "I don't want to, but someone has to. Might as well get this over with."

He turned back to me and, with a gleam in his eye, said, "I have to admit, I'm real curious what the cops will do with this." As I watched Tom go after the other two men, I considered his parting comment. This information would blow the investigation wide open. From his inattentive interviews, Captain Roberts obviously wanted to start only a cursory investigation until he could turn it over to Pierce. But now . . .

Despite my vow to stay out of this, I had to admit I, too, was more than a little intrigued. Who was Jason Hilliard, really? And who tied that fancy knot around his neck? And then removed it before anyone else saw it? I tried to remember what it looked like, but everything had happened so fast that the image was already fading from my memory. I closed my eyes and tried to recall all the details I could. When I finally returned to my office, I'd sketch it out.

Surely the captain would be more interested in the case when he learned Pierce was unavailable for duty. For now, though, I decided that remaining at the scene of the crime was the worst possible place for me. I needed to be out of sight from the police and the hospital administrators until things settled down.

This was probably a good time to see how Pierce was doing. Maybe he'd have some idea—

No. I wasn't going to get involved, I reminded myself.

I took a back stairwell down one flight to 2-West. As much as I dreaded seeing what Ron had done to Pierce, I knew I was safer with him than on the third floor.

Taking the coward's way out, I stopped at the nurses' station first and waited for someone to return.

"How is Matthew Pierce doing?" I asked the fifty-something nurse when she returned carrying a small tray covered with tiny paper cups, the remains of late afternoon medications.

"Pierce. Pierce," she said, checking her list. "Oh. The new back patient in 213. A charming man."

She looked up at me over half-glasses. "Are you a relative?"

That's the problem with weekend crews. They don't know the weekday players. This wasn't the time to mention I worked there. "No, I'm the friend who brought him in. He hurt his back helping me in the garden."

She set her glasses on the desk. "And you feel terrible for his injury, don't you, dear?"

I swallowed hard and nodded, suddenly unable to speak.

"Well, dear, he's stable and resting as comfortably as can be expected," the nurse said. Her eyes were so full of care and concern that I almost cried right there.

"Can I see him now?"

"I think he'd like that," she said as she turned away to start her next task.

As I approached Pierce's room, I realized she hadn't told me anything about what to expect. Stable and resting as comfortably as can be expected was not encouraging. Taking a deep breath, I peeked around the door into Pierce's room. And gasped.

He was in traction, trussed up to minimize movement so his injured muscles could heal. An overhead frame with a single bar ran the length of the middle of the bed. Above Pierce's chest was a trapeze. He was wearing scrub pants so I could see the stiff canvas corset with straps down each side, more toward his bottom than the sides of his hips. The two traction straps were attached by ropes to pulleys hanging off the end of the bed, with cast iron weights hanging on hangers.

I backed away from the door and leaned against the wall with my eyes closed, feeling incredibly guilty all over again. How could I have let him carry so many heavy bags? I should have insisted we wait for Josh. Or at least borrowed my neighbor's wheelbarrow. Why hadn't I thought of that earlier? I didn't need a public flogging; I could do it to myself mentally with more severity.

He must have heard me because he turned. "Robyn Kelly!" he called. I stepped into the room and tried to avoid his scathing scowl. "This is the *good* news? *This* is better than surgery? Better than going home with pain pills and muscle relaxants and lying on the couch watching sports?"

"Well—"

"You see this . . . this . . . this trapeze thing? Can't use that for a few days—how the hell long am I going to be in here?" His voice was reaching a roar. "I can get up to go to the bathroom. That's it. Three days before I can walk or start physical therapy. And this is better than going home?"

This probably wasn't the time to explain, so I wrung my hands. "Oh, Pierce, I'm so sorry. I'll put Josh on restriction until he's thirty."

"It's not his fault." Pierce looked away and sighed heavily. "It's not your fault, either."

"It's just one of those things?"

He grimaced, but nodded. "Accidents. They happen."

I released the breath I had unconsciously been holding.

"Where've you been, anyway?" he demanded. "I expected you back here hours ago."

"Upstairs. You wouldn't believe—" I stopped. Pierce knew nothing about Jason Hilliard, or whoever he was. Nothing about why I'd gone to see this patient or about finding him dead, or the investigation. Nothing about my convincing Ron to keep him in the hospital where he'd be safe from his boss.

"What wouldn't I believe?" Despite the pain meds, his eyes, full of interest, were now focused intently on me.

"I . . . well . . . it's a long story."

"Rob. In case you haven't noticed," he said, nodding toward his traction apparatus. "I'm not going anywhere for a while."

He was right. He wasn't going anywhere, and sooner or later Captain Roberts would find out where Pierce was. Better for me to tell Pierce everything so he wouldn't be caught by surprise later.

"It started on Friday," I said.

He cocked one eyebrow. "Friday. You mean yesterday?"

Yesterday? It seemed like a lifetime ago. "Uh-huh. I got a call from Susan Wong, the nurse manager on 3-West."

"I remember her. She was the manager last fall when Congressman Hamilton—"

"That's right," I interrupted, uneasy about bringing up that situation again. "Well, she called and said they had a problem with this patient and would I come talk to him."

"What kind of a problem?"

You'd think that with all the things Pierce saw in the course of his work he wouldn't want to know more about human behavior, but he always got a kick out of the situations I was involved in. Maybe it was the different perspective of humanity that appealed to him, the conflict and chaos without the violence—most of the time.

"This patient was a bit of an exhibitionist, shall we say. He liked to let his sheet slip at inopportune moments. At least they were inopportune from the female staff's perspective."

"I see. And what were you supposed to do with him?"

"I was supposed to tell him to knock it off."

A hint of amusement crossed Pierce's face. "And if he followed your instructions and knocked his sheet off while you were there?" There were times when Pierce considered himself quite the comic.

"Very funny," I said. "Actually, I don't know how I would have responded. Laughed?"

Pierce clutched his chest. "Oh, woman, you are cruel!"

I was glad to see him in good humor again, even though I figured that was going to change as soon as he heard the rest of the story.

"So what happened?" Pierce asked.

"He wasn't in his room, and I got involved with another patient and forgot until I was on my way home."

"And you hoped he'd be gone by Monday."

"Given what he was in for, I doubted it, but I suppose in a way, I did. But then I had to come in today," I said with a grimace, "and the dietary manager saw me in the cafeteria and complained that her people had problems with him too, so I figured since you were . . . tied up, shall we say, I'd talk to him."

"How did he respond when you told him to knock it off?"

Pierce was enjoying my potential discomfort much too much.

"Well, I didn't have a chance."

"He'd been discharged?"

"Not . . . exactly." I paused. "He was dead."

Silence hovered like a thunderhead cloud between us. I tried not to squirm under Pierce's eagle-eyed scrutiny and decided it was better if I wasn't the one who spoke first.

"Was this death expected?"

"Not exactly," I said. "But he was dead when I found—"

"*You* found him?" Pierce was incredulous. He grabbed the trapeze bar, jerked himself up, then groaned and flopped back down.

I called for the nurse, who came quickly and repositioned him in his corset. Then she lectured both of us on the importance of not messing with the pelvic tilt, finishing with, "How're his muscles supposed to get well if you keep interfering with the treatment?"

We were quiet for a few minutes after she left, then Pierce asked, "You found another dead body?"

"Uh-huh. He was quite dead when I discovered him. And . . . I made the nurse call the police. I wouldn't let her touch anything either, because with the tubing knotted around his neck, I thought—"

"Jeez, Rob. I can't believe this."

Feeling a bit miserable, I nodded my agreement. It had been bad before, but it sounded so much worse in the retelling, especially to Pierce.

"Who responded to the call?"

"Officer Tomlin."

Pierce rolled his eyes. "Your old friend, huh? Who's investigating?"

When I hesitated, he groaned and said, "No. Don't tell me. It's Captain Roberts, isn't it?"

71

"I thought you didn't want me to tell you."

"Cripes. He hasn't been lead on an investigation in years. Well, at least the rest of the team knows the procedures. They'll keep him on track."

"Well, he did seem in a hurry. When he interviewed me, he didn't let me complete a sentence and he didn't write down a single thing I said."

"You're kidding, right?"

"No. I wish I was. I mean the whole thing seemed pretty sloppy compared to the way you do things."

"I'll take that as a compliment."

I nodded.

Then he asked, "Who else did he interview?"

"The nurse on duty, Amanda Whitcomb. She's a long story by herself." I thought for a minute. "I don't remember him talking to anyone else except Officer Tomlin and the crime scene unit."

"Are you sure he didn't talk to anyone else?"

"Well, he spent a lot of time complaining that you weren't answering your pages, and Officer Tomlin and I agreed we didn't want to be the ones to tell him where you were."

"Thanks. That's going to be one ugly scene when he finds out I'm here."

"That's my doing."

"What? I told you it's not your fault."

"No, I mean your being *here* here. I couldn't let Ron send you home knowing your boss would have you taking over the investigation as soon as he found you home in bed, bad back or not. I've done enough damage for one day. Keeping you here, safe, was the least I could do."

Pierce's sharp gaze softened. "Well, thanks for that. Guess I wouldn't have watched much TV after all."

I laughed at the thought of Pierce goofing off.

"So who else did he talk to?" He was all business now, even trussed up like a chicken ready to be roasted.

"The only other person I saw him talking to was Howard."

"Who's he?"

"Howard Knowles. He's the hospital administrator. I wasn't close enough to hear, but I assume they were talking about how Captain Roberts was going to handle the investigation and the media. Howard wouldn't want 3-West disrupted any more than necessary, and he certainly would want to downplay the story as much as possible. But, I think that's going to be hard to do."

Pierce eyed me. "Why do you say that, other than the obvious?"

"I didn't stay to see what happened, but Tom Geralding—you remember Tom, don't you? He's head of security and—"

"Yeah, yeah." Pierce cut me off with a wave of his hand. "I know Tom."

"He was trying to reach the patient's emergency contact, but the people at that number had never heard of him, and—" I caught Pierce's impatient scowl. "And so, to make a long story short, Tom discovered that the patient wasn't who he said he was, that he doesn't exist. Well, he does—did—exist, but he wasn't who he said he was."

Pierce stared at me with disbelief. "How do you do it, Rob? How do you get yourself involved in these messes?"

"Oh, I'm not involved. Really, I'm not. I've told myself repeatedly that I'm not going to get involved. This isn't my problem. It's a police matter. My job is patient relations, not murder investigation."

"You keep telling yourself that, you hear?" Pierce tried to shift his position. I winced at how uncomfortable he looked. "Okay. So you've got this guy who's in the hospital for?"

I hesitated a moment about confidentiality. Pierce was in no condition to investigate Hilliard's murder—I'd decided I'd call him "the dead man" until we knew who he really was—so technically, I shouldn't share information with Pierce. But he was a police detective, the murder had occurred in his jurisdiction, and if he wasn't here in the hospital, he'd be the lead detective. So did that make it okay? Probably not. "All I can say is that the reason he was here is a long story too."

"Is there anything you do that isn't a long story?"

I smiled at his jab. "I could probably come up with something if I really worked on it, but lately nothing's been short and sweet. You probably don't want to know about the mentally ill man who lives in Central Park, the one in New York City, who showed up in my office yesterday afternoon. In fact, he's the patient I was involved with when I forgot to visit Hilliard and his slipping sheet."

Pierce groaned again and covered his face with the covers. "Take me now, God. Take me before she drives me insane."

Laughing, I reached over and tugged the blanket until Pierce's eyes were revealed. "I'm not that bad."

He pulled the covers down to his chest. "I don't know. Some days, Rob." He shook his head. "Now, back to this Hilliard, or whoever he is—"

"Mom! Matt!" My son, Josh, stood in the doorway, dressed in jeans, UW t-shirt, and the ubiquitous baseball cap. Wide-eyed, he glanced from me to Pierce and back again. He gulped hard and snatched the cap from his head to run his hand through dark brown hair long past the point of needing a trim. His tall, lanky frame was beginning to fill out, and he was the spitting image of his father at that age.

"Come in, Josh." I started to say more, but I caught Pierce's warning glance that I wasn't to say anything that could make Josh feel more guilty than he obviously already was.

"Jeez, Matt. What'd they do to you?"

Pierce pointed to the corset, the pulleys, the weights. "Your mother's doctor friend put me in this to keep me from moving. It's supposed to give the muscles a chance to heal."

Josh eyed the apparatus. "Does it hurt?"

"Naw. I'm on pain medicine. But, let this be a warning to you, son. Don't grow up to be a weekend warrior. Either work out regularly or be a total couch potato."

"Okay." Looking slightly relieved, Josh twisted his cap into an unrecognizable shape. "Is there anything I can do for you?"

"Yeah. Finish your mother's flower beds before I get out of here."

Josh nodded. "Sure. Anything else?"

Pierce frowned in my direction. "Keep an eye on your mother. She's gotten herself involved in another murder."

"Mom!"

"That's not really true. I'm not involved in a murder—"

"No," Pierce inserted. "You just happened to be the one who found a patient who died under mysterious circumstances and whose identity is in question."

"Really?" His eyes wide with intrigue, Josh pulled up a chair and straddled it. "You don't know who he is?"

"Oh, no." Pierce covered his eyes, this time with his hand. "Not you too."

"No, no," Josh said waving his hand. "This is way cool, Matt."

"Josh, this is not way cool," I said in my sternest maternal voice. "This is serious police business, and we are going to let the police handle it."

"Yeah, but Mom, Matt's laid up, so he needs our help."

Pierce whispered, "God save me from armchair detectives."

"Now that's not fair," I said. "Didn't I solve the murder last fall?"

"Yeah, and almost . . . Didn't you learn anything from that?"

I wanted to say, *I learned to be more careful,* but I knew that wasn't what Pierce wanted to hear. "I learned to stay out of police business."

"That's right, and—"

"Well, well. Isn't this cozy."

I turned to see Captain Roberts standing in the doorway. He did not look happy. In fact, if the way he was chomping on his unlit cigar was any indication, he was downright furious. He turned his attention to me. "You're . . ." He snapped his fingers to jog his memory.

"Robyn Kelly."

"That's right. You're the one who found the vic."

I gave Josh a warning look. He jumped up and pushed his chair back into the corner. "Ah, I gotta go," he said in a quiet rush. "I'll see you later." He slipped around Captain Roberts, who didn't so much as glance at my son.

"I should go too." I stood and gestured to my chair. "Would you like to sit here?"

"I won't be that long."

I glanced at Pierce and saw that his face had become an expressionless mask. There was nothing he could do to escape the chewing out he was about to receive. Guilt over my role in that returned full tilt. At least I'd done what I could to protect his back from more harm.

"I'll talk to you later," I said to Pierce and nodded to Captain Roberts as I left the room.

"That woman found the body," I overheard Captain Roberts snap at Pierce. "What the hell's she doing in here with you? And what the hell's wrong with you?"

Pierce's response was too quiet for me to hear, so I headed toward the elevators where Josh stood waiting for me.

"I'm sorry, Mom. I didn't mean to be late."

He looked so utterly miserable, I patted him on the shoulder. "It's okay, Josh. Pierce should be fine in a few days. That traction contraption looks terrible, and Pierce was in a lot of pain before they started the pain meds, but there's no permanent damage. Of course, he'll have to do back exercises from now on, and be really careful how he moves and—"

"Mom! Stop. I get the picture."

"Consider yourself the recipient of the full 'being responsible' lecture."

"Yeah. I got it."

He wore his best hangdog expression and my irritation with him softened. He was a good boy, but he was still a kid. "Okay, go by my office on your way out. Get the Visa card from my wallet and stop at the local hardware store on your way home and buy a wheelbarrow. That will probably save both our backs." When I saw the gleam in his eye, I added, "Just the wheelbarrow, Josh, nothing more."

He pretended he didn't have a clue what I was talking about, but I'd been to the hardware store with him before. Changing the subject, I asked "Where are you off to now?"

"I told Chuck I'd be over to study for Monday's test, but I think I'll ask her to come to our house tonight. I have some yard work to do first."

Chuck was Josh's girlfriend, a very smart, cute-as-a-bug's-ear blonde who'd wrapped my son around her little finger without him realizing it. I wasn't ready for Josh to leave the nest, and I could have bristled with jealous loathing when I first met Chuck, if she hadn't charmed me too. "When you call, invite her to dinner."

Josh brightened. "That'd be great, Mom. Then we won't lose time fixing and—" He saw the look on my face. "I mean, we'd be happy to clean up afterwards."

I nodded my approval. "Don't worry, it'll be something simple. You go on home and get started spreading the bark around the flower beds. Use an upside-down rake to start the spreading, but I want you to use your hands around the plants.

I don't want any pulled out plants or broken branches."

"Aren't you coming home now?"

"I have a few things I need to do first."

Josh eyed me with suspicion. "Mom? Didn't you tell Matt you weren't going to get involved with the murder investigation?"

"I wouldn't dream of getting mixed up in that mess," I said with feigned indignation. "It just so happens, I have another patient I need to check on."

"Yeah. Okay. I'll see you at home then." Josh bent down to kiss my cheek, then slapped his cap against his leg to reshape it and settled it on his head.

We both took the stairs, him going down at a gallop and me trudging up. I did want to check on William again. Really. The fact that his room was near the murder scene was beside the point. I wondered how many times I'd have to repeat that to myself before I believed it.

CHAPTER 6

The congestion of investigators had thinned when I entered the unit. Crime scene tape still cordoned off Hilliard's room, and Officer Tomlin stood guard.

"Officer Tomlin."

"Ms. Kelly."

"Why don't you call me Robyn," I said.

"Okay. Call me Roger. How's Detective Pierce doing?"

"He's going to be laid up for a while." I shook my head. "Unfortunately, your Captain Roberts has found him and was beginning to give Pierce a piece of his mind when I left."

Tomlin looked around, then said in a quiet voice, "Captain Roberts better be careful. He doesn't have a lot of mind to share."

"Roger!"

"It's true." He shrugged. "Well, okay. It's not, but let's just say he's not the easiest guy to work with."

"I figured that. So what's going on here?"

"The crime scene crew did its thing. The body's on its way to the M.E. for an autopsy."

"Anything interesting about the victim?" I asked.

"I probably shouldn't say anything, but seeing's how you're the one who found him, and you're a friend of Detective Pierce's I guess it's okay to tell you that I heard there's some question about his identity."

I nodded. "He called himself Jason Hilliard, but so far, all of his ID is fake."

Roger's jaw dropped and his eyes widened. "How did you know that?"

"I have my sources, Officer." I grinned. "A hospital is just one giant information sieve, you know."

"I guess! That's amazing. I mean you weren't even here when the captain got the news. Boy, was he pi—I mean, he was really angry."

"I don't suppose they have any idea who did it?"

Roger shook his head. "Not yet. The captain didn't want any speculation as to the cause before the autopsy either."

"Remember when I showed you the body? When I first found Hilliard, he had IV tubing tied around his throat. It was in some kind of odd-looking knot. I'd never seen anything like it before," I said

"Not the usual Boy Scout square, huh?"

"No, nothing like that, or any of the ones we used on my parents' ranch when I was a kid."

"Hmmm. That could turn out to be an important clue, Robyn. Did you mention it to Captain Roberts?"

"Believe me, I tried to tell him, but he wasn't interested in anything I had to say. He didn't even take notes."

"Why am I not surprised? He was probably treading water until he could turn it over to Detective Pierce. Have you mentioned it to him?"

"Oh, yes. I've been absolutely, positively, no room for discussion forbidden to even think about the case, and it wouldn't be fair to tease an immobile man with a tantalizing clue like a fancy knot."

"Okay. But don't forget what that knot looked like."

"I'll draw a picture of it, I promise. But that won't be much help either. My artistic talent is nonexistent. Well, I'd better check on my other patient. Are you going to be here long?"

"I hope not." He grinned. "I'm supposed to be off shift at six o'clock, and I have plans."

"Well, I hope nothing happens to change those plans." I left him then and took the long way around to William's room rather than the short cut through the family meeting room.

William's room was empty, so I went to the nurses' station, dreading another encounter with the unpleasant Amanda. Instead, I found Susan.

Surprised, I asked, "What are you doing here?"

She scowled at me. "Oh, that Paula. She called and insisted I come in. For what?" She raised her arms in exasperation. "The pervert is dead. The police are gone. The fill-in nurse is off shift. The swing-shift crew is working. So why am I here?"

Swallowing my amusement, I said, "I just asked you that."

Susan scowled at me again. "Paula talks a good line, but between you and me, when a real problem comes up, that woman can punt better than a pro-football kicker."

"Slicker than Teflon?"

"You got it." She sighed heavily. "So, here we go again, huh? My unit. You find the body. Jeez, Rob, what's with us?"

"I don't think it's anything to do with us, Susan. We're just lucky to be in the right place at the wrong time, I guess."

"Well, I could do with a whole lot less luck," she grumbled. "Or maybe have the luck transferred to the Lotto. The jackpot's up to fifteen million bucks. I've got five tickets. If I'm not here on Monday, you'll know why."

"I better buy some on my way home. By the way, the reason I'm here—"

"You want the latest scoop on the murder."

"No, I know all I want to about that, maybe even more. But I promised Detective Pierce that I'd stay out of it, cross my heart and everything. No, I'm here to see William Jones, but he's not in his room."

At the change of subject, Susan's expression softened. "One of the aides took him to the solarium upstairs. He was still upset about the police and everything, so Jeannie thought he'd like to see the plants and waterfalls."

"That was nice of her. I'm sure he'll like that, especially since he's from Central Park." I hesitated, then said, "He's really a nice man, in spite of his problems."

Susan nodded. "I know what you mean. He was really scary at first, but he's so polite. He's like a frightened child."

"That's a good analogy. You know," I said, settling comfortably against the counter, "when I visited him right before I found Hilliard's body, he kept talking about 'the money.' 'It's always the money,' he said. Has someone from the office been up here bothering him about payment?"

Susan shook her head. "If they did, it was before I arrived. They can be doggedly persistent when it comes to collecting a patient's financial information. All their little blanks have to be filled in, even if it says 'none.' "

"Hmmm. Well, it seems that they filled in all of Hilliard's blanks, and the answers were all wrong."

Susan's eyes narrowed. "Uh-oh, Rob. You've got that look in your eye."

"What look?"

"*That* look. The one that says you can't stand having a blank space either." She looked around, then whispered, "Are you going to investigate Hilliard's murder?"

"No!" I quickly lowered my voice. "I know better than that. It's a police matter."

"Sure it is," Susan said smugly, crossing her arms over her chest. "And you never get involved in anything that isn't strictly your business."

"Okay, so I'm the most blatant in-house snoop. That's my job. But admit it. You want to know the deal with Hilliard as much as I do."

"Sure. I'll admit it. But I'm not going to do anything about it."

I took that as a challenge, throwing down the gauntlet. Indignant, I said, "I'm not either. In fact, I'm going home now, and I'm fixing dinner for my son and his girlfriend, and I'll listen to them discuss engineering stuff while I start this really good book I've been wanting to read for weeks."

"Sounds great." She eyed me knowingly and smirked. "Be sure to let me know when you have some new clues."

Rolling my eyes, I left then, determined to keep my word to Pierce not to get involved. Well, maybe I'd check Josh's *Boy Scout Handbook* to see if I could identify the knot. Otherwise, I could—and would—stay out of it. It wasn't as if I had a dearth of other things to do. My to-do list was a mile long, both at home and here at work. I'd have no trouble staying away from the murder investigation.

No trouble at all.

And yet, still I wondered: who was Jason Hilliard?

Monday morning came much too soon. Intent on going to work early, I made a beeline for the kitchen. But in the dining room, I tripped.

"What the—?" I'd stumbled over a soggy piece of wallboard.

Dismayed, I'd looked up to see a gaping hole in the ceiling, wet insulation hanging over the edge. Rain water dripped on my face. I stepped away, and the carpet squished under my feet. Had I been so busy and distracted shuttling between my house, Pierce's condo, and the hospital in a constant downpour, that I didn't notice the ceiling had a growing wet spot.

A murdered patient, Pierce's back, and now a leaky roof? What had I done to deserve this? Or was it all a delayed full moon–Friday the 13th?

Muttering under my breath, I looked up the number for the contractor who'd done my kitchen remodel and built my deck. As I punched in his number, I didn't have much hope. Every contractor in Western Washington was busy after all the spring storms. When Nathan answered his cell phone, he was driving to another client's house, but said my house was on the way. He'd swing by in a few minutes to assess the damages.

Was that the universe's way of countering all the other disasters I'd faced this weekend? I said a fervent thank you to whoever was responsible.

My hopes were quickly dashed when Nathan climbed up his ladder, shaking his head. When he pulled a screwdriver out of his pocket, I shoved Taffy into the kitchen and closed the door, then scrambled to pull the table and chairs out of the way. Seconds later, the floor where they'd stood was covered in saturated wallboard and insulation.

"How does it look," I asked weakly.

"Not good, Robyn. Not good at all." Nathan enlarged the hole and pulled a flashlight out of another pocket. He shined it up to the roof. "See this?"

I looked but saw only a plywood sheet. "Yes. And that means . . . ?

He climbed down from the ladder. "You go up." He gestured for me to climb the ladder.

I don't like high places, and I don't do ladders, but I figured this was important. When my head reached the ceiling, he handed me the flashlight.

"Go up two more rungs."

I really didn't like this, but I gingerly climbed up the two more steps.

"Shine the light along the roof."

From this proximity, even I could tell the plywood was soaked for at least the ten feet illuminated by the flashlight. Not good at all. I climbed down and stepped away from the ladder. "What do you think?"

Nathan shook his head again. "It's bad, Robyn. I'll have to climb up on the roof to be sure, but you've had that leak for a long time. Probably dry rot. The whole thing on this side may have to be torn out and replaced. If we're lucky, the trusses are okay. Otherwise, we'll have to replace the whole roof, not just this side."

I was speechless. A new roof? Where was I supposed to find the money for that?

"When was this house built?" Nathan was back on the ladder, up to his waist above the ceiling. Or, where the ceiling was supposed to be.

"Mid-eighties, I think." A new roof?

He grunted. "Well, at least we don't have to worry about asbestos abatement. That gets really expensive."

"But . . . but, how did this happen?"

Nathan climbed back down. "All those high winds we've had for years? Probably got under a shingle so rain got in under it, and then it spread from there."

"How much is it going to cost?"

"I'll have to take measurements, and get a close look at the trusses. But your insurance may cover it."

"Oh, I hadn't thought of that."

"I'll have my guys come by and start tearing it out."

"But—"

He smiled. "Don't worry, we'll use tarps so nothing else is damaged. I'll have to check everything to be sure we find all the water damage. No point replacing part of the roof and leave dry rot someplace else. Next thing you know, you'll have termites and carpenter ants moving in—"

Bugs in my attic? I shuddered.

"—I'll take some measurements before I leave and get you an

estimate for your insurance company by tomorrow."

Nathan went out the front door. In the pouring rain, he pulled out his tape measure. I didn't want to watch him poke and prod my roof, so I returned to the dining room. Looking at all the debris, I realized it couldn't stay there with Taffy home all day. I quickly changed out of my work clothes and cleaned the mess up. If only the roof would be fixed as quickly as I'd filled the garbage bags.

By the time I sloshed through the employee parking lot puddles, I was late. The view from my office showed that the spring rain that started Saturday night now threatened to flood the patient and visitor parking lot downhill from the hospital.

Shaking my head, I started shifting the files on top of my desk into priority order. Connie and Margie returned with fresh coffee, ready to share weekend stories.

"Good morning, Rob," Margie said when I stepped from my office to greet them. A statuesque African-American woman in her mid-thirties, she seemed particularly animated this morning.

I took the fresh latté Connie offered and leaned against her desk. "How was everyone's weekend?"

"Forget the weekend." Margie leaned towards me with avid curiosity. "What's going on with this murder thing? What do you know?"

"I told you that man was bad news," Connie grumbled.

I laughed at Margie's quizzical look toward Connie before I responded. "Connie, you told me Susan Wong's call was bad news."

"And I was right, wasn't I? I keep telling you I have psychic abilities, but you never believe me," Connie said.

"It's not that we don't believe you, honey," Margie said soothingly. "It's just that your pronouncements are a little vague. But getting back to more important issues. Rob, what have you heard about the murder? The police spokesman on TV would only say they're investigating. He wouldn't even say who the victim was, just a young white male. Your Detective Pierce must be up to his eyeballs in it."

"Well, no." I gave them a thumbnail sketch of how Saturday started and then worked my way up to the unexpected trip to the ER. "Ron Downing admitted Pierce and put him in traction for at least a week."

"Oh, no!" Connie exclaimed. "He's here now?"

I nodded, then took a deep breath. "That's not the worst of it. I'm the one who discovered the murder victim."

Margie gasped. "Rob!"

"Again?" Connie squeaked.

They besieged me with questions. When I had them quieted down, I told them most of what I knew about the murder, which wasn't much. I didn't go into detail about the knot, which I'd checked but hadn't found in Josh's old *Boy Scout Handbook*. Nor did I say anything about Jason Hilliard not being Jason Hilliard. Although I trusted my staff implicitly to be discreet, if the police weren't sharing that bit of news, then it wasn't my place to share it, either.

"So who do you think did it?" Margie asked.

"I haven't a clue. I mean last time we had an abundance of suspects to choose from, but this time . . ." I shook my head. "There was hardly anyone on the floor Saturday afternoon."

Connie closed her eyes and started to sway from side to side and hum softly. I glanced at Margie, who had no patience with anything "woo-woo." She rolled her eyes, and I could tell it was taking all her efforts to not laugh out loud.

"Connie?"

Connie continued swaying and humming as if in a trance.

"Connie?" I asked, a bit louder this time.

"Shhh." She weaved and hummed for a few more seconds, then slowly opened her eyes. "I'm visualizing who did it. I think it was that registry nurse."

Margie looked askance at the proclamation. "Really? And what made you choose her?"

"Bad karma," Connie announced.

"If that's all it took to be guilty of murder, I'd vote for her too," I said. "However, I promised Pierce that I wouldn't get involved. Seriously," I added when their faces fell. "He keeps reminding me it's not my job, and with him in traction, he can't protect me from the murderer, or from his boss who is a real piece of work."

We threw out ideas of who might have "dunnit," some totally ridiculous. I sensed again that Margie was bubbling over with excitement. This was about more than the murder. My attention was drawn to the elaborately slow way she turned her hand as she set her coffee cup down. Her left hand sparkled.

"Margie? Do you have something to tell us?"

"I can't believe it took you two this long." A smile spread slowly across her face as she waved her hand in front of us. "I'm engaged!"

Connie and I squealed and jumped up to hug her and to take a closer look at the ring. The emerald-cut diamond was huge, the largest I'd ever seen, but somehow it didn't look ostentatious on Margie's long, slender finger.

"Tell us everything," I demanded. "All the details!"

Margie beamed. "Well, you know I've been dating Terence for a while. Terence Parnell," she finished with a dreamy sigh. "He's the most gorgeous hunk of manhood you ever laid your eyes on." She looked at me and added, "And he's got a good job too. He's vice-president of marketing for a local seafood company."

I laughed. Of course Margie would pick a good-looking guy

who could also afford her. She wasn't extravagant, but the girl had expensive tastes. "Have you set a date yet?"

"He wants to get married right away, but I told him I'm only getting married once so we're going to do everything right, and a fancy wedding takes months to plan, which puts us into the holiday season, and you know how hard it is to reserve places for a reception."

"I'm sure you'll come up with something wonderful," I said.

The phone rang, and Connie answered it. "Rob, it's for you. Katie Caldwell."

I stepped into my office to take the call. "Hi, Katie. How're you this morning?"

"Fine. I'm calling about William Jones. Susan said I should talk to you about his discharge plans."

"Sure. I haven't seen him yet this morning. I'll come over now and spend a few minutes with him, then meet you in Susan's office?"

"That's great. I'll make some phone calls while I'm waiting."

I grabbed my notebook, pen, and notes for my meeting with Howard and headed out. "Sorry I can't hear more, Margie. Duty calls." I gave her a big hug. "I'm really happy for you. You'll tell me the rest later?"

"Girl, you're going to be hearing me blabber on and on about my wedding for the next six months." She hoisted her cup. "Here's to me and Mr. Parnell."

Her eyes took on a faraway look, so uncharacteristic of her that Connie and I looked at each other in alarm.

"I'll keep an eye on her," Connie whispered.

"Good. I'll be on 3-West and then Admin if you need me."

CHAPTER 7

I crossed the waiting area off the elevators and went to William's room, stopping at the doorway. The room looked different. It took me a moment to realize it was the pictures, three more pictures on the walls than the usual patient room. I had to admit, the room looked better. Was that a good thing?

Then I turned my attention to William, who was sitting in bed with the TV remote in his hand, scrolling through the channels at breakneck speed. An alternative to his gaze bouncing around the room?

"Good morning, William."

Even though I'd spent time with him on Saturday and Sunday since his admission, he still had to stop and think about who I was. My Irish grandmother used to say, "Castles are built stone by stone." I'd have to be patient with William.

He finally smiled in recognition before turning back to the TV. I hoped it wasn't one of those confrontational talk shows.

"I ain't never seen nothing like this before, Miz Robyn. People talkin' like this to each other. Don't seem right for them to be doing it front of all those other people."

Oh, dear, it was one of those shows. Still I was pleased to see him respond so well to good food and medication. He still had a childlike innocence about him, but he seemed more connected. "Is that so? What do you think of it?"

William shook his head. "I don't rightly know. They's good actors. Still shouldn't be talkin' that way."

The concept of reality shows was probably too much for him. "How are you feeling today?"

"I'm doing okay. The nurses, they still look at my leg, but they don't hurt it none anymore."

"I'm glad to hear that." I took a moment to straighten his bed covers. "Are the nurses doing anything else?"

He lifted his arm to show me the IV connection. "They still put stuff in here."

I looked around the room. With the flowers and extra pictures, the room was cozier compared to other occupied rooms. The nurses may have brought the bouquets, but where did he find the pictures? He didn't have them on Friday. I knew homeless people often collected things that no one else wanted, moving them from place to place in shopping carts. This appeared to be more like nesting, turning a sterile-looking space into a little home. Well, why not? He would be here a few days.

"Can I get you anything?"

"No. I'm okay." A delighted expression crossed his face. "Miz Robyn, yesterday a nice lady took me to the park. It had a waterfall and lots of pretty plants."

I smiled. "That was nice for you."

He shook his head as if puzzled. "But I don't think it was outside. How can a park be inside?"

"It's not a real park, William, not like Central Park where you live. It's a pretend one for patients who can't go outside."

He thought about that. "Oh."

"I need to see someone else now, but I'll be back."

William frowned, and I saw confusion cross his face. "The money man, he ain't coming back, is he?"

My heart sank. So much for progress. "No, William. The money man won't bother you."

"I don't know how I'm gonna pay for this hotel. It's got to be expensive."

"Don't worry about that, William. I'll take care of it."

He nodded, but his mind was already someplace else as he started channel surfing again.

I left his room to find Katie, a discharge planner. Her job was to find ways to move patients out of the hospital as quickly as possible. Medicare defined what services it would pay for in a hospital. Once a patient no longer needed a certain level of care from registered nurses, Medicare refused to pay any more hospital bills for that patient. Other insurance carriers had quickly adopted the same standards. In response, hospitals became more assertive about moving patients out when they no longer needed "acute" care, sending them either to nursing homes for "skilled" or "custodial" care, or, if it was safe to do so, to their own homes.

I had a feeling my meeting with Katie was going to be an interesting discussion: what to do with William. Rounding the corner to the nurses' station, I found Katie sitting at the computer, updating a patient's medical record. "Catching up on your charting?"

"Hmm?" She looked up. "Yeah. Even with notes, if I don't do my write-ups promptly on really busy days, some of the patients blur together in my mind."

"I can see how that would happen. You wanted to talk about William?"

"Ah, yes, Mr. Jones." She closed the medical records file she'd been working on and entered the keystrokes to open a list of 3-West's current patients, then clicked on William's name. "Here he is. Interesting case."

Katie's understatement amused me. "Uh-huh."

As Katie scanned William's records, she said, "I talked to Dr. Transel this morning and since the wound is healing so nicely, we could discharge him tonight with oral antibiotics."

"But?"

Katie shook her head. "I'm not sure what to do with him, Robyn. He's homeless with no family, and has an underlying mental health condition that would interfere with him taking his meds like he's supposed to. That's simply not a safe discharge plan. Not by anybody's standards."

We had time. I breathed a silent sigh of relief. "I suppose you're checking with the outpatient mental health clinics?"

"Oh, yes, and my counterparts at the downtown hospitals. They deal with these patients all the time. We really don't have the community resources in Madrona Bay like they do in Seattle and some other parts of King County." Katie leaned back in her chair to look up at me. "Do you have any suggestions?"

"I'm afraid not," I said, shaking my head. "All I can tell you is that since he's been admitted, he's having more moments of being connected, mentally. But you should have seen him when he showed up in my office on Friday afternoon."

Katie laughed. "I bet that was a surprise!"

I smiled and shrugged. "On a full-moon, Friday the 13th? Nothing surprises me on those days."

"Isn't that the truth." Katie closed the file and signed off the computer. "By the way, have you visited Mr. Jones lately?"

I nodded. "I just came from there."

"That's quite a decorating job he's doing."

"I figured the flowers came from the nurses. Left behinds?"

"No, I don't think so."

That stopped me for a moment. "Where else would he be getting them from?"

"Well . . . I think he's finding the flowers himself."

"But how? He's attached to an IV."

"He's getting out of the room somehow."

"Same with the pictures?"

"Pictures? I didn't know about them."

"At least three that shouldn't be there," I told her.

93

"Uh-oh. I hope he doesn't get too settled in. At some point, we're going to have to discharge Mr. Jones out into the real world again. In the meantime, I'll keep looking for something to do with him. He'll be here for at least another day or two."

"Thanks." I glanced at my watch. "Right now I have to keep an appointment with Howard, then go see a patient on 2-West."

"Another problem?"

"Not in the way you mean. It's a friend of mine who hurt his back helping me."

"2-West. Back." Katie looked askance. "Oh, the police detective?"

I nodded.

"He's the one who investigated that murder last fall."

"He's the one."

"I don't suppose he's investigating this one." She nodded down the hall toward Jason Hilliard's room, which was still sealed with yellow tape.

"Not while he's in traction. And neither am I," I added quickly. "Keep me posted on William?"

"I'll let you know what I come up with for Mr. Jones," Katie promised.

On my way to the first floor, I tried to convince myself that what I'd told Katie was true: I was not involved with the murder investigation. But deep inside, I had to be honest. I was dying to find out what was going on.

When I entered the Admin suite and approached my boss's office, I tapped on his open door to get his attention. "Hi, Howard."

Howard had been our administrator for about four months. Before that, he'd been our Chief Financial Officer. What he didn't know about budgets didn't exist. Even though he was a "bean-counter" extraordinaire, Howard was an extroverted teddy-bear of a man. Quick to smile and quick to compliment, it didn't take him long to earn the loyalty of those who reported directly to him, including me.

Howard's transformation of the administrator's office from a stark, sterile environment to one that welcomed and provided numerous distractions still made me smile. Tall potted plants sat in the corners. Vines overflowed pots hanging from the ceiling, draping themselves over the tops of file cabinets and around photographs of men doing manly things, GIs and loggers mostly. The sun-lit room had a jungle feel. Away from the plants, a credenza stood under the window, but piles of paper and folders threatened to block the view. He even had a collection of wind-up toys on his desk. I appreciated the lived-in look, which was much like my own office. My office, however, was considerably smaller.

He glanced up at my greeting, and his round face broke into a dazzling smile. "Robyn! Thanks for coming." He pointed to a chair next to his conference table.

As I sat down, I hid my amusement. This was our regular weekly meeting, yet Howard made it seem like I was doing him a big favor. No wonder everyone loved him.

"How's it going?" He came around his desk and joined me at the table.

"Oh, the usual," I said, then gave him a brief summary of what we were working on. Howard liked numbers, so I always brought him a sheet with statistics he could play with, and I handed that to him. "You'll see we're down in most of the service complaint categories, but with summer coming and the orthopedists blocking out time for their annual conference and vacations, their surgery wait times are growing."

He frowned at the numbers, then at me. "You make it sound like this is an expected thing."

I laughed. "Oh, it is. This year I'd like to do something different. We need to implement the fixes now, not in August when it's a crisis and patients are screaming at my staff."

"What can I do to help?"

God, I loved working for this man. "I'm going to send a memo to Larry," I said, referring to Dr. Larry Bridgeway, our Chief of Staff, "reminding him how we go through this every year and suggesting we start the solution now rather than waiting. It's really a medical staff issue, but when there are problems, it overflows onto the rest of us. If you could reinforce the idea of doing something now, I'd appreciate it."

"Consider it done." Howard leaned over to grab a bright blue sticky-note pad off his desk. He scribbled on the top sheet, peeled it off the pad and slapped it on the table next to a long line of sticky-notes in different colors.

When Howard first took over as administrator, he'd intrigued everyone with his sticky-note system. Different colors for different subjects. Blues were medical staff issues, reds were administrative. Greens were budget, of course. The color intensity indicated the priority. The bright blue he'd used for my request meant I could truly consider it done.

"Now." He turned his intense gaze on me, and I realized his eyes were the same shade of blue as the sticky note. Funny the things you notice over time. "Anything else?"

"Something happened on Friday afternoon that I think you should be aware of." I explained about the contract physician's attempt to transfer William to another hospital. "I'm going to call Larry about it too."

"I don't like that at all, Robyn. Don't get me wrong, financial solvency is paramount to achieving our mission, but we can't dump patients."

"I hoped you'd see it that way. William has his problems, but he's doing so much better since he was admitted."

Howard nodded. "Good. Is he still here?"

"Katie Caldwell is working on finding a safe discharge plan.

We can't let him go back on the streets until that wound is healed enough that he doesn't need antibiotics."

"Makes sense. Now, there are two things I need to discuss with you."

"Sure," I settled back in my chair now that my issues had been dealt with.

"The first is this unfortunate . . ." He sighed. "This murder thing. I'm telling all the managers that they are to continue as normal."

My expression must have shown my surprise because Howard raised his hand and said, "I know, I know. That sounds impossible. But the fact of the matter is, we all have plenty of real work to do to keep this hospital running, and we don't need to be diverted, either our time or our attention, by things beyond our control."

"I understand that—"

"Robyn, I know you found the victim. And I know you were very involved in the investigation last fall when I was away on vacation, and I know you did an excellent job of helping the police identify the murderer. But I've had several meetings with Captain Roberts, and I'm quite confident he can handle this investigation without our help."

It took all my willpower not to leap from my chair and repeat Pierce's assessment of Captain Roberts's handling of the case so far. Instead, I held my relaxed pose, nodded, and kept my mouth shut.

"If Captain Roberts asks you for information, then of course, you're to cooperate," Howard continued. "Otherwise, we are to let the police department handle this their own way." He paused, and then smiled. "Now, as for the second item I wanted to discuss with you. Things are so crazy right now with the investigation and the media and the Board of Directors, that I'm having trouble finishing a couple of things." He ran his fingers through his almost non-existent brown hair. "That's why I really needed to meet with you today."

Let's face it, everyone wants to be needed. I was ready to agree to anything to help this guy. "What is it you want?"

"I really hate to do this to you, especially on such short notice." He stood up, crossed the room to the walnut credenza, and picked up a twelve inch stack of papers piled on top of it. Dropping it on the table in front of me, he said, "It's the quarterly Quality Committee Report, Robyn. It's supposed to be sent out to the members this Wednesday, and I have your section, but my part of it is a mess. Here's all the raw data. It needs to be organized and all that qualitative stuff needs to be written, the things you're probably well aware of from our management meetings. Can you do it for me?"

I looked at Howard in dismay. The Quality Committee was a volunteer community group that reviewed different aspects of medical care and service and how well we did them. Howard was right, I probably could write a big chunk of his section with little trouble, but that wasn't my biggest concern.

Swallowing hard, I asked, "You'll make the presentation, though, right?"

"I may need your help with that too. A lot of this is all new to me and I won't know the answers to the Committee's non-budget questions the way you would."

I thought long and hard. Certainly there were other managers who reported directly to Howard more than capable of doing this, but he'd asked me, which was very flattering. Still . . .

"Look, Howard, I need to level with you. I'll write the report, but I don't think it'd be such a good idea for me to attend the meeting. You see, the chair, Samantha Duke, doesn't like me or my department—"

"Why?" Howard asked. "Is it something I can straighten out?"

I gave him a wry smile. "Thanks for the offer, but it's a bit complicated. Essentially, I investigated a complaint filed by her sister-in-law and we found no grounds for her accusations. Since then, Samantha has accused my department of protecting the medical staff, of cover-ups and all that."

"Can't you talk to her about it?"

"No."

Howard eyed me, then said, "Must be mental health stuff."

His shrewdness impressed me, but even though he was right, I couldn't respond to him without violating patient confidentiality.

"Okay," Howard said. "We'll cross that bridge when we come to it. Right now, I really need the written report ready to courier to the committee on Wednesday. Can you get it to me Tuesday? Arlene will splice it in with the other sections."

"Of course, Howard. Anything for you," I said with a sigh.

Howard beamed at me, and I had to laugh. Shaking my head, I said, "You sure have a way about you. I wouldn't be surprised if you were a carny in a past life."

He chuckled. "I wouldn't be surprised, either. But thanks, Robyn. I really appreciate it."

"If you don't have anything else for me," I said as I picked up the pile of papers, "I better haul this upstairs and get started."

"That'd be great, Robyn." Howard patted my shoulder. "I owe you one."

I turned and gazed at him with a gimlet eye. "I'll remember that at performance review time."

On that cheery note, we parted, Howard heading for his next meeting and me back to my office to see what disasters had befallen us in the past hour.

How in the world I was ever going to weave this new project into an already overwhelming schedule?

Weary and a bit exasperated, I returned from my third visit to

William and realized the morning was basically gone. He seemed to need reassurance every hour that the money man wouldn't hurt him. I'd seen no new additions to his room, so whenever he found them, it wasn't during the day. I doubted he was mentally stable enough for me to probe, and since no one had complained about missing items, I didn't raise the subject. Besides, although I'd grown genuinely fond of William, I was so far behind in the rest of my work that I seriously considered not answering my phone for what was left of the day.

Giving up on accomplishing anything more, I stopped by my office to get the bags of things I'd picked up for Pierce at his condo and went to see him.

I'd been to Pierce's home a few times before, but never without him. The furnishings were definitely masculine: dark leather and overstuffed. Comfortable and good quality. Without the wear and tear of kids or pets. The coffee table was littered with law enforcement journals. A few well-chosen prints, which I wouldn't have minded having, of Pacific Northwest forests and the coastline adorned the butterscotch walls. Old family photos rested on the mantel over a used brick fireplace. Sturdy houseplants that thrived on benign neglect flourished in the corners. I knew he had a housecleaner, so the lack of dust didn't surprise me.

While there, I'd taken a moment to decide what the place said about him.

Solid.

Dependable.

Content being single.

Which was fine with me. I had no burning desire to be seriously involved with any man. I had a career I loved, a son who was almost out the door, and a house I owned more of than the bank, thanks to a hot real estate market in the years since I'd moved here from New York. I could come and go when I wanted, spend a day lounging in my PJs with no make-up, or fix only a sandwich for dinner, if that's what I chose.

Besides, Pierce and I had developed a companionable relationship that was comfortable and low maintenance. If he was involved with a case or I was busy with work or friends, and we didn't hear from each other for a week, that was okay. If either of us needed an escort for an official event, we had one. His impromptu lunch invitation on Saturday was typical. But I still cringed at how that day had unraveled.

On my first trip to his condo, I'd collected his pocket calendar and address book. Another trip was to pick up some books he'd asked for and a CD player.

I figured that at some point he'd want the backlog of work collected from the police station. Just because he was laid up didn't mean his brain had slowed down. He was trying to do everything he normally did, but without moving. I'd leave the work stuff for him to settle with Captain Roberts, who continued to annoy the hospital staff on both 3-West and 2-West, as well as Pierce himself.

I'd also checked the refrigerator to see what was growing and wasn't shocked to find two shriveled oranges, a past-pull-date yogurt, and something mysterious, and undoubtedly toxic, growing in a clear plastic container that I didn't even bother to open before throwing out. The dishwasher was half-full of dirty dishes, so I started it before I left.

Dr. Ron had pronounced that, except for visits with Physical Therapy and occasional brief walks around the unit starting on Tuesday, Pierce would be confined to a hospital bed for at least a week to see if the conservative treatment worked. As if the traction device could be called conservative by anyone who saw it. Pierce was nice enough to the nurses and other hospital staff; he saved all his glowering and grumpiness for me, which I supposed was only fair.

When I knocked and entered Pierce's room, I was surprised to find Officer Tomlin, dressed in uniform, talking with Pierce.

"Hi, guys," I handed Pierce the bag of books and CDs. "Have you solved the murder yet?"

"No," Pierce grumbled. "Did you find that knot?"

"No. I told you yesterday I looked in Josh's *Boy Scout Handbook,* and I haven't had time to check any other sources."

"Well, Roger here has come up with a disturbing piece of information."

CHAPTER 8

I tried not to let my curiosity show too much as I pulled a chair next to Roger's and sat down. "Really? What is it?"

"Rob," Pierce warned.

"Oh, shush." I gave him a "be quiet" gesture. "I'm not going to do anything with whatever he tells me. I just want to know."

Pierce scowled at me, and I saw Roger's mouth quiver as he suppressed a grin.

Pierce waved the officer on. "Go ahead. She's going to find out soon enough anyway." Pierce turned and shook his finger at me. "But, Rob, you have to promise not to tell anyone, okay?"

"You know you can trust me." When Pierce hesitated, I said, "Tell me."

"Your security guy called Captain Roberts this morning," Roger said. "Someone in the business office had told him the victim had left stuff in the safe."

This wasn't surprising news. A lot of patients did. I wondered if he was going anywhere with this. "Okay. Hilliard left stuff in the safe. That's why we have the safe."

"Well, your security guy—"

"Tom Geralding?" I inserted.

"Yeah, Geralding. He went to the office to check it out. Seems the captain forgot to do that on Saturday." Roger glanced at Pierce, who was scowling and muttering under his breath about incompetence.

This time, I was the one who swallowed a smile. The captain's handling of the case was driving Pierce crazy, and there was nothing he could do about it. "Tom must have found something interesting."

"Yeah. In addition to the things you'd expect to find, like wallet and keys, there was a sealed canvas bag."

"Really?" Now my curiosity was piqued.

Roger obviously enjoyed storytelling and knew how to build the suspense with dramatic pauses. He leaned forward and whispered, "The bag had fifty thousand dollars cash in it."

"Fifty—" I squeaked.

"Shhh!" came from Pierce.

I grabbed Roger's arm and looked from him to Pierce and back again. "Fifty thousand dollars?" I hissed.

They both nodded. "As soon as Geralding realized it was a large sum of money," Pierce said, "he called Captain Roberts, who told Roger to witness the counting and bring everything back to the station."

I turned my attention to Roger. "You counted it?"

"Oh, yes, ma'am," he said with a broad grin. "It was twenties and fifties, mostly old bills."

"Where is it now?"

"After Geralding and I counted it, I sealed the canvas bag." He held up a paper grocery sack that had been sitting on the floor next to him. "He gave me this so I could take the money bag without it being seen. I'm taking it to the station where it'll be put into the evidence room."

"Good idea," I murmured.

"Yeah, and I thought it wise to show the detective here so it doesn't get overlooked in the captain's investigation," Roger said. "Well, I better go so I can get back on the street. See you guys later."

After he left, I turned to Pierce. "What do you think?"

Pierce frowned. "I think there is something very strange about this case, Rob. We still don't know Hilliard's real identity. Roberts should be there when the M.E. does the autopsy—which hasn't happened yet because Roberts didn't make it a priority. What's he thinking? But he should be there to get the fingerprints from the M.E. and take them straight to the county lab and make it a priority. Otherwise, the prints may sit in the backlog."

Pierce rattled his traction. "This is driving me crazy. If a murder isn't solved in the first forty-eight hours, the chances of solving it go way down. The captain might be a pain in the ass, but he was a topnotch investigator in his day. I don't get it. He's screwing up this case so bad, what with his interview with you, a delayed autopsy, no identity, and now this bag. And that's just what we know about! But with Nash on vacation, there's no one else to take over."

"Is there anything I can do to help?" I expected an immediate rejection to my offer.

"Let me think about it, Rob."

He wanted to think about it? That surprised me. I left him then, looking like he was struggling to make a decision.

I decided to have my very late lunch with Pierce. He hadn't come out and said he wanted me involved in the investigation, but talking over the murder seemed to help him feel less useless. And, while I held to my resolve to stay out of it, it was exciting to watch his mind work.

"So, what do we know so far?" Pierce frowned as he suspiciously poked a fork at the mystery meat on his tray.

I munched on my chicken Caesar salad and swallowed before answering. "We still don't know what kind of knot was used, but I'll get on it, I promise," I added when he scowled at me.

"What else?"

"We know that Jason Hilliard is not who he said he was, but

we don't know his true identity."

"He's been in here several times since the first of the year," Pierce added.

"Right. For a recurring staph infection that we're reasonably confident he was causing deliberately."

Pierce thought for a moment. "It's as if he *wanted* to be admitted to the hospital. Why would that be?"

"For the food?" I quipped.

"Not hardly," Pierce said in disgust, flipping the napkin across his food tray. "Not unless his taste buds were dead."

"Come on, it's not that bad." I ceased protesting when he cast a withering glare at my take-out box from a nearby restaurant. "Do you have any ideas?"

"Let's think about the commonalities. Was he always assigned to the third floor?"

"Probably. It's the medical wing with some surgery cases, while the unit you're on has the orthopedic cases and the rest of the surgery cases."

"What else do his stays have in common?"

"From what Susan Wong has said, he had the same doctor each time. Dr. Transel."

"What's he like?" Pierce asked.

"Nice guy. Good doc." I shrugged. "His patients love him."

"I wonder if Captain Roberts has talked to him," Pierce mused. Then he scowled. "Probably not, given the way he's been hovering over me. He caught me up to go to the bathroom and got in an argument with the nurse about why I couldn't go back on duty."

Pierce chortled. "I half expected your security manager to come throw him out and tell him to stay out. Not that it would hinder the investigation," he added in a sober tone. "Captain Roberts is handling this case worse than a raw recruit. I can't believe how he's putting the whole thing off, as if he's waiting for me to take over. Or Nash to return from vacation, whichever comes first."

"Maybe he'll surprise you," I said.

"I seriously doubt that, not with the time that's already passed with no progress. I heard the M.E. finally did the autopsy this afternoon, but Roberts wasn't there, so the fingerprints are shuffling through normal channels. If those fingerprints don't go to the top of the waiting list, we can't begin to ID the guy. I mean, how can we investigate a murder if we don't find out who the victim is?"

I didn't have an answer. Except for assisted trips to the bathroom and starting physical therapy tomorrow, Pierce was bed-ridden in his traction contraption, and I'd promised not to get involved. I reminded myself that talking about it didn't mean I was involved; I was merely keeping Pierce company, although I was concerned at how agitated he was becoming.

I gathered up my lunch things. "Well, I better get back to work."

"We need to check during his earlier hospital stays to see if he had a bag when he left his other personal belongings for safekeeping at the office."

Pierce's suggestion surprised me. I gave him a hard look. "*We?*"

"I've been thinking about this, Rob."

"I know, and I'm sorry, Matt. I feel just awful about your not being able to conduct the investigation yourself, but there's nothing we can do."

"Look, Rob, it's driving me crazy, and as much as I hate to say it, I need your help."

"What did you say?"

"Rob—"

"Could you repeat that?" Incredulous, I sank back into the chair.

"If you're going to be—"

"Did I hear you right? You want me to do some sleuthing on your behalf?"

Pierce looked as uncomfortable with the request as I was deep down inside excited about him making it.

"Nothing big, just a few things you could check out in your spare time."

"Spare time?" In spite of my interest in helping, I laughed shortly. After all, I didn't want to appear too eager. "What spare time?"

"Come on, you can't be that busy."

"William Jones has been a full time job all by himself today, and now my boss, Howard, has dumped a major report on me that's due Tuesday night . . . that's tomorrow. It's going to be caffeine city for"—I glanced at my watch—"the next twenty-eight hours."

"Why'd he give you the report on such short notice?" Pierce asked.

"It's his first quarterly Quality Report, and he said he's too busy to write his section, so he gave me all the raw data to do something with."

"Well, if you really wanted to help, you'd find a few minutes to run down to the office and check out Hilliard's back records."

I stared at him in amazement. Talk about throwing down the gauntlet. Pierce was actually asking me to get involved in a murder investigation? He must be really desperate. In spite of my vow to not get involved, I owed Pierce big-time. And I did want to find out what was going on. I grinned and said, "Okay. I'll do it. But just this one time."

Pierce heaved a sigh of relief—at my agreement or the one time, I wasn't sure. "Good. Now it's important that no one knows what you're doing. Captain Roberts can't find out that we're snooping around on our own."

"*We're* snooping? Excuse me, but I'm the one who's sticking her neck out here."

Pierce grinned. "That's even better, because the captain probably won't give it a second thought if he finds out because you'll come up with some legitimate excuse for doing what you're doing. Say it has to do with your report, or something like that. Throw out some big medical terms like, like—"

"Like efficacious?"

Pierce grinned. "Yeah, that's a good one. I don't know what that means, so he sure as hell won't."

"It's a fancy way of saying the treatment produced the desired results." I was still dubious about running into Pierce's boss. "I don't know. He might remember me from Saturday. After all, I'm the one who found the body. And he's seen me in here with you."

"Well, just be subtle," Pierce said. "Try to go to the Office when a lot of people are there—"

"Okay, mister hot shot police detective, you can stop right there. This is my turf, and I know how to do this. For your information, I don't need to go to the Business Office. What we want is in Medical Records."

"Fine. Then go there."

"Fine. I will." I gave him a smug grin.

Pierce scowled in return. I knew he regretted involving me, but he must be even more upset about the way the investigation was being handled than I'd realized for him to even consider asking for my help.

I smiled at him. "Don't worry. This isn't dangerous. I'll be fine."

"You're sure? I wouldn't ask unless—"

I fluffed up Pierce's pillows. "I can do this. Really."

He was trying to decide whether to watch ESPN or MSNBC when I left him to go downstairs to Medical Records and fill out a request for access to Hilliard's charts.

Technically, some might say I was crossing a line. I could be in big trouble because I had no legitimate reason for reviewing Hilliard's records. Even if I explained that I was helping the police, aside from the fact that there was no warrant, Pierce wasn't investigating the case and that could make it sticky for both of us. I rationalized that I wasn't looking at the clinical part of Hilliard's record, the section that was covered by strict confidentiality laws, but just the Business Office's notes from Hilliard's admissions and discharges.

Sari, the records clerk, reminded me of a Polynesian maiden. Willowy with long dark hair hanging down her back, she moved with a slow, easy sway to her hips, never ruffled or hurried, consistently pleasant. A few minutes with her always left me feeling calmer and breathing easier and deeper. She gave me the day's access code a few minutes later. "Here you go, Robyn. Are you investigating this murder too?" she asked with a conspiratorial grin.

"No," I said with a laugh that I hoped didn't sound fake. Or nervous. "I'm doing a report for the Quality Committee and figured I better include some background information on this case for Howard Knowles, since I'm sure it will come up at the committee meeting."

Okay, it was a stretch, a big stretch. But if that was my story to the police, if asked, then it made sense to be consistent about it.

Sari nodded. "Sounds like a good idea. Good luck," she said before disappearing back into the inner sanctum.

The hospital, or inpatient, medical records were all computerized now, and Sari was probably working to input archived charts into the system. I could access the records for current patients from my office, but previous admits required a trip down here. I went to a computer in a back corner where I was least likely to be disturbed . . . or observed . . . and started my search. I found records from four previous admissions for Hilliard.

Beginning with the most recent hospital stay before this last one, in January, I opened the file. The admit sheet was the first page and there it was, for anyone to see, the list of what Hilliard had left in the safe. Keys, wallet, watch, and a sealed canvas bag.

I leaned back in the chair. So, he'd brought a bag before. But had it contained money too? It seemed unlikely that he'd bring a large amount of money, as he had this last time. Unless he paid for his hospitalization in cash. But Tom had said Hilliard always wrote a check, so he didn't need the money to pay his bill.

I clicked to the last page of the chart to the discharge sheet. When he'd paid for his stay, he'd used a check. From his bank account with the fake name. He'd retrieved his things and signed for them. The discharge clerk had itemized them: keys, wallet, and watch.

No bag.

No bag? I frowned. Why would Hilliard have signed that he'd received all his belongings if he hadn't been given the bag? I sent the admit and discharge pages to the printer.

I opened the file for the next previous stay. This one was three months earlier, in October. The admit sheet showed the same items left to be put in the safe: keys, wallet, watch, and sealed canvas bag. And the discharge page showed the same items checked out: keys, wallet, and watch.

July's admit and discharge pages were the same. All listed bags that had been checked in but not checked out. After sending those pages to the printer, I closed the file, then went to the printer to pick up my copies. I stared at them, willing them to confess. What had happened to the bags? Why didn't Hilliard get them when he was discharged? Why had he signed a receipt for receiving all his personal belongings when he obviously hadn't? And, what was in those bags? Where had they gone?

I had an idea, but before I could do anything, a shadow crossed the pages in front of me.

"Robyn. I'm surprised to see you down here."

I turned around to see Paula Rodriguez. As usual, she was impeccably groomed, even late in the day. How did she do it? Starch herself before leaving home?

"Hello, Paula. Just reviewing some medical records," I said as casually as possible and forced myself to smile. "My job, you know."

I flipped the pages over, printed side down and hoped Paula wouldn't notice. As I headed back to Sari to sign out, I prayed she would be waiting for me. But she wasn't.

Paula followed me. She glanced at the pages I held at my side and her eyes narrowed. "Really. How many hospital cases do you have going right now?"

I shrugged. "A few. I really should get back to my office. Sari?" I called.

"Coming," came a muted voice from the back room.

But would it be in time for me to escape Paula?

"You don't have any hospital cases. You're looking at Jason Hilliard's records, aren't you? This isn't a review for your department. You're snooping in his charts."

"I'm—"

"I'm surprised at you, Robyn. You of all people know the rules about patient confidentiality. You don't have written authorization to review these records, do you?"

This was the time to bluff big time. Raising my chin, I said, "Paula, I have every right to review these charts. I'm writing Howard's report for the Quality Committee, and I'm gathering information about Hilliard's case because I'm sure the committee will have questions about it and Howard will need to be briefed." I said it so well that I convinced myself.

Paula gasped. "You're writing the Quality Report?"

Of all the responses I expected, that had not been one of them. "Yes," I said slowly. "Howard asked me this morning to write his section in addition to my own and have it on his desk by the end of tomorrow."

"But why you?"

Ah. It finally sank in. Paula felt slighted. Could I use her desire to be involved? "Would you like to help? I have a stack of raw data and I'd be happy to give you any of it."

Paula harumphed in a most lady-like way. "Well, it seems to me that *I* should write the sections involving hospital nursing."

"Great! Do you want some of the other departments too?"

"Well—"

I jumped at this opportunity as it if were a life line, which it was. "Tell you what, I'll send all the inpatient data to you to analyze. I'll do the outpatient segment and the overview. They'll both be updated versions of what we did last quarter. Send me your parts when you finish and I'll write the summary and give it to Arlene."

"I guess—"

"Great." I clasped her hands. "Thanks so much, Paula. I was frantic, wondering how I was going to get this to Howard by tomorrow night."

Before she had time to pull away from my grasp or come up with an excuse to refuse, I left. It wasn't until I reached my office that I dared to breathe a sigh of relief. And to chuckle at my cleverness.

It took less than ten minutes to pull the inpatient hospital data from my pile, at least half the stack Howard had given me. I plopped the bundle on Connie's desk. "Connie, would you be a dear and take this to Paula Rodriguez's office. She can't change her mind if you bring it."

"Sure, Rob. Should I bring coffee on my way back?"

"That'd be great." I dug my pre-paid card from my pocket. "The usual."

"Got it."

She'd be back in a few minutes. I sank into my chair and spread the pages I'd printed from Hilliard's chart across my desk. Now wasn't the time to bring them to Pierce; too many people were popping in and out of his room. I'd wait until after work when we were less likely to be interrupted.

Connie returned with my coffee, and I told her I needed an hour with no interruptions so I could make some progress on the data Howard had dumped on—ah, graciously assigned to—me. The Quality Report didn't seem nearly as onerous as it had before.

CHAPTER 9

My intercom buzzed. My clock said it had only been half an hour, so it must be important. "Is the fire outside the door yet?"

Connie laughed. "No flames at the door, but Dr. Kyler's on the line for you."

"Put him through." I waited a moment for my phone to ring, then picked it up. "Hi, Stan. What's God's gift to pregnant women up to?"

Stan Kyler, our most popular obstetrician, sighed. "Ah, Robyn. I don't know what to do with this one."

"What's wrong?" Instinctively, I grabbed a fresh pad of paper and a pen and prepared to write.

"I just came from delivering a beautiful baby boy. He's perfect. The delivery went off without a hitch."

I put my pen down. "So where's the problem?"

"The mom says she wants to sue."

"Stan, you have to have a problem before you can sue." I chuckled.

But Stan didn't share my amusement. "The mom says she's calling an attorney unless we give her half a mil for wrongful life."

"What? Wrongful life? I've heard of wrongful death, but—"

"She says this baby shouldn't have been conceived in the first place, so his birth is our mistake. Her husband had a vasectomy a couple of years ago, and she's claiming we botched it, otherwise, she wouldn't have gotten pregnant."

"Hmmm." I clicked the pen against my teeth as I thought about this. "Did she ever say anything during her prenatal care?"

"I don't know. She wasn't my patient. She's John McLean's, but he's on vacation this week and next, and she came in last night while I was on-call."

"Does the chart say anything?"

"I haven't had time to look at the full outpatient clinic records, just the lab reports, ultrasound, that kind of stuff."

"Has she called an attorney yet?"

"I don't think so. She says that's the first thing she's going to do when she gets home."

"I suppose you want me to talk to her?" Why else would he be calling me?

"Either that or call Risk Management. I've gotta go, Rob. They're paging me for another delivery."

"Wait, Stan! What's her name?"

"What? Oh, yeah. It's Sandra Jenkins. She's in an LDR until tonight."

"I'll take care of it, Stan."

"Thanks, Robyn. You're a peach."

I hung up the phone and shook my head. I'm a peach? Sure, when he wanted me to take care of something ugly for him. I'd remind him the next time I needed him to do something for me.

Without having to look it up, I punched in the number for Risk Management.

"Beverly Samm."

"Hi, Bev."

"Uh-oh. I recognize that tone. What's up, Rob?"

One of the positive aspects of my job is that I get to know some very nice people very well. Bev was one of them. The place where my job ended and hers began was sometimes vague, and since we both had more than enough to keep us busy, neither one was interested in turf battles, so we had some latitude on how to handle some sticky patient problems. If Sandra Jenkins had already involved an attorney, it was an automatic punt to Bev's department. But since the patient was still in the arm-waving stage, the case was in that gray zone.

"Stan Kyler just called me."

"Oh, no." She sighed heavily. "I hate OB cases. They're always so sad."

"No, it's not that bad." I quickly summarized the situation.

"Not that bad, huh? Easy for you to say. It's not your half a million dollars she wants." Bev harumphed. "Okay. You do your thing and we'll see what happens. No need to bump it to me at this point."

"I figured that's what you'd say. Want detailed progress reports?"

"Nah. I've got enough on my plate right now. Call me when you've either resolved it or it blows up in your face, not that I think that will happen."

"Works for me." We touched base on a couple of other cases, then said good-bye.

So much for writing the Quality Report. I told Connie where to find me and left the office, taking the stairs up one flight.

Several years ago, the hospital had torn out the old Labor/Delivery unit on the fourth floor and put in a beautiful solarium to attract the affluent "young healthy" target market to Madrona Bay's maternity service. The remodel was a resounding success. The thermopane glass walls and ceiling in the northeast corner picked up the morning light, but not the hot afternoon sun we usually had for two weeks in August. The old labor rooms had been converted to LDR's, combination labor/deliver/recovery rooms. With all the comforts of home, they were luxury suites, including Jacuzzi tubs. The high tech equipment was camouflaged, but available at a moment's notice.

I spotted Sandra Jenkins's name outside one door, knocked and peeked in. The room was empty. I wound my way around the potted and hanging plants that surrounded several artistically arranged waterfalls in the solarium area. I stopped, giving myself a moment to see it from William's perspective. No wonder he'd been confused when the nurse's aide brought him up here. It looked very much like a real park.

I rounded a tall potted plant to see if Mrs. Jenkins was one of the patients resting in the comfortable chairs. A woman who looked to be in her mid-thirties sat in a rocking chair. She wasn't looking at the sleeping baby she held loosely in her arms. Instead, she stared off into space, looking miserable.

"Mrs. Jenkins?"

She started and clutched the baby before it slipped off her lap. Because I was watching her carefully, it seemed to me to be more of an automatic response than maternal concern for the infant.

"Yes?"

"I'm Robyn Kelly. Dr. Kyler called me. He said you wanted to file a complaint."

She gave me the once-over, and her dismissive expression said she wasn't impressed. Maybe if I'd brought a briefcase full of cash she'd be more interested.

"A complaint? I don't want to file a complaint. You complain if the food's bad or if the nurse is rude. No. I'm filing a lawsuit. You're not getting away with this."

Ignoring her opening comments, I sat in a nearby chair. "May I see your baby?"

She shrugged and handed him to me with as much concern as if he were a sack of onions. I peeled the blankets from his face and saw Stan was right. I couldn't stop myself from saying, "Oh, he's beautiful, Mrs. Jenkins. His face is so round, and look at all that hair. And his little fingers." I almost commented on how pleased she must be, but that would be stretching her tolerance too far.

I continued to hold the baby, mainly because his mother showed no indication she wanted him back, but also because I loved the feel of him snuggled up against me. "I understand you have some concerns about—what have you named him?"

Sandra Jenkins stared steadily at the waterfall. "My husband wants to call him Eddy."

"Short for Edward?"

She nodded.

"Is that a family name?"

"My husband's father's name."

"That's nice." I kept my voice pleasant, soothing, but I felt a growing dislike for this woman. "I'm sure he'll be very pleased that you named his grandson after him."

"He won't care. He's been dead for ten years."

I cuddled baby Eddy and figured the time for small talk was over. "I understand you aren't happy about having Eddy."

She glanced at me, a cold, hard look, then resumed her study of the waterfall. "It's simple. My husband had a vasectomy. The doctor screwed it up. I'm stuck with a baby. You pay me for the cost of raising him, and I'll go away."

"And how much do you think that will be?"

"I figure a half a million dollars should do it."

"That's a bit high, don't you think? I think the estimates for raising a child through high school are closer to a hundred sixty-thousand dollars."

"Yeah, but I deserve some compensation for my time. I mean, I could be pursuing my career if I wasn't taking care of this kid."

I did not have a good feeling about this woman's maternal instincts, not at all. I needed to call Social Work to do an assessment before Mrs. Jenkins was discharged, and maybe even find a way to keep her in the hospital for an extra day or two. I'd work through her complaint, just like I did everyone's, but at the same time, I had to protect this precious, defenseless baby.

"I'll need you to fill out some forms, Mrs. Jenkins. And, since it was your husband who had the vasectomy, I'll need his authorization to review his records too. How are you feeling?"

She looked a little pale when she snapped, "How do you think I feel? My life is ruined. I just had a baby. I look like a cow and I hurt."

"Maybe I can arrange for you to stay another day or so. Would you like that?"

"Yeah. Fine. And while you're at it, fix it so's the nurses take care of the kid, okay?"

She stood up and returned to her room, leaving me with little Eddy. I had to wonder what little Eddy's father thought of him. Naming the baby after his grandfather was a good sign, wasn't it? But if Mr. Jenkins was as upset as his wife, then Social Work should talk to them about their options, including adoption. I glanced down at the baby cuddling against me. Plenty of couples were desperate for a baby and would love to give Eddy a home where he was wanted.

I sat with the baby for a few minutes. He seemed to enjoy the attention, and he was a cute little thing, reminding me of when Josh was born. Now there was a child who was wanted. My husband, David, and I were so excited about having a baby, and when Josh came, well, you'd have thought we'd done something no one else in the history of mankind had achieved. I smiled at the memory, then my smile faded as I wondered what kind of life Eddy faced. Unless his mother had a serious attitude adjustment, his future with her didn't look too bright.

"This is interesting, to say the least," Pierce said after I told him what I'd learned from Hilliard's admission and discharge records. "What do you think happened to the bags?"

"I suppose it's possible he removed them before he was discharged."

"What was he going to do? Splurge in the cafeteria? Go on a shopping binge in the gift shop?" Pierce said in exasperation. "I mean, let's face it, Rob. There aren't a lot of places to spend money here, even if you do have a three latté a day habit." He looked pointedly at my fresh cup.

"I buy a pre-paid card and get a free one when I use it up. This one is my reward for surviving the day," I said in defense of myself. "But, you're right. If Hilliard's other bags were full of money like this one was, it would be extremely hard to spend that amount during a week's hospital stay. Especially if he was not feeling well, which he shouldn't have been with a raging staph infection."

"Too sick to get out of bed?" Pierce asked.

"Probably too sick to go wandering around the hospital," I responded. "Do you want me to check with the Business Office to see if they keep a record of patients removing things from the safe before discharge, and where I'd find it?"

"Let's hold off for now. We don't want to alert anyone that we've learned something."

Amused, I rested my feet on the bed frame. "You mean you don't want Captain Roberts to know you're conducting the investigation from your bed?"

Pierce snorted. "You got that right. If he thought I could handle it, he'd be dumping all kinds of work on me. Let's face it, the only reason I can do anything with this murder case is because you're doing the leg work."

I smiled at the recognition. "Glad I can help, even if it is unofficial."

Pierce gazed at me through narrowed eyes. "Yeah, well, don't get used to it. I'm just trying to answer a few questions for my own peace of mind."

"So you can share that piece with Captain Roberts at the right time?" I quipped.

"Rob." He shook his head. "Sometimes you are impossible."

"So where do we go from here?" I asked. "Figure out likely suspects?"

"Sure, why not?" He reached for a pad of paper on his nightstand and divided the page into two columns marked "possible" and "not likely." "Who was there that afternoon?"

"Nowhere near as many as last time." I started ticking off the possibilities. "Connie's choice is Nurse Amanda—"

Pierce's brow furrowed in puzzlement. "Why is she Connie's choice?"

"This morning, when I was telling her and Margie about the murder, I mentioned how difficult Amanda was when I discovered Hilliard's body." I shrugged. "Connie used her psychic abilities to come up with that conclusion."

Pierce chuckled. "Connie's a kick, but I wish it was that easy. What do you have besides opportunity for this Amanda woman?"

"Nothing really. She's a fill-in from the nurse registry's temporary service. Between you and me, with her attitude, I can see why she doesn't have a permanent position. I doubt we'll request her again. She generated a lot of complaints from patients and staff. But, she did have to endure Hilliard's peep show, and that would make anyone cranky."

"Okay, so she was here and nobody liked her. Sounds like the ideal suspect." He wrote Amanda's name down in the "possible" column, then tapped his pen on the paper. "For the sake of argument, contact the registry service and find out when and where she's worked in the last six months. Then contact your counterparts and see if they had any problems with her."

"Sure." I was so excited, I almost left right away to start this next phase of my investigation.

"Anyone else?" Pierce asked.

"Let's see, it was too early for dietary to deliver meals, and Tina, the girl scheduled to serve, was adamant that she wouldn't bring Hilliard his dinner because of the way he'd behaved at lunch."

Pierce put Tina's name in the "not likely" column.

"Captain Roberts has sealed the medical record so I can't check it to see who did what when, but I can ask the lab manager when they last took a blood draw. I doubt Hilliard had any x-rays or physical therapy. I'll call Dr. Transel in the morning and ask him what else he ordered for Hilliard."

Pierce nodded, then frowned. "You know, Rob, until we know Jason Hilliard's true identity, we're just spinning our wheels, coming up with this list."

"You're probably right. But what else can we do?"

Pierce eyed me, then gruffly said, "You go home. We'll talk about this tomorrow."

I looked at him in surprise. Talk about an imperious dismissal! "Okay," I said, gathering up my stuff. "I'll see you in the morning."

He said nothing until I started to leave the room. "Good night, Rob."

I turned to look back at him and saw from his softened expression that he hadn't meant to hurt my feelings. I nodded. "Sleep well, Matt."

He rattled his traction apparatus. "I'll try."

I stepped outside the room and pulled the door almost closed. Then I waited a moment. Sure enough, I heard the sound of cell phone beeps followed a few moments later by Pierce's voice.

"Joe? Pierce, here . . . yeah, I'm still in the hospital . . . listen, Joe, I need to call in a favor . . . fine, get technical on me . . . yeah, it's important . . . okay, two tickets behind home plate . . .

wait a minute . . . Good night, Rob! Close the door, please."

Nuts. Caught in the act. I felt my face redden as I pulled the door until I heard the latch click.

As I left, I felt a twinge of guilt about going back on my promise to myself, and to everyone else, about staying out of the murder investigation. I had enough of my own work to do. I'd learned my lesson last time about how dangerous sleuthing can be. But this was different. Pierce had asked me—again—for help.

Somehow, I would ignore my resolve not to get involved and hope no one noticed that I was really and truly investigating the murder.

The day might have been a bust for getting any of my "real" work done, but I looked forward to dinner with Josh. His girlfriend, Chuck—short for Charlene—worked on Monday nights, which made it more likely that he would be home.

I parked my car in the garage and, with Taffy prancing at my heels, walked through the kitchen toward the humming noise in the dining room. The carpet had been pulled up, and two huge fans were aimed at the wet areas to speed the drying process. Several five gallon buckets sat in the middle of the room collecting water, drip by steady drip. The buckets were over half full and very heavy. I'd let Josh empty them.

Wishing I could pretend my dining room wasn't a disaster area, I headed for my bedroom to change out of work clothes and into comfortable fleece pants and top. I played with Taffy for a few minutes, then sent her outside to explore.

Despite the previous Saturday's promise of spring, the weather was back to cold and damp, and with the gaping hole in the ceiling, the house was as cold inside as outside. This definitely called for a hot, hearty chicken and rice dinner.

While I stood at the kitchen's granite-topped island, I sipped a glass of wine in between chopping and dicing carrots, celery, and onion, and tried to shed the day's events. It was hard because I tried to figure out where I could find time to do my sleuthing with everything else that needed to be done.

Pierce was beyond cranky about his confinement in the hospital and I couldn't blame him. He was getting better, yet I still shuddered every time I walked into his room and saw him all bound up. I shook some seasonings over boneless chicken pieces, poured some wine on top of it, and popped it in the microwave. Then I refilled my glass.

My boss, Howard, had dumped a week's worth of work on me. It wasn't as if I couldn't write the report, it was the total change of mental gears that caused me problems, shifting from empathetic mode to analytical. At least I didn't have to say anything at the Quality Committee meeting. Samantha Duke had hated me since I had reviewed her sister-in-law's complaint against a doctor and didn't give her the answer she wanted. Samantha would use any opportunity, especially a public venue like the meeting, to skewer my department.

Then there was poor William. He had called me all day long. I didn't have the heart to ignore him, but at least I'd started slowing down my response time. Otherwise, I'd never get anything done. As it was, he consumed a significant amount of time, time I didn't have. Thank goodness Margie and Connie were picking up the slack with the other patients calling for assistance.

The stack of unwritten case reports on my desk was multiplying exponentially. That wasn't anything new, and they'd get done eventually, even if it meant going in on Saturday, which I probably would if William and Pierce were still in the hospital by then.

I swiped at the tears that always came when I chopped raw onions. I poured olive oil into a Dutch oven and when it was hot, scraped the chopped veggies into it. Stirring slowly, I considered how to do some sleuthing in addition to all my "real" work.

Time was the problem. Speaking of time, where was Josh? He was due home fifteen minutes ago. I pushed the veggies to one side of the pot, poured in the rice, and stirred while it browned slightly in the hot oil. Then I added broth, waited until it reached a rolling boil, popped on the lid, turned the heat way down and set the timer.

I let Taffy in, and she shook herself thoroughly, then ambled to the door leading to the garage. In a moment, I heard the garage door open and a car pull in. "Good job, Taf." She wagged her tail once in acknowledgement. Otherwise all her attention was on the door.

Josh came in with a blast of cool air. He and Taffy went through their ritual greeting of roughhousing as he crossed the kitchen.

"Hi, Mom," he mumbled, disappearing through the other door to the dining room. "What happened in here?"

"We have a leak, and the contractor's fixing it. After you change your clothes, would you please empty those buckets for me?"

He responded with a grunt. But I heard noises a few minutes later that told me he was doing it. When he returned to the kitchen, he pulled the refrigerator door open and leaned over to scan the contents.

I finally said, "Nothing's changed in there since this morning. Close the door. You're letting all the cold air out."

He grabbed a can of pop and kicked the door closed with his foot. "When do we eat?"

The microwave timer beeped. "Soon." I took the poached chicken from the microwave and set it on the counter to cool before I tried cutting it up.

Josh went into the living room. I followed him as far as the doorway. He turned on the TV and slumped into his favorite chair, an old recliner that his father had loved. He didn't look ready to do anything more. In fact, it struck me that he was definitely acting strange. Why on earth would that be?

I chose to ignore the new mood. "Josh, we'll have to eat in the kitchen tonight. Would you set the table while I make a salad?"

"Okay." He heaved himself out of the chair and ambled into the kitchen. He still didn't say anything so it was up to me to initiate tonight's conversation.

"How was your day?" This was usually the time I loved, time with my son, talking and sharing. We didn't have near enough of it these days, not with our hectic schedules and his social life. But I had always cherished these times with him and wanted to hold on to them as long as I could. He would be gone too soon.

He shrugged. "It was okay."

That was when I realized he hadn't looked at me since he'd come home. He'd glanced in my general direction, but no eye-to-eye contact. Clearly tonight wasn't going to be one of those cherished evenings. When we sat down to eat, he dug into his food and finally started talking, but not without prodding. He rambled on about this class and that professor. Josh was a mechanical engineering major, and most of the time I didn't have a clue what he was talking about, but I always listened attentively and tried to keep up with his life. Tonight, it seemed more like busy chatter, to forestall other questions.

He stopped talking as we finished eating. He frowned and stared at the pop can as if it held the secrets of life. Now he was gearing up to talk about what was bothering him.

"What's up, Josh?" I braced myself.

"I've decided to do something different this summer."

That surprised me. "Really? You mean you don't want to

127

work on Grandpa's ranch?"

He shook his head, but still didn't look at me. That worried me, but I still couldn't imagine what he thought I'd consider to be that bad.

"So, you found something here where you can make more money?" I prompted.

He shrugged. "Not exactly."

My mom-antennae now stood on full alert. "Is it the found something here or the make more money that's not exactly?"

"Both." He looked up at me, his jaw firm and jutting out slightly, an expression that did not bode well for how he thought I was going to take this.

"Josh. Are you going to tell me or do I have to guess?"

"I'm going to Africa this summer."

CHAPTER 10

I sat there in stunned silence. I wouldn't have been more surprised if he'd said he was going to the moon. Surely I hadn't heard him right. Finally, I managed to sputter, "Africa?"

"That's right. There's this organization, Humanity For All, that takes college students to the bush to help villages build wells and houses and schools and roads. It will look really good on my resume if I apply for graduate school and look for a job."

"But . . . why . . . why do you have to go all the way to Africa to do this?"

"That's where the organization does its work." Josh was now sitting on the edge of his seat, vibrating with excitement.

A hundred questions filled my mind while I struggled to find ones I could ask that wouldn't turn him defensive. "What a . . . what an interesting opportunity. What does this job pay?"

Josh stiffened. "It doesn't pay anything. It's volunteer work, Mom."

"Yes, well, I can understand that. I'm sure it will look good on your resume," I choked out. "But at least they'll cover your travel and living expenses?"

Now he was starting to glower. "No, Mom. I told you. This is a charity. I have to pay my own travel expenses, but I get to live with a native family."

"I see." But I didn't, and everything he said only made it worse. "And you heard about this how?"

"A guy was in the HUB, handing out information and

answering questions."

"A . . . a guy?" I took a deep breath and tried to put on my calm, empathetic hat, the one I used day-in and day-out at work. "This organization, Humanity For All, wants you to go half way around the world, spending your own money to get there. I can understand how important that work sounds. I am concerned though. We need your summer income to help pay next year's tuition." That was the least of my concerns, but it was a start.

"But, Mom, think about the experience." He still looked hopeful, but I could see in his eyes that he knew he wasn't selling me on this scheme. "You've always said travel is a broadening experience. Think about all the things I'll see and do."

My calm, empathetic hat slipped off and I turned one hundred percent parent. "Josh! What are you thinking? Don't you watch the news or read the newspaper? They have horrible civil wars going on over there."

"I know, but we're not supposed to be in those areas."

"Not supposed to be? What kind of assurance is that?" Although I had tried to keep my tone neutral throughout this conversation, I failed miserably. "You have to know where you're going. Some of the countries are in terrible states. These . . . these so-called armies of drug-crazed soldiers cut off peoples' arms. And . . . and there's genocide. And awful diseases. Like Ebola."

"I knew you wouldn't like it," Josh snapped. He shoved himself off the chair and headed toward his room.

"I'm trying to understand," I hollered after him. If he thought storming off to his room was going to help his cause, he was sadly mistaken.

He returned and waved a handful of flyers at me. "Here. Read these. They explain everything."

I flipped through the leaflets, dismayed at the pictures of sad, destitute people and starving children sitting in squalor. College students were so susceptible to materials like this. The cynic in me questioned if it had been done deliberately for the highest emotional response. I scanned the text describing in glowing details the projects planned for this summer. Surely a group with ambitious projects like these would have name familiarity. But I didn't recognize the name of the organization.

"Who are these people, Josh? Who sponsors them? And this tells *what* you'd be doing, but where exactly would you be?"

"I don't know yet. I just heard about it last Friday. I didn't say anything this weekend because I knew you wouldn't like it." There was that pugnacious jaw again. Where was the son happy to seek his mother's counsel?

"Okay, I can understand that," I said much more calmly than I felt. "Why don't you get some more information about who they are? Where exactly are you going? Who is supervising? What are the living conditions? How many of you will be there? Can you get a passport in time? What shots do you need?"

That last one made him blanch, but to his credit, he didn't back down. "I have to sign up by Friday."

"Friday? Why the rush?"

"The guy said they're visiting as many colleges as they can, so they can't wait long for people to make up their minds."

I bit my tongue. "The guy" again. I'd like to get my hands on "the guy," preferably around his neck, and tell him what I thought about him tempting my boy to go halfway around the world. "You know, if working to help the poor this summer is something you'd like to do, there are a lot of similar projects here in the States."

"They don't need it the way these people do, Mom. We have all kinds of programs to help people here." He stood up and carried his dishes to the sink. "I never realized it before. You're prejudiced."

With that, he left the kitchen. Dumbfounded by his parting shot, I watched him go. My son had just called me prejudiced! It simply wasn't true. We lived in a diversified neighborhood. I worked with all kinds of people every day. The ones I might possibly be prejudiced against were people like Mrs. Jenkins. But I still did my best for them.

This was different. He could be sent to any of the strife-ridden areas in Africa! I'd feel the same way if he'd named any war-torn part of the world. I'd always believed it was important to help people in need. I donated regularly to a number of highly regarded organizations that did good work around the world. Some of it was similar to what "that guy's" organization said it did.

While I was thrilled that Josh wanted to help those less fortunate, I also wanted him to do it in a safe place. Was that unreasonable? I didn't think so. In fact, it was a totally normal motherly reaction.

Still, I had this niggling thought that maybe I only wanted to help people if I could stay in my comfort zone, working with people like me and sending money to others to work with the people who weren't like me. I had to think about that.

While cleaning up the kitchen, I mentally rattled off a long list of destitute areas in this country that desperately needed help. And he wouldn't need a passport or shots to go there.

A dark black cloud hovered over me. I didn't think I was an overly protective mother. I mean, I worried about all the usual stuff, like sex, drugs, and friends driving drunk, but I certainly didn't obsess every time Josh left the house. Okay, so I still waited up for him to come home at night, partially to be sure he came home safely and partially because Taffy made such a fuss I'd be awakened anyway.

The phone rang and I grabbed it like a life preserver saving me from my mental downward spiral.

"Robyn? Is that you, dear? It's Lois," said the woman on the other end. She was a neighbor of my father's, as close to a lady friend as he'd ever had. She wouldn't call unless there was a problem.

"Lois! What's wrong?"

"Oh, don't worry. Everything's okay now. But I thought you should know that your father collapsed on Saturday."

I gasped, then the questions tumbled out. "What's happened? Is he okay? Where is he now?"

"He's fine now. I saw him this morning, before he rode out with his crew to check on the herd. He thinks he'll have a good—"

"Lois. What happened?"

"Oh. Yes. He was at the corral with his foreman when he lost consciousness. Wayne drove him to the ER immediately, then called me."

"Did they do tests? What did the doctor say?"

"Your father didn't tell me about any tests. He said the doctor told him he was fine, but it might be a good idea to take a baby aspirin every day." She sniffed. "You can imagine what he thought about taking children's medicine—"

"What was the diagnosis?" Keeping Lois on track was sometimes a problem.

"Oh, your father would never share that with me." She gave a little giggle. "But when he wasn't watching, I sneaked a peek at the paper he got before I took him home from the ER. It said he had a tia."

"A tia?" What in the world was—"You mean a T-I-A?"

"I suppose that's what it could have been."

"Lois, thank you so much for calling me. Da never would have told me a thing about this."

"You aren't going to tell him I told you, are you?"

"No. I'll figure out another way to bring up the subject. But it certainly explains why we didn't talk on Saturday like we usually do."

After we hung up, I leaned my head against the wall. First Josh, and now this. I'd been worrying about Da living alone and so far from town. He could have died before Wayne got him to the hospital in town.

And the treatment plan? Maybe a baby aspirin? I wasn't a physician, but I did know that a TIA was a mini-stroke, and even if there were no residual symptoms, he should be treated.

Da was definitely at the top of my list tomorrow, murder or no murder, quality report or no quality report.

The next morning, I was in no mood to be pleasant. Josh had pronounced I was a bigot, and my father's health was in doubt. When I reached the hospital, I ran into Judy Francis, the O.R. manager in the espresso cart line while I ordered my double tall skinny, Seattle lingo for two shots of espresso and nonfat milk.

"Hi, Judy," I said, then turned to the barista and handed him my card.

"Have you seen the latest?" Judy rolled her eyes and thrust a piece of paper at me. "It's another Bloomingdale letter."

A couple of years before, someone inside our organization had created the imaginary Bloomingdale family as a way to irritate Admin and the physician leadership by pointing out problems. Every now and then a "Bloomingdale" wrote a letter and circulated enough copies throughout the building that the letter couldn't be ignored. Despite everyone's best efforts, the identity of the real writer had not been uncovered, making it the best kept secret in the hospital's history.

I juggled my purse and attaché bag so I could take the paper and read it.

To: Howard Knowles
From: Lonnie Dermat Bloomingdale

RE: Laundry

It has come to my attention that a quality control problem has occurred with Madrona Bay Hospital's laundry. More specifically, instead of receiving pristine clean sheets, towels, and scrubs clearly labeled "Madrona Bay Hospital" from Unified Laundry, we have received not-so-clean sheets, towels, and scrubs clearly labeled "Mercy Hospital" from Spiffy Clean Laundry.

This is creating identity crises for the staff, patients and insurance companies. All are confused about where they are working, or where they are being treated, or if they are paying the correct hospital for the already-disputed charges.

I suggest three possible causes:

1. The Russian mafia is no longer satisfied running highly successful chop-shops in Seattle and has decided to diversify by taking over commercial laundries. Attempts to contact Ivan Igorovich have been unsuccessful as Immigration & Naturalization does not know he is in the country.

2. Mercy Hospital, which does not exist in the Puget Sound area, is a cover for a large hospital corporation that is planning a hostile takeover. By creating brand-confusion, it will be easier to make the change without our staff or patients noticing, let alone the state's hospital commission.

3. Our laundry was originally mislabeled and no one noticed, in which case, we should be talking to the Purchasing Department.

I trust you will investigate and resolve this situation before our community image is soiled.

I handed it back to her. "Really?"

"Tall mocha, whole milk, triple shots," she said to the barista, handing him her punch card. She took the letter from me and shoved it into her surgical scrubs pocket. "Really. Look at this."

She held her scrubs top out, and I could see the imprint *Mercy Hospital.*

"What do you make of it?" I took my coffee and card and stepped aside to wait for her.

"Oh, I don't know." She took her card and steaming hot latté from the barista and joined me as we headed for the elevators. The doors were open so we stepped in and pushed the button for our floor. "You know how it is, occasionally some laundry gets mixed up, but this is weird because there really is no Mercy Hospital in Washington."

"So the Bloomingdales are on to something?"

"There's always some truth in these things, but this isn't a big enough deal for us to get too excited. But of course we're curious," she added as we reached our floor and stepped off the elevator. "Rob, something else." Judy glanced around, and I followed her gaze. The lobby area was empty. She beckoned me towards the windows.

"What's up?"

"Patients are canceling surgeries, Rob."

"Why?"

She looked at me as if I was daft. "The murder, silly girl, the murder. Patients don't want to be anywhere near it, especially since no one's been arrested yet."

Somehow, between Da and Josh and the dining room ceiling, the murder had slipped my mind. Hard to believe, but it had. "I'll see what I can do."

"Thanks, Rob. I knew I could count on you to come up with something."

Cheered by her confidence in me, I sipped my coffee as we went in different directions. Walking down the hall, I wondered what the Bloomingdales had uncovered this time, and what Admin's reaction would be.

When I reached my office, the Bloomingdale letter fell off my list of things to think about. My first priority was to call Dr. Swanson, one of our neurologists, to discuss Da's case. I'd helped him deal with the parents of several patients, turning him from a skeptic of my department to a fan.

Fortunately, I caught him between appointments. I said, "My father collapsed on Saturday—"

"What happened?"

I reiterated what Lois had told me, then asked, "Does that sound right to you?"

"Did he see a neurologist?"

"I have no idea, but optional baby aspirin doesn't sound like it."

"I agree. The standard of care in Seattle is to order an EKG and blood work, including cholesterol and diabetes. We often order a carotid Doppler and an echo cardiogram. Has he had other episodes?"

"I don't know. Why? Is that important?"

"If it's happened more than once, I'd order a MRI of the brain and a MRA to get a 3-D look at the brain's arteries."

"I seriously doubt he had any of those tests, except maybe the EKG and blood work. It's a small county hospital. And if he saw his regular physician, I doubt it."

"Hmmm. Sounds like a story there."

"I'll tell you all about it sometime. But right now, I need to get him to see someone."

"Want me to work him into my schedule?"

"I appreciate that, but I think it'll be easier for him to stay in downtown Seattle and take Seattle Hospital's shuttle to and from the hospital than to stay at my house. Besides, I think his lady friend will come, too, and she'd love to shop in the big city."

"Don't wait too long to get him in, especially since we don't know how serious his condition is."

We hung up and I punched in the number for Elizabeth, the patient rep at Seattle Hospital.

I told her about the situation and my discussion with Dr. Swanson. She asked, "When do you want me to schedule the appointment?"

"Let's go for Thursday." I gave her Da's information and promised I'd have the records faxed to her before the appointment. I hoped I sounded more positive than I felt. Getting Da to travel to see another physician, let alone sign the release form, would be a challenge.

After hanging up the phone, I felt a little better. I wasn't happy about what I'd learned from Dr. Swanson, but he and Elizabeth had assured me that I was right to be concerned.

The next thing I needed to do, before anything else distracted me, was follow-up on Pierce's request for more information about Amanda Whitcomb. If she had behaved at other hospitals the way she'd behaved here, patients must surely have complained.

I picked up the phone and punched in the number for my counterpart at Hillsbrook Memorial Hospital. The patient rep there was a friend, but also president of the local chapter.

"Patient Relations. This is Sharon."

"Good morning, Sharon."

"Rob? Is that you?"

"It's me."

"What are you doing over there? I heard there's been another murder."

"*I'm* not doing anything. Except becoming an expert at discovering murder victims," I said more glumly than I'd meant to.

"Oh, Rob," Sharon said with a compassionate sigh. "Are you okay?"

"Of course I am. But I have to admit I'm tempted to submit

a workshop proposal to the convention planning committee about investigating murder." Like most professional groups, patient reps from all over the U.S. and Canada gathered once a year to learn new skills.

Sharon laughed. "You'd pack them in, Rob. Standing room only, if just for the 'there but for the grace of God go I' factor."

"You're probably right. *I'd* go to that workshop for the very same reason. Maybe if I gave it a boring title not as many people would come."

"Maybe, but someone would leak the real subject and no one would want to miss it. Let me know if you need help with the outline. I know what I'd want you to cover."

"Why do I think 'recognizing a murder' and 'preserving the crime scene' would be at the top of the list and 'inclusion in the management report' would be at the very bottom?"

"Because," Sharon said with a laugh, "we all crave the gory details, not practical stuff. You know the real reason we get together is to swap stories and tell lies."

I rolled my eyes. "Unfortunately, this wouldn't be a lie."

"No, but it would be a hard workshop to top for years to come. So, tell me what's been going on."

I gave her the abridged version, expanding a bit on what the press had already reported, but held back details such as the bag with $50,000.

"Hmmm. So you don't know who the victim is?"

"Not yet. We're hoping to identify him by his fingerprints."

"We? Does this mean you're trying to solve this one too?"

"No, Sharon. I'm not involved in the investigation," I said with my fingers crossed so the fib wouldn't count. "But the detective who handled last year's case—"

"That darling man, what's his name?"

I smiled at Sharon's reference to Pierce as "that darling man." She'd met him at the state patient reps' holiday party last

December and had obviously been smitten. Too bad her husband of twenty-five years had been standing right next to her. Otherwise, I think Sharon would have tried to hustle my date.

"Yes, Sharon, Detective Pierce. That darling man is in our hospital for a few days and—"

"Whatever for?" Sharon's voice was filled with concern.

I skirted around the patient confidentiality issues by telling her about how he'd tried to carry the bags of bark and potting soil at my house.

"Ah, I bet it's back stuff. Poor baby. Should I send some flowers?"

"I don't think that's necessary. Seeing anything that reminds him of a garden would probably make him all the more cranky. And I'm smuggling food in from the outside, so he's as happy as can be expected." I didn't think I should mention that he was going nuts because of the way the murder investigation was being handled.

"Well, tell him I hope he feels better soon." Sharon paused. "I assume you didn't call just to chat. What's up?"

"We've had some problems with a registry nurse and I'm checking with you and some of the others to see if you have any history with her."

"Sure, be happy to help. What's her name?"

"Amanda Whitcomb. She's—"

"Go no further, my friend. The name rings a bell. Let me check my files and get back to you."

"Anything you can tell me would be great. Can you call or e-mail me?"

"I'll try to get something to you before the end of the day."

"Great. I appreciate it."

After I hung up from Sharon, I called patient rep buddies at three other local hospitals. They all said they'd get back to me as quickly as possible.

Check Amanda off my list. I turned on my computer and e-mailed Howard and Larry Bridgeway about the surgery cancellations. This was a big issue that their management level needed to worry about. I had other, truly important, things to work on.

That taken care of, I looked around my office and spotted the Quality Report data. And groaned. Damn. It hadn't written itself overnight, and it was due on Howard's desk by end of work today. I had a bunch of cases, including William and that Mrs. Jenkins's "wrongful life" complaint to deal with, but I had to keep Howard happy. An hour. I'd spend an hour on it.

My luck was changing. I had two full uninterrupted hours to work on the report before emerging from my office to stretch and start the next task.

"Have I missed anything?" I asked Connie.

She shook her head. "Just the usual. Nothing Margie and I couldn't handle."

"Good. I'm going upstairs to pick up Mrs. Jenkins's complaint form. I'll be back in awhile."

The phone rang so I left before Connie could say it was for me. But instead of going directly upstairs to see Mrs. Jenkins, I went downstairs to the Business Office.

I found Becky working in the back. Since I knew she was already aware that something peculiar was going on with Jason Hilliard, it wasn't much of a stretch to ask her for more information. In her early thirties, Becky was smart and ambitious. In two years, she'd gone from weekend front desk receptionist to day shift supervisor, and I'd heard she was working on a college degree.

"Hi, Robyn. What brings you here?" She saved the computer file she was working on and then looked at me over the top of her reading glasses. She patted the chair next to her desk, and I slid into it.

"I need your help." That phrase had extricated me from so many quagmires that I never hesitated to use it. "Remember that patient Tom Geralding talked to you about last weekend?"

Her green eyes danced with excitement. "You mean the one who wasn't?"

CHAPTER 11

"That's the one."

"Tom called me to come in and document that he was taking the patient's personal belongings. He said he was going to try to find out his real identity."

So Becky didn't know about the money. I'd have to keep that information to myself. I glanced around to see who might overhear us, then said in a quiet voice, "Yes, and some questions have come up about the bag he left in the safe when he was admitted. Apparently he left a bag with his other personal belongings on his other admissions. According to the discharge sheets, the bags weren't in the safe when he was discharged, but he never complained about it."

"Really? That's odd."

"Is it possible for a patient to remove something during their stay here?"

Becky shrugged. "Sure. You know, women leave their wedding rings with us before surgery, and then they feel naked without them, so as soon as they can walk, they toddle on down here, trailing their IV behind them."

"How do they get things back?"

"Patients come in and sign a release form, then we give them the item they want."

Feeling a tingle of anticipation at uncovering a new clue, I moved to the edge of my seat. "And the release form would be kept where?"

"Well, it should be entered into the chart, but it happens so seldom and the information is on the discharge page, which makes it hard to document before the patient is discharged, and the chart is electronic, so it would be filed here. Then, if a question comes up later, we'd have a record of it. Do you need it right now?"

I tried not to appear pathetically eager.

Becky laughed. "Okay. Let me see what I can find. Come back in an hour."

"It's a date."

Reassured that I was making some progress on Pierce's investigation, I decided I was on a roll. Finally. I left the Business Office and stopped by the Lab. The manager, Mark, was out, but his assistant, Ted, was more than happy to answer my question.

"Sure, Robyn, I can look that up for you. As long as you don't want to know what we were testing for, I guess it's okay to tell you when we did blood draws."

He entered Hilliard's name into the computer and watched the lab activity screen open. "Okay, says here that his last blood draw was at eleven A.M."

"That was quite awhile before he was murdered. Can you tell me when the next one was due to be taken?" Was the phlebotomist on the unit when Hilliard died?

Ted threw me a look.

"Okay, maybe crossing the confidentiality line. Can you tell me if it was scheduled before five o'clock?"

"Yes."

"Before four o'clock?"

He bobbled his head back and forth. That meant I was getting closer.

"Before three o'clock?"

Ted frowned. So not before three o'clock. I'd have to be satisfied that the next draw was probably scheduled to be done between three and four o'clock, well after the time I found Hilliard's body. That took the lab tech off the suspect list.

My next stop was Dr. Transel's office, but he was attending an infection control seminar in Seattle. I'd wait until I talked to Becky before reporting back to Pierce. With whatever I learned from her, I'd feel I was giving Pierce a lot of new information. That should keep him happy for at least a few minutes.

I took the elevator to the third floor and went to William's room. I hadn't seen him yet today, and I was sure Connie had a stack of "please come see me" messages from him waiting for my return.

He was eating lunch when I entered his room, looking up to give me a happy grin.

"Hello, William. How are you today?"

"Just fine, ma'am. Just fine." He returned his attention to his sandwich and sliced apple.

My heart sank. He didn't recognize me again. "William, do you know who I am?"

He looked at me again, more closely this time. His face lit up. "Miz Robyn! It sure is nice of you to come see me again."

"I wanted to stop by and say hi and see how things are going."

"They's going just fine. The nurse, she took me to that park again. You said it's inside?"

"That's right," I said with a laugh. "Takes some getting used to, doesn't it?"

"It sure does."

I took a moment to glance around the room. No more new pictures since the three he'd added over the weekend. Two fresh bouquets of flowers rested on the windowsill. In the corner under the window stood an end table with a table lamp. That stopped me. Where in the world—? And there, in another corner where the bathroom wall jutted out into the room, sat a matching table and lamp.

"Ah, William?"

"Yes, Miz Robyn?"

"I like your new tables."

His expression turned guarded as he watched me closely. Was he afraid I'd take them away? Or report him to the police? I didn't want to say anything that would upset him further, so I said, "You've made some nice improvements to your room."

His wariness visibly relaxed, but he did nothing more than nod.

I'd probably been here long enough. "I better be going then. I'll come by to see you later, okay, William?"

He nodded again.

This time I took the stairs to the fourth floor. Mrs. Jenkins had left the signed complaint in a sealed envelope at the nurses' station. It was brief and to the point: *you screwed up my husband's vasectomy so now you owe me money.* No misunderstanding what the problem was or how she wanted it resolved. I sighed and shoved the form back into the envelope. I needed one more thing before I could start my review of Mr. Jenkins's vasectomy: his signature on a medical records release, the form Mrs. Jenkins hadn't included in the sealed envelope.

But first, I wanted to check on Eddy. When I found him in the nursery, he wasn't alone. A nice looking man, about the same age as Mrs. Jenkins and wearing a surgical gown, was holding Eddy in a rocking chair. Under his surgical gown, I could see some kind of a uniform. His large hands looked red from a recent scrubbing, but still some black traced the lines around his knuckles. His dark brown hair was in need of a trim, and a five o'clock shadow covered his angular jaw.

"Mr. Jenkins?"

He looked up at me, dark brown eyes surrounded by long lashes, and I saw myriad emotions cross his face. Sadness. Frustration. And fierce protection.

I smiled and introduced myself, and watched the wariness ease from his eyes. "How's little Eddy doing today?" I asked.

"He's good. The nurses say he's a fine little feeder and doesn't make a fuss."

"I'm sure he's a very good baby, Mr. Jenkins."

"Call me Nick, okay? 'Mr. Jenkins' sounds so formal." He smiled shyly, transforming his face.

"Okay, Nick. Are you on your lunch hour?"

"Yeah. I work at an auto mechanics place not far from here. My boss said I could make up the extra time later."

"That was nice of him." I hesitated, not quite sure for a moment how to proceed, then decided the best way was to jump in with both feet.

"I have your wife's written complaint," I said, holding up the envelope.

He frowned. "What complaint's that?"

He didn't know his wife was demanding half a million dollars? That stopped me. I'd assumed that they'd talked about it. Perhaps a Plan B was in order. "Oh, it's nothing."

I reached over and let Eddy grab my finger. "He sure has a good grip."

"Yeah, he does." Nick Jenkins beamed with paternal pride. He didn't look like a man who was livid about his unexpected progeny. Along with him not knowing about his wife's complaint, I'd have to think about what that all meant. For now, I wouldn't say anything more about it.

"Are you happy about the baby?" I asked in as casual a tone

as possible. I didn't look directly at him, but I caught his puzzled expression.

"Of course. I mean, it's a surprise and all, what with—"

I glanced at him again and saw he'd turned beet red. "Yes, well I'm sure the doctor told you it's not completely foolproof."

"I'll tell you, Ms. Kelly, if I'd had any idea what it would feel like to have a son—or a daughter too, I bet—I'd never have gone along with it. It was Sandra, my wife's, idea. She wasn't interested in having kids. 'Snot-nosed brats' is what she called them. Bored her stiff when friends'd pull out the pictures or talk about their kids' games and stuff."

I jiggled Eddy's hand and smiled. "Well, that's not unusual, Nick. No one's kids are as fascinating to others as they are to their own parents."

"Well, maybe." He didn't look convinced. "You know, Sandra and me, we've been having a rough time of it for a while. I don't know, but she wasn't happy. It was like she was restless, wanting more than I could give her."

"Hmmm," I said.

It still surprised me, even after all these years, how many intimate conversations I'd had with patients, telling me things about themselves and their families that they wouldn't share with someone they knew. Sometimes, I felt like a mother confessor. I was glad Mr. Jenkins had opened up to me because it would help me figure out how to handle his wife's complaint.

"I love my wife, Ms. Kelly. I'd do anything for her. But I'm not a rich man and won't ever be one. I'm good at repairing cars, and I can fix or build most anything she wants for the house. But I can't take her fancy places or give her expensive jewelry. I'm doing good if I can take her to Denny's once a month."

He looked at me with so much pain in his eyes, my heart ached for him. His gaze returned to the baby, and his expression was transformed by love for his child. "I'm hoping little Eddy here will make her happy. I've already talked to my mom about taking care of him during the day while I'm at work, and I'll do what needs to be done at night if Sandra's too tired. She'd have all the fun part of having a baby, you know what I mean?"

I nodded. "I think I do." Underneath his hopes for a happy life with his wife, this man was a realist. He knew better than to expect an outpouring of maternal love from her. He had the plans in place for the "just in case" things didn't go as he wished.

I stood up to leave. "You know, Nick, since you had a . . . ah, surgery here that didn't seem to take, I can schedule an appointment for you to have it redone at no charge."

Nick Jenkins's attention was totally focused on his son. "I'll think about it, Ms. Kelly. I'm in no rush."

When I left, I couldn't help but smile at the charming picture that man made with his child. My smile turned to a glower. How had a woman like Sandra Jenkins hooked a nice man like him? And then, not to appreciate what a good man she had.

She and I were going to talk again before I did anything with her case.

I returned to the Business Office to see what Becky had found. After winding my way around the low-walled cubicles, I reached her desk.

"Hi, Robyn. I found those discharge pages you wanted." Becky handed me several pieces of paper.

I sank slowly into the hard-backed chair next to her desk as I scanned them. The only notation on each sheet was a totally indecipherable signature for taking the bag from the safe. I pointed my finger at the lines where the patient is supposed to sign. "Can you tell if these are initials or a signature?"

She studied them, then said, "Hmmm. I can't tell."

I realigned the pages. "How do these compare to Jason Hilliard's signature when he was admitted?"

"That's in another file. Hold on a minute."

While she went to retrieve those documents, I read the discharge pages again. On each of the earlier admissions to the hospital, Jason Hilliard had signed to remove those bags from the safe while he was still a patient.

Becky returned and her pursed lips weren't encouraging.

"Well?"

She tucked her skirt under her as she sat down. "You're not going to like this. *I* don't like this. The signatures on these discharge sheets have absolutely no resemblance to the signature on his admit paper." She shook her head. "I'm going to have to schedule another training session for all three shifts."

"Something else is odd, Becky. There are no initials from someone here in the office as a witness."

"What?" She snatched the papers from me and studied them before slumping back in her chair. She looked at me in dismay. "This can't be, Rob. Someone has to open the safe to take out the contents, and initialing these sheets is mandatory." She arched an eyebrow. "How much do you want to bet no one signed the safe log?"

"Given what we've already found, I'm not going to touch that one."

"Follow me." Becky led me to a back room filled with shelves stocked with office supplies, a mini Office Depot. When we reached the square metal safe in the back, she retrieved an old leather-bound ledger book from a nearby shelf.

"That looks like something Bob Crachet used for Mr. Scrooge," I said with a laugh.

"Just about," she said ruefully. "It was bought long before we had computers, and since this is a manual process anyway, we've kept using it."

After setting the book on top of the safe, she opened it. "Let's see what we've got here. What were those dates again?"

"They were all a day or two after our mystery patient was admitted." I read off the dates as Becky flipped through the logbook.

When she finished, she closed the book with a resounding whomp and turned to me, throwing up her arms in disgust. "I can't believe this! Signing the logbook when opening the safe and indicating that a patient's belongings were taken out before discharge is one of our most basic procedures."

Glowering, she returned to her desk with me following behind. "I can *maybe* understand missing either the logbook *or* the discharge sheet one time, but not *both* on four different occasions."

"It sounds deliberate," I said quietly.

She nodded slowly and heaved a sigh. "It certainly does. I guess I'd better call Tom to initiate an investigation."

"Was it only Hilliard's bag that was taken all four times? Have any other patients complained that their belongings were missing?"

"Not that I can remember. Maybe before I call Tom I'll review all the discharge sheets during those same time periods. I'll see if they're initialed and then compare them to the logbook." She frowned. "This is really weird, Robyn. I mean, why would Hilliard be the only one this happened to, and why only the bag? And why every time?"

Knowing about the most recent bag's contents, I figured the reason must be something illegal, but said, "I have no idea. I'll be interested to hear what you learn from the other discharge sheets. Thanks, Becky."

"No, thank you, Robyn, for bringing this to my attention. The last thing I need is a bad audit from Risk Management. How would I ever explain that this had gone on for a year and not been detected?"

When I stood up to leave, Becky looked at me over the top of her reading glasses. "And I suppose I'm not to mention this to anyone yet."

I nodded. "But you'll be one of the first to know when we solve this mystery."

"Well, I just hope you don't get hurt in the process."

"Don't worry. I have no intention of doing that." I left her then. I couldn't tell her about the money, but I was sure Pierce would find my discovery very interesting.

I returned to my office and shuffled papers around until I couldn't put off calling my father any longer. This wasn't going to be fun. In fact, it would require all my persuasive skills. All I had to do was stay calm. Right.

I speed-dialed the number on my cell phone.

"Kelly Ranch."

"Hi, Da."

Silence blanketed the airwaves. Finally, he said, "Robyn Anne. Lois told me she called you. It was nothing to worry about."

Predictable. "Da, a T-I-A isn't something to ignore."

"I'm seventy years old and can do more in a day than the twenty-five years olds who are working for me."

Still predictable. "That may be true—"

" 'Tis true!"

"Okay, it is true, but I'd feel much better if you came to Seattle to be checked out."

"I won't be losing a week's work just because you're worried, Robyn Anne."

A gross exaggeration, but predictable. "It's not a week, Da. If you fly in tomorrow afternoon, you'll be seen on Thursday and can go home Friday."

"Robyn Anne, you been setting this up already?"

"As a matter of fact, yes. You have an appointment at Seattle Hospital. It's the big regional hospital for the Northwest and has a terrific reputation. A friend of mine who works there has gone to a great deal of trouble to make the arrangements."

"Then she can just be canceling those arrangements. I'm not coming. Dr. George checked me out in the Emergency Room and said I was fine."

He'd hit the hot button. "Yeah, the same Dr. George who kept telling Mom that the lump was nothing, and since she felt fine to come back in a year? A year for the cancer to spread to her bones and leave her in terrible pain? He let her die."

The silence felt different this time. Not defensive, but resigned. "Ah, girl, that was a sad day for us."

I snapped back, "I don't want a sad day for me again any time soon."

He was quiet for so long that I thought we'd lost connection. Finally he said quietly, "I'll come to Seattle and let them run their tests."

"Oh, Da, thank you." I sagged with relief. "This means a great deal to me."

"Well, you won't be getting a big birthday present with what this'll be costing me."

"That's fine. Having you around to harass will be the best present you can give me."

He harumphed. "Fine way to treat your father."

"You'll have to go to your hospital and sign a release. Tell them to fax your records, including any test results—if Dr. George could be bothered to order any—"

"Robyn Anne!"

"Sign the release, Da," I said with a sigh. "Have the records faxed to Seattle Hospital at 206-555-5161. My friend will make sure the doctor has them before your appointment. Did you write that number down?"

He mumbled something, so I waited until he had pencil and paper and was able to repeat the number back to me.

"I don't want to be trouble."

"It's no trouble, Da. Just go in today—"

"—another day's work lost—"

"Sign the form, Da!" He grumbled, but I ignored it. "I'll make the airline and hotel reservations for you and e-mail the information to you. Bring Lois too. She'd probably enjoy some time in the city."

"She'll have to bring an empty suitcase for all she'd be buying in those fancy stores."

"The stores will ship the things for her, Da. You won't have to tote extra luggage."

"Good thing, too."

"I love you, Da. Call me when you reach the airport."

"I love you too, girl."

I flipped my cell phone closed and sighed in relief. That had gone reasonably well. I was sorry I'd brought up my mother, but sometimes Da exasperated me to the point that I lost my objectivity. The same way I had with Josh about going to Africa. Well, let's face it: dealing with family over sensitive subjects was very different from dealing with patients.

I saw Pierce after work. I didn't want to watch him push the hospital food around his plate, so I had called and ordered two take-out lasagna dinners from my favorite Italian restaurant, complete with antipasto salad, garlic bread sticks, and tiramisu, and brought it to his room.

When I carried the bags into his room, you'd have thought I was bringing chateaubriand and champagne. He grabbed his trapeze bar and raised his bed to a sitting position. Assuming he was okay to sit up while eating, I set his food on the tray table and wheeled it in front of him.

We chatted about this and that while we ate. When he finished, he eased the tray away and sighed with contentment. He lowered his bed to a prone position. "That was outstanding, Rob. Only a glass of chianti would have made it better."

I laughed. "Yes, and that would do wonderful things to you when it mixed with your pain meds."

"Well, there is that, I suppose," he said with a shrug. "So. Now that we've eaten, tell me what's going on."

Before he started his barrage of questions, I asked, "Have you gone for all your walks?"

He scowled at me. "I missed one."

"Well, let's do it now. Then we'll talk."

It was quite the ordeal getting him disconnected from his traction. He inhaled sharply at the pain when I helped him swing his legs over the side of the bed to sit up.

"Oh, I'm sorry, Matt. It's my fault. Do you want me to call the nurse?"

"No, it's not your fault. And no, don't call the nurse. It hurts when they help me too." He looked at me with a woeful expression. "The physical therapist said that in a day or two, it'll stop hurting every time I move. That's supposed to be consoling, I guess."

There was nothing I could say to improve the situation, so instead I said, "Now that you're up, let's go."

I held his arm, more for moral support than anything else, and we strolled slowly down the hall and back. He concentrated on each step, limiting conversation.

"That's enough," he said.

I glanced at my watch. "It's only been eight minutes."

"Yeah, and a full loop is four minutes. I'd rather stop two minutes short than go two minutes too long."

"My, my, grumpy this evening aren't we? And after I brought you that nice dinner too."

He glowered at me. "It's just that—"

"—it hurts. I understand. Let's get you back into bed."

This time I did call for the nurse's assistance in getting Pierce trussed back into his corset. We sat quietly until the pain medication kicked in again.

CHAPTER 12

"Okay. Now tell me what's going on."

"Do you want the long version or the short one?"

"Rob. I want all the gory details. Otherwise, it's going to be an interminably boring evening."

"I shall do my best to entertain and enlighten you," I said with a grin. I launched into a detailed explanation of what I'd learned from Becky and the lab.

Pierce frowned and plucked at his lower lip while he thought about what I'd told him. "Tell me again what's supposed to happen."

"The patient gives his possessions to the admitting clerk who logs them in on the admit sheet and puts the items in the safe. When he's discharged, the items are returned to him, and he signs a form acknowledging he's received them. But if he wants something while he's still here, he has to sign a special form, and the Business Office employee is supposed to co-sign that form and file it, and sign and date the safe's logbook."

"And none of that happened during any of Hilliard's admissions when the bag was removed?"

I shook my head. "Becky said she could see maybe one deviation from procedure during one admission, but not all the procedures completely ignored every time."

"Hmmm. What does that suggest to you?"

He had his own ideas, I was sure, but it was fun to play Watson to his Sherlock. "I have no idea, but it can't be anything legal."

Pierce nodded his agreement. "My thought too. What else can you tell me?"

"What do you mean?"

"Details. Where is the safe located?"

"In the back storage room."

"It's not visible from the public part of the Business Office?"

"No. You'd have to know it was there."

"Okay then. Who has access to the safe?"

"I suspect most of the office employees. They all rotate doing admits and discharges so they'd have to be able to open the safe when needed."

Pierce scowled. "Great. Another cast of thousands."

"I don't think it's quite that bad," I said with a laugh. "Maybe twenty people when you figure the Business Office is staffed twenty-four/seven."

"Does it take a key or a combination to open the safe?"

"I don't know."

"Well, find out. If it's a key, find out where it's kept. If it's a combination, how often is it changed—if ever—and where do they keep a written copy of it?"

I could see where he was going with this. How hard would it be for someone outside the Business Office to gain access to the safe and its contents? If it was too complicated, it had to be an inside job. "I'll talk to Becky tomorrow and ask her."

"Another thing. When were these items removed from the safe? What time of day was it done? Was it in broad daylight when the Business Office is crawling with people, or in the dead of night?"

"I don't know, and I don't know if we can find out since the procedures weren't followed." I was beginning to feel my performance as assistant detective was not very good.

"Well, there's signatures on one of those forms. See if it's time-stamped and dated." He clasped his hands together and tapped his index fingers against his lips as he considered the situation. "The other thing you might check for me is who admitted and discharged Hilliard. Was it the same person each time, or a different person?"

By this time, I'd pulled a piece of paper from my purse and had started making notes. "What do you think so far?"

"I don't want to jump to conclusions before I have some answers to those questions."

"But . . ."

"It has to be an inside job. A non-employee would stand out like a sore thumb, especially since the safe's away from public view."

"As much as I hate to think one of our employees is doing something illegal, there doesn't seem to be any other answer."

"Right. So, what we have to do is look into the backgrounds of all the Business Office employees and find out who had a connection with Hilliard."

"That sounds good, Matt, but there's one big problem."

"What's that?"

"Hilliard isn't really Hilliard, remember? If we don't know who he is, how can we make a connection?"

Pierce scowled at me. "You're right. For a moment I'd forgotten that the investigation is being handled by a . . . Go home, Rob. There's nothing more we can do tonight. Maybe tomorrow we'll find something else useful."

"Something that doesn't generate more unanswered questions." I gathered up the remains of our take-out dinner and put them in a plastic bag. "I'm sorry, Matt."

"Ah, it's not your fault." He jangled his traction apparatus. "I'm just frustrated to be here. And I'm worried about how much I'm asking you to do. I don't want to put you at risk."

"I'm being very subtle," I assured him.

"Yeah, but the problem is, you don't know for sure whom to be subtle around, and every time you ask questions or probe deeper, you're in danger of attracting the murderer's attention."

I patted him on the shoulder. "I promise to stay below the radar. I'm talking only to people I trust completely."

"Just the same, be careful. Very, very careful."

"I will. Sleep well, and I'll see you tomorrow."

Pierce was grumbling and mumbling under his breath when I left. I appreciated his concern for my safety, but I was the one who'd landed him in the hospital, leaving me obliged to act as his eyes and ears on the investigation. I wasn't worried that anything I had done so far had put me in danger.

I pulled my car into the garage with a heavy heart. Josh's car wasn't there, and I didn't know when he'd come home.

Taffy greeted me at the door, and I was reassured to see she'd been fed and had fresh water. Josh had been home and left again. That was a good sign that he wasn't rejecting everything. Just his mom.

I lingered in the kitchen for as long as I could, but I had to walk through the dining room sometime. I might as well get it over with. I'd noticed blue tarps covering part of the roof as I drove up the street and a pile of debris on the ground below. Inside, there were other signs of slow progress. The buckets were gone, and the carpet had been rearranged so the rest of the wet areas faced the fans.

In the midst of everything that had gone on today, calling my insurance agent had completely slipped my mind. Let's face it, there are only so many personal crises a person can handle at one time.

After spending a long day inside the hospital and worrying about Josh, Da, the murder, William, and Baby Eddy, I should have been too exhausted to move. But sitting on the couch was the last thing I wanted to do. I needed some fresh air. Maybe it would help clear my thinking too.

I changed clothes and in a few minutes, Taffy and I were walking briskly to the corner and on to our regular route. Fortunately, the rain had stopped.

It felt grand to be outside, moving energetically along the quiet residential streets, nodding a greeting to the other dog-walkers we passed. When at last we returned to our cul-de-sac, some of the weight on my shoulders had slipped away. Now it was okay to slow to a more leisurely pace. Taffy enjoyed the chance to savor the sniffs and I wanted to think beneath the cloudless sky while gazing at the stars above.

Josh. What would we say to each other after last night's outburst? His accusation that I was prejudiced had hurt me deeply. It was the antithesis of everything I believed.

Taffy brought me to a halt, and I looked at the houses around mine. When I'd first moved here, ours was the first single parent household. I'd been viewed with suspicion at first; was I looking to snare one of the married men away from his home? It took a few months of greeting both husbands and wives over front yard gardens, a few spontaneous conversations in the middle of the street, and some shared cups of coffee with the other moms in each other's kitchens for me to be completely accepted.

But then the East Indian computer programmer arrived with his family and received the same reaction. After them, the single mom Hispanic accountant. By the time the African-American lawyer and his partner moved in, no one batted an eyelash. With exposure came familiarity, then acceptance, and finally friendship. I was stopped in front of a house for sale. Who would move in here? Would they be like "us?" Whatever "us" was anymore in this eclectic neighborhood.

I thought about Margie, who was African-American. Like most boss-employee relationships, we didn't socialize outside the office, but we considered ourselves friends. I'd do anything to help her if she needed it, and she would return the favor. And let's face it, healthcare was such a diversified employer that I worked with a wide variety of people.

So Josh's criticism hurt. Reluctantly, I remembered my initial encounter with William. It was a natural reaction to a potential threat, right?

The real issue I had to deal with now, though, was Josh's plan to spend his summer in a hostile country in Africa. Whatever I did, I couldn't rush, despite "the guy's" Friday deadline.

I had a few days left. I'd find subtle, meaningful ways to get my point across without Josh feeling backed against a wall. I'd take the same approach I used at work, non-confrontational, supplying information to help the decision-making. All those jargon-laden, process things we did every day.

It started to rain again, so we scurried home and entered through the garage's side door. After drying Taffy's feet and shaking water off my raincoat, we stepped back into the kitchen. I took Taffy's leash off and gave her a biscuit. She gulped it down, then eased her way around the dining room to the living room and her pad.

Seeing she was content, I tugged off my heavy sweater and headed for my computer. In a few minutes, I'd made airline and hotel reservations for Da and Lois and e-mailed the flight information to them.

Signing off, I leaned back in my chair. What should I tell Josh? I had to tell him that Da was coming to Seattle. But I wasn't sure how much detail I wanted to share at this point.

The last thing I wanted was for Da's health issues to interfere or cloud the discussion about Josh's summer plans. For now, I wouldn't say anything.

Early the next morning, in a distracted dash, I finished the Quality report and handed it to Connie, rationalizing that I'd met the Tuesday P.M. deadline. Howard's administrative assistant never stayed a minute past five o'clock, and Connie would have it on Arlene's desk before nine. After sending a hurried e-mail to Paula to let her know the report was in and to say I was glad we could work together on it, I reshuffled some of the work on my desk, and even managed to finish a few things and toss them into my out-box.

It was almost noon when I emerged from my office and slipped into my raincoat. "I'm off to the patient rep meeting, Connie."

"Okay. Will you be back?"

I hesitated at the doorway. "Probably not. I have to pick up my dad at the airport this afternoon and bring him to downtown Seattle."

She nodded. "You're right. You'd never make it across the bridge by that time. We'll see you tomorrow."

I stopped by William's room before I left the hospital. I had to see him every day, for his sake and to reassure myself that he continued to do well.

When I walked into his room, his new decorations no longer surprised me. Today, I spotted two scented candles, one on each end table. The cinnamon spice and pine were out of season, but the room certainly smelled nothing like a typical hospital room. Of course, open flames were not allowed in hospital rooms, but William wasn't using oxygen, and if the nurses hadn't snuffed them out, why should I?

"Hi, William."

"Morning, Miz Robyn."

163

He recognized me. Definitely a good sign.

We chatted for a few minutes about the lunch he waited for with great anticipation, his trips to the indoor park, how he was feeling. Neither of us mentioned the additions he continued to make to his room.

Before leaving 3-West, I swung by Susan Wong's office.

When I knocked gently on her open door, she looked up at me and sighed. "What's wrong now?"

I laughed. "Nothing! Can't I stop by to say hi?"

"Well, I guess," she grumbled. "It's just that you never do."

"Maybe I should change that. With everyone. Might take away some of the automatic cringe reception I get."

This time, Susan laughed. "No, it'd make us more paranoid because we'd wonder which is it *this* time, the nice Robyn or the trouble-making Robyn?"

"Susan! How can you say 'the trouble-making Robyn?' "

"You're right, that really isn't fair. You don't make trouble." She grinned. "It just follows you wherever you go."

I had to admit she had a good point. And if most people still greeted me in a friendly way, despite their concern about why I was coming to see them, then I could accept that.

"I suppose you've seen William?" she asked.

"Yes. He's continuing to make interesting additions to the room."

"I know! We haven't a clue where he's finding these things. Has anyone complained to you or Tom that they're missing them?"

"Not to me. I didn't think to ask Tom, what with everything else that's going on." Josh. Da.

"Yeah, who has time with a murder to investigate?" She gave me a smug smile. "I heard there's a mysterious bag he left in the safe."

I shouldn't have been surprised that she knew the bag existed;

that would fly through the hospital grapevine. But I seriously doubted she knew about the contents, and certainly not about the other bags Hilliard had brought with him to the hospital. I had to respond to her comment. "Tom mentioned that to me."

"Do you know anything more?"

"Why, Susan, don't you remember? I vowed not to be involved in the investigation."

She eyed me sharply. "Yeah, but with your detective friend in the hospital, I'd think he'd be tempted to ask for your help."

Her astuteness surprised me. I had to back my way out of this one, and fast. "Don't be silly. Oh, gee, look at the time. I'm going to be late for my meeting. See you later."

"See ya."

I trotted down the stairs and took the exit door leading to the staff parking lot. It had stopped raining for a few minutes at least, but I had to dodge several deep puddles. The last thing I needed was to spend the rest of the day in wet shoes.

I started the car and headed toward I-405. Given everything that was happening, I was sorely tempted to skip the meeting, but I hoped to learn something from my compatriots about the registry nurse, Amanda Whitcomb.

Besides, I'd be making this trip today anyway to pick up my dad and Lois. Maybe we would have dinner together before I came home.

The traffic gods were on my side for once. After a brief slowdown on I-405, I found myself breezing across the Highway 520 bridge toward Seattle, enjoying the cloudless blue sky and bright sunshine reflecting off Lake Washington.

The official opening day of yachting season was coming up fast, the first Saturday in May. Boats line up to enter Puget Sound through the Chittendon Locks, sometimes days earlier. By opening day, the boats are so thick on Lake Union, the Montlake Cut, and into Lake Washington that people hop from one boat to another. When Josh was younger, we'd take a picnic lunch and sit on the grassy slope overlooking the Locks and pick out our dream boats. Maybe we could do it this year?

That thought was dashed when I remembered our unresolved argument. Surely we'd have patched things up by then, but Josh was moving in different directions now. He didn't have time to spend a whole day with his mom, even for long-standing traditions. Maybe I'd talk to Chuck and if she was interested, perhaps they'd both come. They probably wouldn't want me tagging along, though, even if I did pack a great picnic lunch. They'd have friends they'd want to go with.

So fine, I grumbled to myself. I have friends. I'll call some of them and pack a lunch they'll enjoy eating with me.

Feeling a little better, I glanced at the lake. Today, a few boats were out, and one brave soul was waterskiing. I took the Lake Washington Boulevard exit, drove along the edge of the Arboretum, and turned south. I reached Charity Hospital in almost record time. The patient reps from Seattle-area hospitals met here once a month to discuss common concerns and ways to handle difficult complaints.

There is something special about walking into a room full of people who totally understand what it is you do and don't think you're crazy. I was pleased to see that most of the patient reps I'd called about Amanda were present. Hopefully I'd gather some information Pierce would find useful.

The basic meeting was just starting, and there wasn't time to talk to them beforehand. But I was pleased that after Sharon called the meeting to order, she brought up the topic of registry personnel, those who came to fill in shifts not covered by regular employees. For the most part, we had no problem with them, but we agreed that temps like Amanda Whitcomb, difficult and unprofessional types, needed to be weeded out.

Sharon said she'd invite the registry to send someone to speak at our next meeting to see what process could be used to solve this problem. I was appointed to a subcommittee to meet with the registry representative to explain what we wanted to cover at the meeting. Like I needed another thing on my to-do list. But I had brought the subject up.

The guest speaker talked about the uninsured in King County. It was frightening to learn the number of children with virtually no access to healthcare.

But despite how compelling he was with a lot of statistics and distressing case studies, I was in a hurry to talk to the others about Amanda Whitcomb. Finally, the meeting was over, and I moved to the back of the room.

Melinda from Mountain View Hospital was the first to join me. "Hi, Rob. Boy, am I glad you asked me to check out that registry nurse. When I reviewed the complaints about nurses, Amanda Whitcomb was involved in eighty percent of them. I couldn't believe it—she was yelling and swearing at the patients. I let my Director of Nursing know, so I doubt we'll see Amanda again."

"I found the same thing," said Jena, the patient rep at Lakeside Hospital, entering the discussion. "Most patients love our nurses, but Amanda definitely wasn't on that list. How come we didn't pick up on her sooner?"

"Probably because she was registry, not regular staff," said Elizabeth.

Sharon joined the group. "She was more than rude to my patients."

We all turned to her. "What'd she do?" I asked.

"I had a couple of complaints about her being rough enough to cause bruising."

"Hmmm. That sounds like someone with anger management issues," said Melinda.

Was it serious enough that she'd commit murder? I wondered silently.

Sharon nodded. "Our Nursing Director has already contacted the registry to say we wouldn't take her back."

We left the meeting at one-thirty, more than an hour before Da's plane was scheduled to land. That extra time gave me an idea. I stopped by the Patient Relations office and asked Megan to let me see her telephone book.

It took some looking, but I found Spiffy Clean Laundry in the gray section, the alphabetical listing of businesses, but not in the Yellow Pages under "commercial laundry." That in itself was interesting. Why wasn't it advertising for business? I jotted down the address and left the phone book with Megan's assistant.

As I exited the parking garage, I turned down James Street to the I-5 south-bound on-ramp. Maybe I'd learn something to explain the Bloomingdale letter. As I approached the exit, I questioned what I was doing. Did I really want to know? I had time, and I had the address. I remembered my grandmother's expression, "You cannot know what's around the next bend until you start walking."

CHAPTER 13

Following that advice, I started the new adventure by taking the Michigan Street exit and wound my way around Georgetown, the light industrial district in south Seattle. Georgetown is a confusing area, with straight streets and diagonal streets and railroad tracks and dead ends.

It took me a while, and much consulting of my *Thomas Guide* map book, but I finally found Spiffy Clean Laundry. The first time, I drove right past. To backtrack, I tried going around the block, hit another dead end, and finally got myself turned around and back to the right address. I pulled into the small parking lot. After turning off the engine, I sat in my SUV and looked around. If I hadn't double and triple checked the address, I would have sworn the place was deserted. The asphalt parking lot was riddled with cracks filled with thriving dandelions. The squat one-story building was much smaller than I would have expected for a commercial laundry, was badly in need of a paint job, and there was no signage. Despite the grime, I could see lights on through the small, high-set windows.

This wasn't amusing anymore. Not sinister, exactly, just . . . weird. I thought about chickening out, but I'd come this far already. There really was nothing specifically scary that I could see. Still, my sense of unease continued. Taking a deep breath for courage, I left the security of my car and opened the metal door that I assumed was the main entrance, since it was in front, near the end.

Stepping inside the building, I was assailed by the heat, humidity, and powerful aromas of detergent and bleach. Yup, no doubt about it; this was a laundry. But I had to walk down a hall that ran the length of the building before I reached another door. When I stepped into that room, I saw a young woman, feet propped on an army surplus metal desk, watching a small TV attached to the wall above her. Her hair was turquoise, purple, and a brassy red, and she had to be sweltering in that black leather jacket decorated with metal studs.

Not wanting to startle her, I said "Hi" as I stepped forward. Then I noticed a security camera monitor on her desk. There was my SUV, so she knew I was coming in.

She turned in her chair, but her eyes stayed on the TV screen. "Whatchyawant?"

"I understand you're a commercial laundry?"

"Yeah, but we're not taking new jobs." She still hadn't looked at me.

"I see." I looked around the room, surprised at how few washing machines there were, and how small. None of them were running. "Is this all the capacity you have?"

"Uh-huh."

I didn't know what else to ask. "Okay. Well, thanks for your time." I left and returned to my car. Since I now knew about the security camera, I had to wonder if it videotaped as well. And, if so, who would view it later? Feeling more than a bit paranoid, I drove away rather than stay and be observed. Or videotaped. I was thoroughly confused by what I'd seen. This was the cause for the latest Bloomingdale letter? There was no way that facility could possibly handle one hospital's laundry needs, let alone two. What was going on?

I had to concentrate on the traffic for the drive to the airport. To reduce the traffic near Baggage Claim, the airport had designated a parking lot a short way from the terminal for people to wait until their travelers called to announce their arrivals. I parked in the lot for maybe fifteen minutes before Da called on my cell phone to say they'd arrived at the gate. I gave them a few minutes before driving to the airport's lower level to pick them up.

Since Lois's call and my brief conversation with Da, I wasn't sure what to expect. He was a burly man, tall with broad shoulders and narrow hips, just what you'd expect from a man who'd spent his life herding cattle. Always in excellent health, he scoffed at vitamin pills and flu shots. I wondered if this had been a major scare for him. I knew it was for me.

I climbed out of my car and scanned the faces of the people exiting the terminal. When I spotted Da, my heart sank. He'd aged so much. Was that from being in the hospital or was travel too hard on him? Surely he looked better at home. Although he still had his thick silver hair, his face was drawn, and he had a gray look about him that scared me. I'd done the right thing, insisting he come to Seattle for tests and treatment recommendations.

When I waved, Lois spotted me first. She waved in return, then tugged Da's jacket and pointed at me. He turned in my direction, and his face lit up, transforming him into the father I adored.

Rushing to them, I gave him a big hug and found myself enveloped in a tight embrace. I almost couldn't breathe, but that was okay; it meant Da still had his strength. When he released me, I hugged Lois, whom I hadn't seen in at least a year, then grabbed their suitcases.

Wheeling them to the back of my Explorer, I called over my shoulder, "How was the flight?"

Lois smiled. "Fine—"

"Terrible—"

I swallowed a grin as I hefted Lois's suitcase into the car. My mother had always deferred to my father's opinions on everything. Lois was the opposite, wanting to debate everything. Da was obviously fond of her, and I think he found her entertaining too. She certainly kept his mental faculties sharp.

After settling them in the car, Da riding shotgun after a brief verbal skirmish about wanting to drive, and Lois content to sit in back, I said, "I made your reservations at the Four Seasons—"

"Saints in heaven, girl! How'm I supposed to be paying the bill for that?"

"Now, Patrick," Lois said. "You and I both know you can well afford it."

"You be looking in my checkbook while I was in the hospital?"

Instead of being offended, Lois laughed. "Of course not. Who'd want to snoop through your old things? Besides, you told me how much you're making in stud fees for that old bull of yours."

"Ah, the Four Seasons?" I interjected. "I have your rooms reserved."

"Thank you, dear," Lois said. "That was sweet of you to take care of all that for us. We don't get out much you know."

Glancing in the rearview mirror, I saw her make a face at the back of Da's head. Then she winked at me.

"Well, it's good to come to the big city once in awhile," I said. "You need to see what's really going on in world."

"I know what's going on, Robyn Anne. It's going to the devil, that's what it is."

"Don't listen to him," Lois said. "He's been cranky ever since he had his spell."

"A lot of fuss about nothing," Da grumbled.

"Lois and I thank you for letting us fuss you into coming here to see a doctor."

"Going to be costing me a fortune," he continued. "And all the work that'll be piling up. Catching up's going to be killing me faster than any sickness."

The conversation continued until I pulled up to the hotel, helped them from the car, handed the car over to the valet, and escorted them inside. It took only a few minutes for them to register, and then we went up to their room.

"Would you like to go out for an early dinner?" I asked.

Lois glanced at Da. "No, dear, I'm tired after the flight and would like to take a little nap before going out. Is that okay with you, Patrick?"

He nodded his agreement, but I knew from the way she'd looked at him that this once, she'd taken her cue from him.

"There's a terrific restaurant downstairs, and there are lots of them up and down the street," I said.

"Don't worry, dear. We may just order something light from room service—"

"And I'll be paying the extra for that service—"

"Or we may go out. It has been a long day. Traveling isn't fun like it used to be," Lois said with a wistful sigh.

I left them to work it out for themselves and collected my car from the valet. I probably wouldn't be able to come back to drive them to the doctor's appointment, but it was easy enough to catch a cab to go up the hill and get one to come back.

The rush hour traffic was going full tilt by the time I started to cross the I-90 bridge. Between construction and a disabled vehicle, I-405 was a worse mess than usual, and I reached the hospital after office hours.

I picked up a well-deserved latté—Da would have a fit if he knew how much I spent on those every day—from the hospital's espresso cart. By the time I returned to my office. Connie and Margie were long gone. I settled into my chair and dug through my desk drawer for the Bloomingdale letter. I finally found it and headed for Pierce's room.

It was time for his evening walk, so I put down my latté and joined Pierce in his journey to the end of the hall, around the corner, and up the other side. What would normally take me only a few minutes, took us fifteen.

He clenched his jaw in concentration.

"Does it hurt?" I asked.

"If I move wrong."

"So no talking?"

"No."

"The stuff I want to talk about should be behind closed doors anyway."

He turned to look at me, his expression full of interest, quickly followed by severe wincing. He faced forward again.

"That hurt? To look at me like that?"

"Uh-huh."

"Okay. No more talking until you're settled again."

When we reached his room, I called for the nurse to settle him in and adjust the traction to the right tension.

When she was finished and left, he let out a deep sigh. "That's over for a while." His face was pale, and he still looked like he was in pain.

"Feel better now?"

He shifted slightly. "Hard to believe, but yes. This apparatus really does help."

"Good."

"Okay, now I want to know what you found out at your meeting."

"The meeting was very interesting." Settling into a chair with my latte, I took a sip; cold, but I needed the caffeine. "I knew the uninsured were a problem, but I had no idea how widespread it was—"

"Rob!"

I grinned at him. "Okay, here's what I learned. Several of the other patient reps went through their complaint records and found that Amanda Whitcomb was the primary source for complaints involving nurses."

"Anything serious?" He looked so hopeful.

"Most said it was attitude issues, but we found that Amanda has been accused of not only yelling and swearing at patients, but also of being too rough with them. Bruising them even."

Pierce looked taken aback. "Really. I guess I'm surprised that she was that bad. It seems so . . . so . . . ."

"Un-nurse like?" I offered.

"Yeah, un-nurse like. But if she has a short fuse—"

"And had motive and opportunity—"

"She's on my short-list."

"*Our* short-list."

"Yeah, okay, *our* short-list." Pierce's brow was furrowed as he considered this new information.

"I found something else. It means nothing to the murder, but it is puzzling. Maybe you have some idea what it all means," I said.

He pinned me with his eagle-eyed stare. "What?"

"Well, since you asked so nicely, read this." I handed him the Bloomingdale letter.

He took it, glanced at it, and said, "What's this?"

"It's a Bloomingdale letter. Someone inside the hospital randomly sends these letters to Admin to tweak their noses. No one knows who's behind them, but they're distributed every-where at once so there's no way for Admin to keep them secret."

Pierce scanned the letter, then handed it back to me. "So?"

"With Bloomingdale letters, we never know the truth behind them. Since I was already on First Hill, I checked out the ad-dress and found it wasn't that far away. So I went to George-town to take a look at the laundry. It was really weird, nothing at all like I would've expected."

"How so?" He definitely appeared interested now.

"Well, the parking lot was deserted and in disrepair, the building was small and needed paint. Inside, there was only one person, and she was watching TV. There were only a few household-sized washers and dryers, and none of them was running. You know those big canvas-sided carts we use for dirty laundry?"

"Uh-huh."

"There weren't any, not a single one. And there were no stacks of clean folded laundry waiting to be delivered either. Not from here or from the mysterious Mercy Hospital."

Pierce shrugged. "Maybe all the clean laundry was being delivered and the dirty hadn't come back yet."

"I don't know," I said hesitantly. "It was as if . . . it was as if the machines had been run empty to create the ambiance of a commercial laundry—the heat and humidity and the smell—but it wasn't really a laundry."

Pierce looked askance at me. "Robyn, that's one of the most ridiculous things I've ever heard you say."

My feelings were hurt—well ruffled, maybe, by his words, but I wasn't going to argue. "I suppose."

I let it go at that, but it really did make me wonder what was going on at the Spiffy Clean Laundry and why Madrona Bay Hospital did business with it.

I reached home long after the sun had disappeared behind the Olympic Mountains. More of my roof was covered by blue tarps, and it appeared that four-by-fours had been laid across the edges to keep the wind from blowing them away.

The house was quiet when I stepped into the kitchen from the garage. Taffy greeted me with her welcome dance, twirling and barking in delight. Exactly what I needed after a very long day: no-strings-attached love from my dog and the normality of home.

"Hello, Taffy." I dropped my things on the kitchen counter and ruffled her fur.

I crossed the kitchen and checked the dining room. The fans were still going, but the wet areas on the carpet felt close to dry. I needed some good news for a change.

When I opened the sliding door to the deck, Taffy was more interested in me than in going out. Finally convinced I was staying home for a while, she let me push her eighty pounds of fur out the door, and then she proceeded to check out the backyard.

I stood at the window and watched her for a moment. Josh and Da were on hold, awaiting further developments, so my thoughts drifted to the murder. I mean, here it was four days after the murder and I didn't have a single viable suspect except that registry nurse, Amanda. I'd done much better last winter when I'd found myself in the middle of a murder investigation.

That was it, wasn't it? Not having time to solve the murder was bugging me. I hadn't had time to look for clues. All those little tidbits of information I'd picked up at the Patient Rep meeting about the registry nurse, Amanda Whitcomb, were interesting, provocative even, but should we consider her a serious suspect? My visit with Becky in the Business Office, which I'd thought had been a successful foray into real detective work, had turned out to be seriously lacking, according to Pierce. I hadn't been able to do anything yet about his long list of questions.

And what was going on with Spiffy Clean Laundry? That was the most curious because I had no idea how it fit in with the Bloomingdale letter. Sometimes those letters were so esoteric it took someone far smarter than I was to figure out what they really meant. At least Spiffy Clean had nothing to do with anything I was working on.

No more thinking about work! Take the rest of the night off!

I went to the kitchen and poured myself a glass of wine, a sauvignon blanc a friend had recommended, saying the hints of pear, melon, and peach were perfect for warm spring days. The weather certainly wasn't warm, and dampness permeated the house. I took a sip. My unsophisticated palette could only discern grape, but the wine still tasted good.

I kicked off my shoes and puttered for a few minutes, checking the mail—bills and things addressed to "resident"—and listening to telephone messages, a little more personal than my mail. A charity group wanted to pick up stuff I didn't need anymore and the library was holding a book I'd requested.

When I let Taffy back inside, she raced off to find a toy, and I played with her for a few minutes, taking care her nails didn't scratch me while we each sought possession of her stuffed pig. When she grabbed her toy and took it to her pad in the corner of the living room, I knew I was really off duty for the rest of the day.

After changing clothes, I contemplated dinner, but nothing sounded exciting. When you're alone, who wants to fix a big meal that you have to clean up all by yourself? With a sigh, I went out to the garage to see what was in the freezer that I could defrost and reheat in the microwave.

My body was half in the chest freezer when I heard the doorbell. I grabbed the first plastic container that looked like it had potential and rushed back into the house. When I looked through the peephole and saw who was standing on the other side of the front door, I opened it.

"Hi, Andrea," I said.

She looked me up and down. "You okay? You're out of breath."

I guess you could say Andrea is my best friend. We'd met at a Friends of the Library used book sale about eight years ago, both reaching for the same book at the same time. That led to introductions, sharing favorite authors over a cup of coffee, and a deep and abiding friendship. Whenever we get together, we always have a grand time. We're close in age, but opposite in looks. While I'm average height and build, she's short and round. I have black hair, and she's a blonde.

"I'm fine." I held up my frozen plastic container. "I was rummaging in the freezer for something to thaw out for dinner."

"I have something better." She held up bags from our favorite Chinese restaurant.

"Take-out. You're a goddess!" I opened the door wider for her to pass, then led her into the kitchen.

"Uh-oh!" she said as we passed through the dining room. "What's going on here? It doesn't look like a remodel."

"It's not. My roof leaked and damaged the ceiling."

"You're kidding!"

"I wish I was." I briefly described my roof saga, then said, "But tell me, how did you know I hadn't eaten?"

"I called you at work, and Connie told me what your schedule was like, so I figured out the best time to show up."

"Connie would say you were psychic," I said with a laugh.

"Nothing psychic about it, Rob. Not if you were picking up your dad." She set the bags on the counter. "How is he?"

"Oh, his usual cantankerous self."

"Rob . . ."

"He looks awful, Andrea, just awful."

"Good thing you brought him here."

"We'll see. He'll probably argue that every test is a waste of time and money."

"I know what you mean. My parents were the same way. You'd've thought they had no insurance and no money rather than a Medicare supplement that paid every bill, along with fabulous pensions." She started pulling white take-out boxes from the paper bags and set them on the kitchen table, then sighed. "We should be so lucky."

"Andrea, my retirement is the least of my problems this week."

She went to the sideboard in the dining room for some place mats. When she returned, she asked, "Isn't Josh home? I brought enough for him too."

Scanning the bags spread across the table, I said, "So I see. No, he and Chuck are studying at her place." I poured her a glass of wine.

Her eyes widened as she accepted the wine. "At her place? Are you sure it's engineering they're studying?"

"Andrea." I gave her a mock scowl. "We've had the talks, and at this point in his life, it's none of my business."

"Hmmm. If you say so."

I love Andrea dearly, but she's never been married or had children, although that doesn't stop her from giving me parenting advice on a regular basis. Changing the subject, I asked, "Why tonight with the take-out?"

"I got back into town late last night, so I didn't know anything until I watched this morning's news. Naturally, when I saw your hospital featured on every station, I wanted to know more. So, spill the beans!"

"Oh, I don't even know where to begin with that one." I popped the frozen plastic container into the refrigerator to wait for another night's dinner, and then gathered flatware and handed it to her. "Let's see. You left Friday after work, so you don't know anything, do you?"

"You mean there's more?"

"I better start with the homeless man from New York City." When her eyes widened, I knew she was hooked. I took a sip of wine and proceeded to relay a brief description of William and the nurses' complaints about the flashing patient without crossing the confidentiality line.

Andrea laughed, a deep belly laugh that had me chuckling in response. "Just can't stay out of trouble, can you? How do you do it?"

Then I told her about Pierce hurting his back.

Shaking her head, she said, "He's the closest thing you've had to a boyfriend in all the time I've known you, and here you ruin him?"

I rolled my eyes at her assessment of my non-existent relationship history. "He chose to lift those bags, Andrea," I called back. "I told him to be careful."

"Hmmm. Well, we'll see if he comes calling again after he gets out of your hospital. But you still haven't filled in the details of the murder. What happened?"

Since I hate putting hot food on cold plates, I warmed two dinner plates in the microwave while I told her about finding Hilliard's body and how he'd used false identification.

"Really? I couldn't imagine what they were talking about on the news when they said the victim still hadn't been identified," Andrea said. "I mean, aren't hospitals notorious for not dispensing so much as a Band-Aid until they have your whole life history so they can be sure they get their money?"

After removing the warmed plates, we refilled our wine glasses and settled around the kitchen table. "The murder victim gave all kinds of information, but unfortunately, none of it was true. And since he paid his bill with checks from a legitimate account and they didn't bounce, the Business Office had no reason to verify any of it."

I opened the first white box of Chinese food and breathed deeply. Broccoli beef. I opened the rest of the boxes and tried not to swoon at the sight of BBQ pork, chow mein noodles, and sweet and sour prawns as I stuck a big spoon in each one. Andrea had definitely been thinking of Josh when ordering all this food.

"But what about the police?" She pulled chopsticks from another bag. "Why haven't they ID'd him yet? Didn't they run his fingerprints or something?"

"That's part of the problem. Apparently, there's a backlog of prints, so they have to wait."

Andrea was quiet for a few moments while we passed around the boxes of food and helped ourselves to hearty portions. "Doesn't that strike you as really odd?"

"Yes, it does." I took my first bite of moo shu pork wrapped in a tiny pancake with a dab of plum sauce and moaned with contentment. "And, it's driving Pierce insane. I've never seen him so crabby since . . ." I sighed. "He hasn't been this crabby since the last time we had a murder at the hospital."

"But that time he was annoyed with you for snooping on your own."

"That's true. This time he's upset because he isn't handling the investigation and there's nothing he can do about it."

Andrea was quiet again. "Rob. Are you snooping, or did you learn your lesson last time?"

CHAPTER 14

"Well, yes and no, I guess."

"What's that supposed to mean?" Andrea demanded.

I hesitated. "It means I'm looking into a few things for Pierce. Very quietly, mind you. No one knows he and I are involved."

"You wish!" She harrumphed, then pointed a chopstick at me. "Face it, Rob. If you're talking to people about it, somebody else will notice. I just hope it's not the wrong somebody else." Then she gave me a solemn look. "I know you'll do what you want, regardless of what I say. But, be careful, okay? Pierce can't protect you this time if he's all tied up like a Thanksgiving turkey."

"I know. Believe me, I'm being very careful."

Avid curiosity quickly replaced her caution. "So, have you found anything good?"

"Nothing I can share."

She grunted in disappointment. "I suppose I'll have to wait to hear about it on the eleven o'clock news?"

"I might be able to tell you something before the reporters hear it, but no promises at this point."

Andrea mumbled something about what was the point of having a best friend in the middle of the action. I changed the subject to the books we were reading now. But as I carried the leftovers into the kitchen, I considered Andrea's warning that somebody would notice what I was up to. She wasn't the first one to make that observation. Both Pierce and Susan had warned me about the same thing this afternoon. I remembered the danger I'd been in the last time I was embroiled in a murder investigation. And I thought of my responsibilities: my son and my ailing father. Was it worth the risk?

After Andrea left, I cleaned up the kitchen and put the leftovers in the refrigerator for Josh. I didn't want another blow-up with him. Was it possible for us to get past this looming problem and go back to the easy-going camaraderie we'd always had? At this point, I wasn't hopeful, but I'd sure give it my best try.

On my way to get a book from my bedroom, I walked past Josh's room. The door was open, as usual, and the room was a disaster area, also as usual. Saddened by this rift between us, I continued on down the hall to my room and picked up the book I wanted. Returning to the kitchen, I paused at Josh's room. Looking past the chaos and confusion of clothes, books, and papers, I scanned for something specific.

For some reason, "the guy" had touched a nerve with my son, and before Josh came home, I needed to know more about why *this* organization and why Africa as opposed to all the other places in the world. I couldn't remember the organization's name, so doing my Internet sleuthing before I left the office hadn't been an option.

At last, I spotted the brochure resting on the corner of the bookshelf about three steps into the room. I'd always respected Josh's privacy, but this was not a private matter anymore. He'd discussed it with me and had waved the paper in my face when we'd argued. I crossed the threshold, grabbed the brochure, and returned to the kitchen.

I turned on the computer, and while it hummed itself awake, I put a note on the refrigerator door telling Josh the leftovers were for him.

Tonight, I wasn't interested in e-mails from family and

friends. I was interested in only one web site, the one for Humanity For All. As I waited for the web site to download, I wondered who came up with these names.

Finally, the web site popped open, and I was greeted with appalling pictures of abject poverty and despair. I shook my head in dismay. Who wouldn't jump at the chance to help these people? It was terrible. I skipped around the web site to pages that talked about their projects in different locales. All were in the middle of nowhere, with no electricity, no clean water or sanitary systems, and certainly well outside cell phone tower range.

I leaned back in my chair and thought. I'd tried to raise Josh to be a caring person, to see the needs of others and do something about them. If "the guy" had posters with these sorts of pictures, I could understand Josh's reaction.

But years of dealing with people had made me question if things were always as first presented. So, I dug deeper. I found the page of financial data, and from what I could see, at least ninety percent of the revenues were put into programs. Okay, that was good, given the costs of administering projects in such remote locales.

Although I easily found opportunities to send money, I had to really work to find volunteer opportunities. When I did, alarm bells went off in my head. Volunteers had to pay all their own transportation expenses, they had to pay room and board to their host family, the idea being this was a step toward teaching the people modern commerce, including encouraging development of a tourist trade. Volunteers signed up online and paid up front with a credit card, and the organization would e-mail travel plans and destination information. No wonder they kept their expense percentage down.

Despite diligent effort, I found no phone number, and the only snail-mail address was a post office box. Then I went to a web site that rated charitable organizations. But Humanity For All wasn't on their list. Habitat For Humanity was there, of course.

Was "the guy" pulling a scam by using a name similar to a well-respected organization to confuse college kids? This had to be fraud. But how did I explain that to an idealistic nineteen-year-old who suddenly saw me as the obstruction?

Exhausted after my trying day, I couldn't wait up for Josh to come home. And quite frankly, it was too late in the evening to start a long discussion.

At this point, all I could do was leave a note on his bedroom door about my findings and reference the web sites. Maybe he'd be more open to my opinion after he'd checked it out for himself.

The next morning, my first priority was to call Lois as soon as I reached my office. She quickly answered her cell phone. "Lois? How's Da?"

She chuckled. "Good morning to you too, Robyn Anne."

"Sorry. Good morning, Lois. How's Da?"

"Oh, as well as can be expected for a cantankerous old man who doesn't want to be here."

"Has anything happened yet?"

"Not so far. We're at the clinic and your dad's gone into the exam room." She chuckled again. "We had a huge argument over breakfast about my being there when the doctor talks to him."

"I hope you won. I know him well enough that he'll turn on his selective hearing."

"That's very true. He'll listen to all the good things and ignore anything that represents a change in what he currently does."

"Well, let's hope the doctor doesn't come up with something

like no more red meat or whisky."

"If that's the case, your father will ignore that and anything else the doctor recommends. His attitude these days is that he's going to enjoy the time he has left, not be miserable only to buy himself more time."

"If I put on my impartial, objective hat, I can understand that. But he's my dad, and I want him around for a long time." I smiled. "Maybe even long enough to bounce his great-grandchild on his knee."

Lois gasped. "Is Josh serious about this girl?"

"As serious as any almost-twenty-year-old can be about anything," I said with a laugh.

Lois chuckled. "I'll pray that that wish comes true. And that I'll still be here to see it."

We said our good-byes, with Lois promising to call me the minute she knew something. As far as I was concerned, confidentiality laws were for other people. The rules didn't matter when it came to my dad's health.

Before I was bogged down, I paid my morning call on William. Since my last visit, he'd added two shag throw rugs, one on either side of his bed. They didn't look new, but still, where was he finding this stuff? Between the added pictures, flowers, furniture, and rugs, the only thing that still looked like part of a hospital room was the bed. Of course, if he somehow found a chenille bedspread, the transformation would be complete.

"Good morning, William."

We chatted for a few minutes, then I asked him a question, trying to sound as casual as possible. "Did you ever see the patient on the other side of that door?" I pointed toward the family conference room.

William thought for a moment, then slowly shook his head. "No. I didn't see no one staying there. Lots of other people's been going in and out. The nurses, they's happy he's gone."

So he'd overheard the nurses talking about Hilliard. "Thank you, William. That's all I need to know. I'll see you later."

"Bye, Miz Robyn."

William was very honest. He'd tell me if he'd seen Hilliard and not understand that it could implicate him. If William said he never saw Hilliard, then there was no way he was the murderer.

I'd been in my office not more than an hour when the phone rang. I grimaced as I lost the train of thought I'd been working on to sort out a case. Resigned, I answered the phone.

"Rob?" It was Katie.

"Hi, Katie. What's up?"

"Get over here now. William's room."

"I'll be there in a minute."

"Faster." Katie hung up. Usually one of the calmest people around, she sounded frantic.

As I left my office, Connie said, "Leaving already? Come back when you can stay longer."

I didn't have time to explain. As I hurried across the elevator lobby area to 3-West, I wondered why Katie had called me. She'd sounded so urgent on the phone. What was going on with William?

I started down the hall to William's room and heard Katie's raised voice.

"You can't take him!" she said.

"You can't tell me what I can and can't do," boomed a man's voice.

I reached the doorway and gasped. Wearing surgical scrubs and handcuffs, William stood between two police officers. One of them was Officer Tomlin who looked as if he wanted to be anywhere else but this room.

Katie was talking to Captain Roberts. His dark brown eyes

were narrowed as he faced off with her. This was not a man I relished preserving and protecting me. I could see why Pierce didn't like working for him. I didn't like dealing with him.

I stepped into the room. "Is there something I can help with?" My gaze went from Katie to Captain Roberts, then back to Katie.

"The captain wants to arrest William for the murder." Katie crossed her arms over her chest, clutching her leather notebook as if it were body armor.

I turned my attention to Captain Roberts. "You can't be serious."

"Very. Not that I owe you an explanation." He pulled himself up to his full height. As if that would intimidate me. But he wasn't one of the unhinged patients I occasionally saw who wanted to take a swing at me. Captain Roberts might throw his weight around, but he wouldn't do anything physical. I hoped.

One glance at William and my heart nearly broke. Gone was the lucid man I'd talked to only a short time ago. He had deteriorated to the state he'd been in last Friday, gaze darting around the room, mumbling to himself. I held my ground. "William is a risk only to himself. He has problems, but he's not a threat to anyone else."

"The man's a homeless transient. From New York City. They are cunning and can be extremely violent, Ms. Kelly. I put in a call into the NYPD for his records. I'm sure they have a long file on him." He signaled for the officers to bring William along.

"That's ridiculous," I snapped, stepping in front of him to block the doorway. "He's far from cunning, and certainly not violent. If he were, we would have transferred him to a hospital better equipped to handle him."

Captain Roberts towered over me and bellowed, "If you had sent him to a locked unit, the vic would still be alive."

The man's logic baffled me. Did he have so little experience with the homeless that he couldn't tell the difference between the dangerous ones and the lost souls? Granted, we didn't see many in Madrona Bay, but if you looked closely, you could see them on the fringes of the parks, trying to blend in with the shrubbery. As far as I knew, for years City Hall had pretty much ignored them and their needs for social services.

"You can't take him," Katie insisted.

"How're you gonna stop me?"

"William can't leave without a safe discharge plan."

"Safe discharge plan?" Captain Roberts laughed derisively.

But Katie persevered. "A physician's on his way—"

"What the hell's going on here?" Dr. Transel walked into the room. He quickly sized up the situation. "Get those handcuffs off that man. Who do you think you are?"

"What do we look like? Circus clowns?" The captain's bluster had diminished, but only a little. Although lean, Dr. Transel matched him in height.

"I said take off those handcuffs. Now. Katie, call Legal and tell them what's going on." Dr. Transel turned to Captain Roberts. "You'll have to get a court order to take him, and our attorneys will tie you up for days."

The captain glared at us, then nodded slightly.

I hurried to William as Officer Tomlin quickly slipped the handcuffs off William, and we both helped him get back in bed. I whispered to William, hoping to calm him down, but he had no awareness of his surroundings and just moaned quietly.

"You're impeding my investigation," Captain Roberts said.

I returned to stand next to Katie. "No, we're trying to protect an innocent man from moving to a hostile environment. Look what you've done to him before even leaving this room."

"Stop wasting time on William and go find the real killer," Katie lashed out, amazingly out of character for her. Everyone had limits, though, and Captain Roberts must have really upset her before I arrived.

The captain's gaze moved from Dr. Transel to me, then to Katie. "This isn't the end of it. That man's going to jail for murder. Others will be charged with obstructing justice."

He glared in my direction, and a frisson of fear shot through me.

"You can't stop me from arresting him forever." With a final glower, he left the room. He had to push through the small crowd that had gathered in the hall. Officer Tomlin patted my shoulder as he and the other officer passed.

"Whew! Glad that's over. Thanks for paging me, Katie," Dr. Transel said.

"Hasn't there been enough trouble on my floor already?" Susan Wong stood in the doorway. "Now you're brawling with the cops?"

William whimpered, cowering away from an invisible threat. While Susan reconnected his IV, I tried to offer what comfort I could by holding his hands and making shushing sounds.

Dr. Transel shook his head. "C'mon, Susan. I need to order some meds for this poor man. We'll need someone to stay with him, too."

After they left, the others in the hallway dispersed. Katie stood on the other side of William's bed. He seemed calmer now.

"Thank you so much for coming when you did," Katie whispered. "I don't know how much longer I could have held him off."

"You were incredible, Katie. I've never seen that side of you."

She blushed and looked at the floor. "Well, I don't like it when people try to use their size or their position to intimidate me."

"I agree. We've both seen that before. Captain Roberts is nothing more than a bully."

"Yeah, but this bully has the law on his side. Good thing Dr. Transel came when he did." Katie shook her head. "I'll document all of this and William's condition in the chart just in case it goes any further."

"It's good to be prepared. Better send copies to Legal and Risk Management so they're aware of the situation."

Susan arrived with medication to add to William's IV and a nurse's aide to sit by him.

I didn't want to leave him alone with a stranger, so I leaned against the door until he settled into sleep. Dr. Transel and Legal would protect William from any further harassment. But, who would protect me? Captain Roberts's threat to charge me with obstruction of justice was thinly veiled, and the menace in his eyes couldn't be ignored. Should I tell Pierce, or keep it to myself, hoping we uncovered the murderer before the captain carried through on any of his threats?

I didn't have an answer for that.

I'd been in my office for maybe an hour, working on a complaint about medical care, combing through the medical records to follow the threads. Reconstructing that train of thought I'd lost when Katie called. Totally immersed, I didn't pick up the phone until the fifth ring.

"Robyn? It's Howard. Thanks so much for pulling that report together for me."

"Sure, no problem."

Howard laughed. "You say that every time, but I know that was a lot to dump on you."

"Well, I'm just glad I could get it done for you in time."

"Listen, Robyn, I have another favor to ask of you."

Scrunching my face, I said, "Oh? What's that?" Would he see through the confidence in my voice to the thinly disguised despair at another big assignment?

"I'd like you to attend the Quality Committee meeting with me and do the presentation."

I suppressed a groan. Barely. This was my worst nightmare.

"It'll be good experience for you. You know the ins and outs for the discussions."

"The meeting's tonight."

"Yes, at seven o'clock."

Stalling for time, I flipped through my calendar, praying I had something else scheduled. Something so important I couldn't possibly miss it. The space was blank. Nuts! "It looks like I'm free."

"That's great, Robyn. Just great." He paused. "Ah, Robyn, there's something else we need to talk about."

At his tone, my stomach fell and my brain went "uh-oh." Might as well charge into it. "Is something wrong?"

"Not wrong exactly, but . . . I'm worried about you."

"Me? Why would you be worried about me?"

"I talked with Captain Roberts of the Madrona Bay Police Department."

My stomach sank even lower, and I sensed I was in really deep doo-doo this time. "What did the captain say?"

"Well, I had called to ask him about the murder since it's still in the news. It's terrible PR for the hospital, and I talked to Larry about your e-mail that patients were canceling surgeries. I told Captain Roberts that we needed this investigation wrapped up as quickly as possible."

Leave it to me to raise the issue about the murder's impact on other patients. "So what did Captain Roberts say?"

"He told me he had a list of possible suspects and . . . I'm not sure how to say this, Robyn."

"Did he say I opposed him arresting William Jones this morning for the murder?"

"He did say you and two others were 'interfering.' I think

that was the word he used. Interfering with his investigation, he said."

"I wasn't interfering. Katie called and asked for my help. Arresting William Jones for the murder is outrageous. Captain Roberts is grasping at straws. There's absolutely nothing to link William to the murder, except for being a patient on that unit. Besides, William told me he never even saw Jason Hilliard."

Silence. "Robyn, the only way you'd know that is if you asked Mr. Jones." Howard sighed. "I'm afraid the captain was right. He implied that you're so involved in this case that now he's suspicious of your interference."

"Suspicious of me?" I squeaked. This was worse than I'd thought.

"Yes. Not only did you interfere with the arrest, you were the one to discover the body."

"So? I discovered the body last time too." Not that it was something I was proud of, but this was a different situation, one that required some clarification and defense.

"But last time there were lots of people around, and a police officer outside the door, and a way to determine how long you were in the room. Definitely not long enough to kill someone. Even if you did have a motive, as I found out much later."

I winced at that one. "This time was different."

"Well, yes it was. Captain Roberts says there was hardly anyone around and you would have had plenty of uninterrupted time to do it. There was one nurse on the floor. She'd just given the afternoon meds and wouldn't be expected to return to the room for another hour or two."

"And how was I supposed to know that? Where's the motive?" This was all so circumstantial that it was ridiculous. But how could I convince Howard that Captain Roberts was only trying to make trouble for me? "I was on the other side of the unit talking to William when the murder occurred."

"Yes. Well, that may be true, Robyn. But Captain Roberts thinks your actions have been suspicious. Obstruction of justice would be an easy charge to file against you, compared to arresting you for murder. He's pulling the paperwork together and plans to make an arrest by Friday night. I don't want that someone to be you, for either charge."

I gasped. "He wouldn't dare."

"Stay away from Captain Roberts and his investigation," Howard said. "You're too valuable to me, and I don't want your reputation compromised in any way by this investigation."

"But, I—"

Howard continued as if I hadn't even spoken. "How could you deal with patients after that? I mean, public memory may be short, but they do remember some things, and the name of a Patient Relations manager arrested for murdering a patient would stick in their mind, whether charges were dropped later or not."

His words stung me. The captain was getting back at me for standing up to him. Furious, I couldn't believe that Captain Roberts would stoop so low as to make these accusations to my boss. "In my defense, I'd have to say that Jason Hilliard was strangled with IV tubing that was knotted in a way I've never seen before. It had to be a very specialized knot for a specific purpose."

"The IV tubing no one else saw and that hasn't been found?"

Moaning silently to myself, I realized what an untenable position I was in if I was counting on Amanda Whitcomb to be my corroborating witness. If she said she saw the tubing, she'd probably imply that I had tied the knot, waited until Hilliard was dead, then called her to see the body. "What would you suggest I do, Howard?"

"Be sensible, Robyn. I repeat: stay as far away from Captain Roberts as possible. No sleuthing or snooping on your own."

"Howard! I would never—"

"Rob, Paula told me about finding you looking at Jason Hilliard's medical records—"

I winced. "But I—"

"I'm sure you had the most altruistic motive."

"I did. It was to pull together information for you in case the Quality Committee asked about him. You know they will," I insisted.

"That's probably true. But the fact of the matter is that I didn't ask you to do that. I'm sure it won't even come up tonight. The agenda's packed with presentations."

I grumbled to myself that he didn't know the committee as well as I did. "I wanted to help by anticipating a problem."

"And I appreciate that. But, Robyn, stay out of it completely. Really. I mean it. I depend on you." I heard him shuffle some papers in the background. "I'd like to meet with you before tonight's meeting. Maybe we can grab a bite to eat in the cafeteria and go over the report."

"Sure. That'd be fine."

CHAPTER 15

I hung up the phone, still stunned that Captain Roberts's threat to include me on his suspect list was more than an idle one. And to then tell Howard I was on the list of most likely to be arrested in thirty-six hours!

I don't murder people. It's not in my nature. It's not in my job description. I'm supposed to be nice, and calm, and take a lot of verbal abuse while acting as if it wasn't happening.

I resented Captain Roberts for even planting the seed of suspicion and for causing trouble between me and my boss.

I was still seething after I hung up the phone. It seemed I'd spent most of my time this week fuming about something. Captain Roberts intended to arrest someone by Friday night, despite the cursory investigation. And not knowing the victim's true identity!

I took off to see Pierce. He'd know what our next step should be. If we had anything to say about it, neither William nor I was going to jail.

I opened the door to his room and was relieved to see he was alone. Slamming the door shut behind me, I said, "You are not going to believe this."

"I seldom believe anything you tell me at first. It's usually so bizarre." Pierce grinned his amusement.

"What? You're so happy on your pain meds that you can't see I'm really upset?"

He shifted in his bed. "What's got your knickers in a knot this time?"

I scowled at the "this time" comment. "I just got off the phone with Howard—"

"Who's he again?"

"The hospital administrator. Best boss I ever had—"

"So what's the problem?"

"If you'd let me finish a sentence, I'll tell you!"

"Geez, Rob, you really are upset. I'll listen until you're done."

Skeptical he'd be able to keep that promise, I started again. "I got a call from Howard. He was very pleased with the Quality Report—" Pierce opened his mouth to speak, but I shushed him. "But he also said he'd had a phone conversation with *your* Captain Roberts—"

"He's not *my* Captain—"

"Would you be quiet and let me talk?" This man could be so exasperating!

"All right, all right. I'll listen. My lips are sealed." He made a zipper motion across his mouth.

"So Captain Roberts tells Howard that he thinks I'm interfering with the case—"

"How'd he find out you were investigating for me?" Pierce grabbed the overhead bar and struggled to sit up, but finally collapsed back in defeat.

"He didn't find out about that. When he tried to arrest William, the homeless man, this morning, Katie and I insisted that William was in no condition to be transferred any place, especially jail."

"Why would he think William is the murderer?"

Relieved that I now had Pierce's full attention, I said, "William has the room across the hall. It's not directly across the hall because it has the family conference room in between, and one or both of the doors that connect the room to the two halls outside William and Hilliard's rooms are often closed."

Pierce shook his head as he tried to follow my detailed explanation. "Does William have a motive for killing Hilliard?"

"Heavens, no! The man's as gentle as a kitten. I told you before how agitated he was when he first showed up in my office, but after he was admitted and started on medications, he's been very happy about everything. And I asked him if he'd ever seen Hilliard and he said no."

"And suspects never lie." Pierce gave me a sardonic look.

"William doesn't know how to dissemble."

"Hmmm." Pierce thought for a moment. "Okay, so the only thing Captain Roberts has on William is that he was on the unit at the time."

I nodded my agreement.

"But there's no motive?"

I shook my head.

"No indication that this William is or can be violent?"

I shook my head again. "That's right. It's as if Captain Roberts is going for the easiest suspect, one who has no ability to defend himself." I looked at Pierce and frowned. "William wouldn't last the night in jail."

"Okay, I get why you're upset."

"Oh, that's not all."

Pierce sighed and straightened his sheet and blanket until they were neatly folded across his chest. "Of course not," he mumbled. "It never is."

"Matt!"

He lolled his head from side to side. "Sorry. But it's true, Rob, nothing's ever simple with you." He grinned wryly. "That's what makes you so much fun."

"If you say so." I gave him my skeptical raised eyebrow. "No, the other part is Captain Roberts implied that I was a suspect, and then he went and told my boss he suspected me."

"Why? Oh, because you found the body? Again?"

I winced. "Well, he does have a point. I was on the scene, but I was with William. Not that anyone would believe him. I suppose I had a motive—a very weak one—if you think strangling a man who'd made a spectacle of himself and annoyed the staff to the point that they didn't want to enter his room is a motive."

"You've convinced me you're the real murderer, Rob."

"Thanks a lot! If that was the case, we'd have had dead bodies strewn around the hospital for the last ten years. My job is to make these people less annoying, not murder them. Besides, the thing that saves me is that I haven't a clue how to tie that knot that was around Hilliard's neck."

Pierce shrugged. "It's awfully hard to prove that you didn't know something. Was Josh in Scouts?"

"Yes, but I told you, this knot isn't in the handbook. Remember? I checked that out first thing when I got home Saturday night."

"But still, Roberts is watching you." Pierce eyed me speculatively. "Have you had a chance to get back to the Business Office with those questions I asked you about the safe?"

"No. I'm sorry. I probably shouldn't talk to Becky right now. Howard told me to stay far away from Captain Roberts and the murder investigation."

"As much as we need that information, I don't want you taking any chances. The last thing I want to see is you arrested, Rob."

"I don't either. And I don't want William arrested either." I sighed heavily. "We have less than thirty-six hours before one of us goes to jail."

"What?" Pierce barked. "Roberts set a deadline to arrest you?"

"I nodded miserably. "William or me, and it doesn't seem to

make much difference to him as long as he makes an arrest."

Pierce rattled his traction apparatus. "I have got to get out of here."

"We need more information. I'll find a way to cruise below Howard and Captain Roberts's radar."

"Be careful, Rob. The captain's always been a competent detective, despite being totally worthless on this case. He can also be perverse when he gets his back up. You need to stay flat on the ground, not flying low. And you'll be in trouble with your boss if he catches you."

"Yeah, you're right." I stood up. "I'd better get back to my office. Howard keeps adding to my workload. Now I have to attend a meeting tonight, and if I'm not fully prepared to answer questions, he'll get suspicious and ask why."

"Stay away from situations where you might have to lie. You don't do it very well, you know."

"I'll take that as a compliment," I said wistfully. "And even without Howard's assignments, there's more than enough work in my office to keep me out of trouble."

"You go off and be a good girl, then. I'll see you later. Don't worry about it, Rob. We'll figure out another way."

Pierce's sympathy was the last thing I needed right now. It rankled that I hadn't followed up on his questions as quickly as I should have and now I might not have another chance. Friends weren't supposed to let friends down, yet I had to protect my job, and I didn't want to go to jail. What should I do?

Despite the clock ticking down to Captain Roberts's arrest deadline and my frustration at not being able to investigate, I couldn't stop thinking about the murder. Something William had said niggled at the edge of my consciousness, something important. The harder I chased after it, the more elusive it became. If I ignored it, maybe it would come to me.

I forced myself to concentrate on things I could do something about. First, I called Lois to find out how Da was doing, but the call went straight to voice mail. No progress for me on that one.

Next, I told Connie I needed to work like a demon to catch up on everything that I'd ignored for too long. Between William, the Quality Report, Pierce, the murder, and worrying about Josh and Da, I hadn't had time to do my "real" job. Since the murder investigation was now off limits, thanks to Howard and Captain Roberts, and the Quality Committee report was finished, I could finally address the ever-growing piles on my desk. In no uncertain words, I made it clear to Connie: no interruptions. Even if flames were at the door.

When my door opened a half hour later, I started to snarl, but it wasn't Connie. It was Stewart Fromm, one of my regulars who would have ignored Connie and marched straight into my office anyway. Stewart was a classic case of the walking wounded if ever there was one. In his fifties, his face was deeply lined from myriad troubles, most of them self-imposed.

Today he was wearing a polyester jacket left over from the 1970s, a dark green plaid that matched his dark green polyester slacks, both with numerous snags. If it had been March, I'd have said he was dressed as a leprechaun. But this was Stewart, so the outfit was normal for any time of the year.

He sat down at my little conference table, running his hands through his thinning gray hair. Completely oblivious to the fact that he'd arrived unannounced, and that I was working at my desk, he started talking. "It was those nurses that started it. Breathing that cigarette smoke on her when she was just an infant. Tobacco addicts are the cause of it all."

I sighed and turned my chair to face him.

"If it hadn't been for them," Stewart continued, "they'd have stayed away from the alcohol and the drugs."

As I always did, I let him ramble on for five minutes before my first attempt to focus him. "And what can I do for you today, Stewart?"

"Then it was the marijuana in high school, along with the alcohol. And they'd sneak cigarettes from my wife. She didn't smoke when we got married, you know. It wasn't until after the baby was born and all those tobacco addict nurses breathed on her. That's what got her addicted, you know, the nicotine in the smoke. By the time she came home, she needed cigarettes of her own."

"Yes, we've talked about that before, Stewart. What can I do for you today?" Attempt number two.

"If the girls hadn't been breathed on by those tobacco addicts right after they was born, they never would have started themselves. And now the three of them sit around every evening and all weekend, smoking cigarettes and drinking beer."

I was tempted to ask how many beers, one or three or a case? Or if his wife and daughters were happy during these times, but that one didn't seem appropriate. Besides, how could they have fun with him hovering around, carping at them?

Instead, I asked, "Stewart, we've talked before about the hospital nurses when your daughters were born. There's nothing I can do about that now. What can I help you with today?"

He stopped talking and stared at me, blinking owl-like behind his magnifying glass lenses. "I talked to those people you sent me to."

I had to rewind my memory tape to recall whom I'd referred him to months ago. It wasn't clear in my mind, but I took a guess. "The people in the Insurance Office?"

"Yes. They're the ones. I talked to them about what I could expect them to pay for my wife and daughters to get treatment for all their addictions. They told me if it was alcohol or drugs, they could have ten days in the hospital and then they'd have to go to AA."

"Well, that sounds like a good plan."

Stewart glared at me and fumed. "It's not enough. The ten days in the hospital don't include tobacco addicts."

"What about a nicotine patch or gum? Did you ask if those medications would be covered?"

"Wouldn't matter. My wife and daughters wouldn't use them. They don't want to quit."

"Well, then we have a bigger problem, don't we, Stewart?"

"What do you mean?"

"I mean that if they don't want to quit, it doesn't matter if the medication or the hospital stay is paid for by insurance. We can't force them to do either one. *They* have to be the ones who want to change."

"But it's not right. It's your fault they started, so it's your responsibility to fix them."

I sighed, knowing the concept of personal decisions and responsibility wouldn't make a dent in Stewart's arguments. Stewart had probably been a happy young man until he'd been sent to Vietnam. Now he was still haunted by the images he'd seen there. He'd had bookkeeping jobs over the years, but never seemed to be able to settle down to one employer for very long.

That he'd married and stayed married all these years was a testament to both him and his wife. He hadn't given up and moved to the streets like so many other vets. But they each seemed to be in their own private hell and only long-term therapy had any chance of making a difference. At this point, though, Stewart was as unwilling to consider that as his wife and daughters were to leaving the cigarettes and beer alone.

"Look, Stewart, there's nothing I can do to help you with this problem. If they don't want to quit, we can't force them. The only thing we can do is try to help you. Would you like me to make an appointment with Dr. Baker?" He was one of our psychiatrists, but I wasn't about to mention his specialty to Stewart.

"Why would I want to see him?"

"You could talk to him about your problems and how you can deal with your family's addictions." I hated to use that term, but it was what he related to. "I don't like to see you so miserable all the time over something you can't change."

He sat quietly for a moment, his face scrunched up as he considered my offer. "No. I'm okay. I'm not the one with the problem, so I don't need to talk to anybody about it. If you can't help me, then I'll just go find someone else who can."

He stood up and gave me a sad look. "I was counting on them nurses to take good care of my wife and my babies. It's always the people you trust who let you down."

As quickly as he'd arrived, he disappeared out the door again. I leaned back in my chair, knowing there was nothing I could do for him. Some problems simply couldn't be solved.

Then I thought about the first time Stewart had come to my office. I'd been unnerved, of course, but he'd marched in, unannounced, sat down, and started his spiel.

The same way William had a few days ago. But Stewart hadn't frightened me, whereas the first sight of William had. Well, maybe not scared me, but reminded me of an earlier experience when I'd been in danger. He'd made me uneasy in a way I couldn't remember feeling with other patients.

Why was that? Was it because his clothes were dirty? Because he smelled? Because he was "different" from any of the people I usually came in contact with? I was accustomed to dealing with various types of mental illness, but William *was* different, although not in the way Captain Roberts implied. I'd never really had any contact with the homeless, with people so poor or so mentally ill that they couldn't cope with life at any level.

The ones I dealt with might dress oddly, but they were reasonably clean and lived in houses and usually had insurance that afforded them medical care when they needed it. So that made them more like me. I supposed that made them "safe" as opposed to those who lived under entirely different circumstances.

My neighborhood and my workplace were full of people who were different, and yet they were the same. Which meant I felt more at ease around them.

I'd never thought of myself as prejudiced, as Josh had charged. What was it that made me react so strongly to Josh's plan to go to Africa? Was this my dirty laundry? I thought hard about it for several minutes, searching deep into my soul before coming to a conclusion.

My reaction to Josh's plan wasn't a racial or ethnic issue. It wasn't even that they were poor because I'd have been pleased if he'd chosen to work with the poor here in the States.

No, my reaction was maternal, fear of the uncertainty, of the dangers I knew Josh would face. I did not want my son injured . . . or worse.

Now that I'd thought it through for myself, I was prepared to talk to Josh again. I had nothing to feel bad about, nothing to be ashamed of. I was Josh's mother first and foremost, and that was what guided me.

Another call came in from Arlene, saying Howard wanted to see me right away. I figured he must have some urgent question about the Quality Committee meeting that couldn't wait, so I picked up my copy of the report and headed toward his office.

"Go on in," Arlene said. "He's waiting for you."

I paused at the threshold. "Hi, Howard."

He looked up and a broad grin crossed his face. "Robyn. Just the person I've been waiting for."

Let's face it, after the last few sessions with him, I was now a bit cynical. I looked for ulterior motive behind Howard's cheerful greeting. I waved my folder and said, "I brought my copy of the Quality Report. Did you want to discuss it?"

"That's fine, but I have something else to talk to you about right now."

"Oh?" I tried to smile with delighted anticipation, but my heart wasn't in it. In fact, my internal alarm was dinging like crazy. I sat down in the chair across from his desk and laid the folder on my lap.

He leaned forward, hands clasped and resting on the desktop. "I need your help with something."

I swallowed my sigh.

"The tri-county hospital administrators group met yesterday, and I mentioned that situation last week with the uninsured homeless man."

"That was William."

"Really? I didn't make the connections. Anyway, we decided to set up a task force to study the impact of indigent care on our Emergency Rooms. I said you would be our representative."

"Me? You want me?" I was flattered, to be sure, but these task forces tended to be very long on meetings and short on results. Didn't I have more than enough on my plate already? Was this one of those "other duties as assigned" that was in my job description? Or was this Howard's way of keeping me out of Captain Roberts's way and out of jail? I supposed I should be thanking him.

"I think you'd be terrific, Rob. You'd bring a fresh perspective to a room full of number crunchers."

Did he hear me groan? Did he see my body twitch at being assigned yet another big project?

"I see." I was familiar with the topic after the Patient Rep meeting and knew whom to call for more information. But how could I tell my boss that participating in a large task force like this one ranked right up there in my top ten worst nightmares.

As if reading my thoughts, Howard said, "This task force is different, Robyn. It's to meet weekly for a month, then present a report to the tri-county administrators group, with problems clearly defined and a list of solutions that we can take to the state legislature."

"Okay." Weekly meetings. A complete report due in a month. I tried to remember if my medical insurance covered anti-depressants and antianxiety meds. Then I wondered if I could be depressed and have panic attacks at the same time. Hmmm. Something to ask Dr. Baker the next time I talked to him.

"It's a lunch meeting tomorrow at Seattle Hospital, noon to one. Check at the front desk for the room. And, I've asked Ar-lene to get our numbers to you by the end of today so you have time to review them before the meeting."

"Tomorrow afternoon. Great. That's great." I forced myself to smile. "Do you have any questions about the Quality Report?"

"I haven't had time to read it yet, but I'm sure it's terrific, Robyn. You always do such good work. We'll talk about it over dinner in the cafeteria before the meeting, okay?"

"Great. That'd be just great." I scooted to the front of the chair, spring loaded to escape before he came up with another assignment. Still, I heard myself ask, "Anything else?"

"Not right now, but I know where to find you." Howard beamed.

I tried to smile back, but couldn't manage it. Rushing from the Admin suite in a most unseemly manner, I hurried back to my own office, completely forgetting to pick up my afternoon latté, a sure sign of how bad off I was. I went into my office and shut the door.

Ticking clocks everywhere. I'd take Da and Lois to the airport after the meeting. Then Da wouldn't be able to sneak away without telling me what was going on.

But after that? Seattle traffic on a Friday afternoon was notoriously gridlocked. Would I get back before Captain Roberts arrested William? Would a squad car be sitting in front of my house, waiting for me to come home?

I shuddered at the thought of my neighbors watching as I was taken away in handcuffs. I'd be the new pariah.

Resting my head on the desk, I wondered how I was ever going to extricate myself. Worry about Da. Checking on Pierce and William. I still didn't know what to do about Josh's African mission plans. Patient cases and phone messages were stacking up on my desk, and we still didn't know who Jason Hilliard really was.

Groaning, I sat up and looked out the window. It was raining, a gentle spring shower. Bright spots of color dotted the parking lot landscaping, tulips and daffodils signifying the arrival of spring. Maybe the dark days of winter were behind us. I tried to take cheer from that. This wasn't the first time I'd felt overwhelmed by my workload, and it wouldn't be the last. I'd get through it, all of it.

But what was it that William had said? It continued to stay out of grasp, and that bothered me.

CHAPTER 16

I sat at my desk, intent on drafting a letter. Doing my best to stay away from the investigation was tying me up in knots. A little over twenty-four hours remained before Captain Roberts arrested someone. I tried focusing on work, the only thing in my life that I felt I had any control over.

That meant tackling Sandra Jenkins and her wrongful life complaint. Today was her fourth day in the hospital, and I wanted to resolve this and send her home before someone started yelling at me about what this prolonged stay was costing the hospital. I needed some advice, so I called Bev Samm, the Risk Management Director.

"So, what you're telling me," Bev said, "is Sandra Jenkins wants nothing to do with the most beautiful baby you've ever seen, and she still wants us to pay her all that money for wrongful life, but she hasn't said a word to her husband about filing a complaint, let alone suing us, so we don't have a signed release from him to review his vasectomy records."

"I know. It's weird." I leaned back in my chair. "Nick Jenkins, on the other hand, has a fierce protectiveness about that baby that tells me little Eddy's not in danger when he gets home."

"So what's your next step?" Bev asked.

"I don't know. I can't really do anything about her complaints until he signs the medical records release." I sighed and doodled on a pad of paper. "There's something not right here. Any suggestions?"

"You've still got her there, and she's not being charged for the extra days, and she hasn't called in a lawyer, so I still don't want it." She laughed and I begrudgingly joined her.

"Why am I not surprised? I can't stall her discharge much longer. I have to come up with something before the end of today."

We said good-bye, and I hung up. I'd told Bev the truth. Katie Caldwell had already called twice this morning about discharging Sandra Jenkins. I'd tried stalling her until the social worker's assessment of the mother/baby relationship was written and filed in the chart. I thought about calling Social Work to find out how the review was coming along, but decided not to. I knew what it felt like to have someone literally breathing down my neck.

I stepped outside my office. Margie's door was closed, and I could hear the murmur of voices that told me she was with a patient or someone on staff. Connie was on the phone. I signaled that I was going upstairs, and she nodded.

I hadn't seen William yet this morning, so I stopped by his room first for a short visit. William had seemed okay when I saw him yesterday, but I wanted to be sure he wasn't traumatized by Captain Roberts's threat of arresting him.

When I stepped into his room, the first thing I saw were framed photographs of smiling people in groups of twos and threes. I could only shake my head. Where on earth had he found those? The next thing I spotted was a table-top water fountain on the window sill between the potted fern and the potted azalea covered with hot pink blossoms. The gurgling sound added to the park-like ambience. A few more plants and his room would be an arboretum. Maybe it felt more homey to William. Whatever it was, he was responding well to his created environment, and as each day passed, it was harder to think about discharging him back to the streets.

"Good morning, William."

He looked up from a tangle of rope, then back. My breath caught in my throat as I approached his bed. Was he tying knots?

"Hi, Miz Robyn."

"What have you got there?"

He snatched it from my sight, shoving it under his sheet, and his gaze started darting around the room.

"It's okay, William. I'm not going to take it away from you. I'd just like to see what you're working on."

He stared hard at me for a moment, and then it was as if a switch flicked on in his brain and he smiled. " 'Course you're not gonna take it away. You're always nice to William." He brought the lump of thick yarn from under the covers.

I picked it up and let it dangle. "Is this macramé, William?"

"I don't know what you calls it, but I thought it'd look pretty holding one of my flowers."

Where in the world had William found this? Avocado green, harvest gold, and burnt orange, it was definitely left over from the seventies. Spreading the tangled mess of yarn across my hands, I studied the knots. Although I couldn't name a single one, none matched the one I'd seen around Hilliard's neck.

I worried about asking a lot of questions for fear of throwing William into a tizzy, but in good conscience, I had to ask at least one. "Are you making the knots yourself, William?"

"No, I'm just taking the tangles out so's it hangs right. Do you think you might find a hook I can put in the ceiling?"

I struggled not to smile. Captain Roberts and his threat of arrest weren't even on William's radar, for which I was thankful. "Yes, I'll see what I can find. I have to go now. Will you be all right until I come back?"

"I thinks so."

I left his room, and my smile quickly soured. Taking the stairs, I thought about Sandra Jenkins's almost-case. I'd met her once and hadn't been impressed with her attitude. And I'd met Nick Jenkins once and had liked him immediately. But why hadn't his wife told him about her complaint? Something was not right about this situation. I couldn't put my finger on it yet, but it would come to me. I hoped it would come sooner rather than later.

I reached the fourth floor and found her in her room, sitting in a rocking chair and staring out the window. Baby Eddy wasn't in the bassinet, so I assumed the nurses had him in the nursery.

"Mrs. Jenkins?"

She turned from the window, and I caught a look of despair, so quickly replaced by smoldering anger that I thought I might have been mistaken.

"Did you bring the check? I want to get out of here." She sounded bored by the whole thing. So that was her act for today.

"I'm sure you're ready to leave. Even a nice room like this can't compare to being in your own home," I said in a more friendly tone than I felt.

She'd turned to look out the window again. I pulled up a chair and sat facing the same direction. Without looking at her, I said, "I'm puzzled, Mrs. Jenkins."

"About what?" Her voice was wary.

"Well, you're so convinced that we botched your husband's vasectomy, and you want us to pay for the baby you don't want."

"That's right. You owe me for ruining my life."

"If that's the case, then why doesn't your husband know about the complaint?" I turned to face her.

She glared back. "It's my life that's ruined."

"I understand that, but you're basing it on the medical care he received from us."

"So?"

Now she was so angry, so defensive. I tried another approach.

213

"Look, Mrs. Jenkins, I understand. A child is a huge responsibility. It's a big job, and if you'd taken steps to avoid that responsibility, then I understand why you're angry."

"You're right. This isn't what I wanted."

It might have been my imagination, but I thought the chip on her shoulder had melted a tiny bit. "I want to help you with this." I tried to sound as genuine as I could, even though I couldn't relate to her on this at all.

"Then why are you here, yammering at me, when you should be out there getting my money?" she yelled, glaring at me in defiance.

"Well, believe me, I'd like nothing better than to give you a check and send you home." I kept my voice calm and at a normal volume. "Unfortunately, I have to follow some procedures. That includes reviewing your husband's medical record, and that means he has to sign a release form authorizing me to do that."

She slumped in her chair, as if it finally sank in that nothing would happen without her husband's involvement. "Oh."

That's all? Just "oh?" A niggling thought entered my mind, and I wondered why I hadn't considered it earlier. Maybe the murder had rattled my usually clear-thinking brain. Following my suspicions, I said, "You know, even if the medical records review doesn't tell us what we need to know, we'll have to ask your husband for a semen specimen."

She blanched. "Why would you need that?"

"Besides determining whether or not there are viable sperm, we need to run a paternity test."

Her now ashen face told it all.

I looked at her sadly as the final piece of the puzzle snapped into place. "Mr. Jenkins isn't Eddy's father, is he?"

She burst into deep, heart-wrenching sobs. A nurse came to the door, but I signaled her away. I picked up a box of tissues from the nightstand and handed one to Sandra. She'd gone through a half dozen before she hiccuped her way to stop.

After she took a few ragged breaths, she turned to me. I saw the face of a woman who had loved, and risked it all, and lost. Her anger had been a facade for despair.

"Do you want to tell me about it?" I asked as I handed her another tissue.

She shook her head, shrugged, raised her hand, then let it fall back into her lap. The gestures all screamed defeat. "Nick and I started dating in high school. Back then it was cool to have a boyfriend who worked on cars. We got married, then after a while, I couldn't stand to have him touch me." She shuddered. "It didn't matter how hard he washed, or what he used. There was always grease. He smelled like car oil and diesel."

"Why didn't you leave?"

"Bunch of reasons, I guess. My family pressured me to stay. They wouldn't help if I left, so I didn't have no place to go. I had a job, but it didn't pay so good. I couldn't leave and expect him to support me. Wouldn't be right, you know?"

After I nodded, she continued, "I convinced him I didn't want children, and talked him into getting a vasectomy so there wouldn't be any mistakes. Then, about two years ago, this man came into our office selling office supplies. He came at least once a month, and he always spent a few minutes talking to me. Flirting, actually. He was so clean."

She looked at me as if willing me to understand. In a way, I did. "And one thing led to another?"

Nodding, she mopped her eyes. "First it was a flower or a chocolate truffle. Then he'd arrive just before my lunch break, and we'd eat together. It was months before anything happened. He told me he loved me."

As if that made it okay, I wanted to say. Instead, I responded,

"I take it he was not pleased when you told him you were pregnant."

"Not pleased? He was furious. He told me I was a fool for not taking precautions, like going on birth control pills—what did he expect? My husband'd had a vasectomy; if he found the packet, how would I have explained taking the pill?"

Her logic annoyed me. She was having an affair with a man she thought she loved, and obviously thought she had a future with, yet she didn't want her husband to find out until *she* was ready. Instead of saying what I really thought, I said, "Yes, that would have been difficult."

"I thought he loved me. I thought when I told him about the baby that he'd ask me to marry him, and then I'd leave Nick. But he said that was ridiculous. He was already married. But he wasn't wearing a ring," she wailed. "He lied to me. And now I'm stuck with a baby. And Nick."

"Look, Sandra." I took her hand and looked directly into her tear-filled eyes. I wanted to tell her that she'd fallen for the oldest line in the world. "This has been a terrible ordeal for you. And I understand that you're hurting."

I paused to think about the best way to say this. "Would you say Nick's hands started to bother you only in the last two years? After you met the salesman and began going to lunch with him?"

Her eyes widened in comprehension. "Yes," she whispered.

"You have some decisions to make about your life, and what you decide will have an impact on your husband and baby Eddy." I pulled one of my business cards from my pocket, wrote a phone number on the back, and held it out to her.

"Here's the phone number for the Mental Health Department. A therapist will help you sort through the process so you can make some decisions. Will you call them?"

"I'll think about it." She shrugged and reached for another

tissue before looking at me. "Will Nick know about this?"

"No. It's all between you and me. It won't go into your medical records either."

"Oh. That's good. I don't want some doctor or nurse spilling the beans before I'm ready."

Disgusted, I stood up. I set the card with Mental Health's phone number on her nightstand. "Get your things together. I'll call Dr. Kyler and have him write your discharge orders. You'll be out of here in a few hours."

She nodded and climbed out of bed, her silence dismissing me from her presence. I wondered which path she'd choose. Would staying with Nick and little Eddy work out for her? Or would she be on her own?

I left her then, but decided to swing by the nursery to see Eddy. I wasn't surprised to find Nick in a rocking chair holding the baby. "Hello, Mr. Jenkins."

He looked up. "Call me Nick."

"That's right. I forgot. How are you doing today?"

Nick turned his attention back to Eddy. "He's doing just fine. The nurses say he's a good feeder and has a good disposition."

He had responded to my question about him with an answer about Eddy. Interesting.

"I just came from your wife's room." He looked up at me, a flash of anger in his eyes, and I wondered if he'd figured it out. Anybody could count back nine months. Ah, well. He seemed to have staked a claim on Eddy, so I wasn't worried about him. Now it was up to Sandra to work things out with her husband. Or not. "She's ready to go home today."

"She said that? She said she wants to come home?"

I hesitated about answering that one. "She's excited to be leaving, so I guess so." A lame response, but I couldn't lie and raise his hopes. I wasn't sure if he caught my hedging, but he didn't argue with me or ask questions.

"Thanks, Ms. Kelly. Thanks for everything."

I left him holding Eddy and appearing a bit more relaxed, as if a burden had been lifted from his shoulders.

Sandra had aired her dirty laundry to me in private; only she and I knew the truth. Stan may have made a notation in the chart that I'd been called, but other than that, nothing would go in her file, or Nick's, or Eddy's, that there'd ever been an issue. And since her complaint had been about Nick's care and he didn't know anything about it, there'd be no record in my office either. I left the unit and hoped that I'd done the right thing for them, and for Eddy. Only time would tell.

And I'd never know the answer.

With two meetings in two days and two major projects dumped in my lap, I had everything to dread when Arlene called with yet another summons for me to see Howard. But there was no getting out of it. We were supposed to get together for dinner in another hour to discuss the Quality Report before he went to the meeting, so why the urgency? At least I'd followed orders and hadn't done any sleuthing since he'd told me to stay out of the investigation, so what did he have in store for me this time?

As I entered the Admin suite, Arlene gave me a look that was half pitying, half encouraging, and waved me through to Howard's office without a word. My stomach sank even lower. Oh, boy. I was in for it now.

I hesitated in his office doorway. I wanted to leave, but there was no excuse. He was my boss, after all.

"Robyn! Thanks for coming so quickly."

Immediately suspicious of his jovial manner, I smiled weakly and took the chair across from his desk.

"I'm in a bit of a bind, Rob."

Now why didn't that surprise me? I kicked into full cynic mode.

"I have to leave town," Howard said. "An emergency. And there's the Quality Committee meeting tonight."

Cynicism fled. This was worse than I'd expected. "But—"

"I know it's short notice. However, you've done a fabulous job with the report and you're already presenting it. I haven't been able to reach Samantha Duke to tell her I won't be there at all, but I'm positive she won't have any problem with your standing in for me as the management rep."

"But—"

"Great. I knew you'd help me out."

"Howard, I can't do this." I couldn't believe I was actually saying no to my boss, but there it was.

Howard smiled his "you can do anything you set your mind to" smile. "Of course you can, Robyn. You know the material inside and out, and—"

"I can't present the Quality Report to the committee, Howard. Samantha Duke hates me."

He leaned back in his chair and rubbed his hand across his mouth. "Hmmm. That's right. I remember your saying something earlier about that."

"It's an issue with the department, and with me in particular. I'm not exaggerating when I say she hates me. Trust me, Howard, if I'm the one presenting, she'll rip everything to shreds and . . . and, it'll be a disaster for everyone."

"Well, that poses a problem, Robyn." Howard looked troubled. "I need team players, regardless of how tough it is. I always thought you were one of my best team players."

The rebuke stung. A surge of icy heat flushed through my body. How could he criticize me after all I'd done? What was I supposed to do? How could I explain to him that sending me to take his place at the meeting was throwing me in the lions' den?

Samantha could—and would—say anything she wanted, just shy of slander, and maybe even a little over that line, while I had no option but to bite my tongue and say nothing.

It wasn't that I didn't have anything to say. Oh, I did. I had plenty. The problem was, I couldn't say it because the issue wasn't between my department and Samantha, but between my department and Samantha's sister-in-law, Emma Jamison. Not only that, it involved mental health, and so the confidentiality rules were even stricter. Samantha used every forum possible to share her complaints, while I was legally and morally bound not to air the other woman's dirty laundry in public.

Besides, I had other things to do. Identify the knot around Hilliard's neck. Find the real murderer so I didn't go to jail in twenty-four hours. Talk to Josh, if he was home and speaking to me. Check on my dad. Now was not a good time to spend the entire evening in a meeting. But, of course, I couldn't say any of this to Howard.

So what was I going to do? Howard started tapping his foot. Was I a team player who'd knowingly attend a meeting where I'd endure a very public verbal flogging? Or was I the maverick?

I took a deep breath and looked him straight in the eye. "I'll do my best. But I want it understood that the citizen chair of the committee views me, my department, and anything I say with hostility."

"That's what I wanted to hear." Howard grinned broadly. "I knew I could count on you. Samantha usually comes early to prepare, so you can tell her about the switch before the meeting. Like I said, you already know the material, and that's the major item on tonight's agenda. And I'd like you to stay for the rest of the meeting so you can report back to me."

"All right." The last thing I wanted to do was spend the entire evening with Samantha Duke, but Howard wasn't leaving me much choice. I couldn't bring myself to look at him. "I hope things turn out okay for you."

"Huh? Oh, yes, thanks. I'm leaving right away."

I didn't ask where he was going. I didn't care. I only knew I was going to a barbecue, and I was going to be the one on the rotisserie.

Only ten minutes into my presentation and I already felt bent, folded, spindled and mutilated. Especially the last two. Would I survive the evening?

Samantha Duke had been furious when I told her before the meeting that I was taking Howard's place. And then I'd seen this look in her eye. An ah-ha, now she had me, kind of look. I'd kept a pleasant expression pasted on my face, but deep inside, I wanted to throttle Howard. And I wanted to throw up. I didn't, of course. I was much too professional to let that happen. I hoped.

These meetings were held in a small conference room intended to be cozy. Tonight, it felt claustrophobic. How was I going to spend hours in this tiny space with a woman who detested me? The committee members and presenters sat around a table large enough to seat ten people.

Usually, the presenter would stand and do his or her thing, and then committee members asked questions. Not tonight. I'd barely said two sentences, introducing myself to the committee, even though they all knew me, and then explaining Howard's absence, when Samantha interrupted with a question.

She was in her mid-fifties, dressed professionally in a suit and heels, with short light brown hair deftly streaked to hide the gray. She worked for a big stock brokerage firm and was a whiz with numbers. Heaven help the manager whose numbers didn't add up. "Ms. Kelly, who wrote this report?"

"I wrote part of it, and Paula Rodriguez wrote the other part.

As I was saying, this report covers January through March of this year."

"Which part did you write?"

"I wrote the outpatient narrative, and Paula wrote the inpatient narrative. As in previous reports—"

"Are the hospital numbers from Paula?"

Oh, no, here it was. "Not all of them. I supplied her with the complaint data."

"So you contributed the tables and charts?"

"Yes, that's correct. As I was saying—"

"Ms. Kelly, please turn to page thirty-four."

I turned to the page and scanned it. I didn't know what Samantha had, or thought she had, but I was confident my numbers were accurate. By this time, the other committee members were looking uneasy, glancing from her to me as if wondering what was going on between us.

"What would you like to know?" I asked as pleasantly as possible through gritted teeth.

"On this page, you have a chart that shows the data over the last year, by quarter, for complaints."

"Yes, that's true. We've found that helpful for the committee and for management. And the two columns on the far right you'll see are the rolling totals for the four quarters and the previous comparable four quarters."

"Perhaps you can explain why the hospital numbers don't match the numbers from last quarter's report?"

Flustered, I didn't know what to say. I didn't have last quarter's report with me. But I couldn't let her browbeat me in a public setting. It would undermine everything that came to the committee from me in the future.

"Perhaps you would clarify which numbers you're referring to."

"The hospital's service complaints were significantly higher last quarter in that report than they are stated in this report."

I panicked for a moment. I did a spreadsheet that automatically carried numbers forward. Was it a glitch in the software? Then I remembered. With a sigh of relief, I asked, "Do you have a copy of last quarter's report with you?"

Samantha shot daggers at me. She hesitated, as if trying to decide how to answer. Then she said smugly, "No, I don't. I left it at home."

CHAPTER 17

My heart sank. I could offer to go upstairs and get a copy, but my credibility would be in tatters by the time I returned. I didn't dare leave Samantha alone with the rest of the committee until I had this issue resolved to everyone's satisfaction.

"I have a copy." Mrs. Wilson, a long-time committee member I'd known for years, waved a stack of papers in my direction. She cast an annoyed glance at Samantha, and held out the report.

"Thank you, Mrs. Wilson. I'm sure I can clear up this confusion in just a moment." I leaned across the table to accept the report, and Mrs. Wilson winked at me. Startled, I looked at her more closely and realized she had a gleam in her eyes. Was she enjoying the opportunity to put Samantha in her place? I could only hope.

Quickly flipping through the report, I found the table I wanted and smiled. "The answer to your question, Mrs. Duke, is in the footnote. You may remember that last November we had to cancel all the scheduled surgeries one day to make room for the victims for that big car crash on I-90 near Snoqualmie Pass?"

All the committee members nodded and began whispering to each other. All except Samantha. She looked ready to kill me. Again.

"As a result, some patients complained about having to wait for their surgery to be rescheduled. I included those numbers in the fourth quarter report, but added a footnote to explain how many complaints were directly related to that disaster, a one-time event, and that they would not be included in future reports."

Samantha glared at me. "I see. That would explain it. Continue with your presentation."

I began again. Mrs. Wilson gave me another wink and a broad smile, while Samantha sat in silence, arms crossed, looking ready to spit nails.

I sailed through the rest of my presentation and was thankful to have only a few questions at the end to clarify. Then I sank into my chair and pretended to be engrossed in the other two presentations. Instead, I started a mental list of all the things I should, and could, be doing if I wasn't trapped in this meeting. I had less than twenty-four hours to solve a murder, and if Howard was really out of town, I could do my sleuthing without worrying about him finding out. If I uncovered the murderer, he couldn't be mad at me, right?

At last the meeting was over. I made polite conversation as I rapidly shoved my papers into an attaché case and tried to leave. But those closest to the door were painfully slow to walk out, chatting and continuing to ask the other two presenters more questions about their work.

I reached the door, escape within my grasp, and there was Samantha, ready to exit at the same time. I hesitated, then stepped back to let her pass ahead of me. But she didn't. Instead, she blocked the doorway and turned on me.

"You think you're so clever, don't you? Always ready with the glib answer."

Her attack, especially now that there was no audience, caught me off guard. "I don't know what you mean."

"If Mrs. Wilson hadn't brought that copy of last quarter's report, you wouldn't have looked so good to the committee.

And you made me look foolish."

"You think I did that deliberately?" I blurted out without thinking. I wanted to ask what she thought she was doing to me, setting me up like that, but I didn't. It wasn't my place, and I didn't want to antagonize her any more than she already was. "I only wanted to confirm that my numbers were right. I don't fabricate the data, Samantha."

There. It was out on the table. She could ignore it, or she could respond. In a way, it would be a relief to get this over with once and for all.

"Don't you? You're just a pretty mouthpiece for the medical staff. You protect them every step of the way. There's no way you'd ever admit they did wrong."

"That's not true!"

"Then give me an example. One example. Prove that I'm wrong."

Exasperated, I held out my arms. "Don't you read my annual report? Don't you see where I detail how much we wrote off or credited in charges because of problems?"

"Right, the old 'good faith gesture' line. You never admit there was a problem."

"Yes we do. But it's not always clear cut. Often it turns out to be a communications problem on both the patient and the doctor's part. Besides, I'm not Risk Management. I am not involved in malpractice suits. I work with the patient to get them the information they need to understand what happened. If it's clear we really blew it, I send it to Risk Management for settlement. But we do not whitewash problems."

With her arms crossed, Samantha still didn't seem convinced.

I took a deep breath and said, "Look, I think this is all because of your sister-in-law, Emma Jamison."

Samantha opened her mouth to speak, then snapped it shut again.

"I know she wasn't happy about the results of our review."

"Wasn't happy? She's made our lives a living hell!" Samantha hissed. "Do you have any idea how hard it's been for me to serve on this committee, let alone be the chairperson, with her complaining all the time?"

"I suspect she can be a challenging person to live with."

"Challenging?" Samantha burst out laughing, and I stared in amazement. I'd never seen her even smile before, and even though this laugh had a bitter edge to it, I could see the person she probably was to everyone except me. "God, if you only knew."

After my few encounters with Emma, I had a pretty good idea. In her mid-forties, she'd come into my office, dressed like a doll, frothy petticoats and all. She'd accused a physician of touching her inappropriately while doing an exam. During the review, it'd become clear the woman had long-term emotional problems. The Chief of Staff, Larry Bridgeway, and I had talked in depth about how to respond to this patient.

"Yes, well, like I said, we don't make this stuff up, Samantha. I can't go into the details without violating confidentiality rules, but I think it's okay for me to say that what she says happened couldn't possibly have occurred. There was a nurse standing next to the doctor the entire time."

Samantha's eyes widened. "There was?"

I nodded.

"I didn't know that. None of us did. She never told us."

"Did you see the letter I wrote to her?"

Samantha nodded.

"I couldn't say a nurse was present without sounding like I was calling your sister-in-law a liar. I had to soft-pedal it so she wouldn't come back with a different complaint."

"She didn't like that letter at all. She's the one who first said it was a cover-up, and after reading the letter, I agreed."

"Perhaps it was a communications problem on both sides," I said with a slight smile.

Samantha shook her head. "Stick to your story if you must. But I know the truth and no matter how long it takes, others will too."

I was livid with Howard for putting me in the center of the bull's eye tonight. Had he done it on purpose, pretending to be called away on an emergency? Did he think that maybe this was the way to solve the problem between Samantha and me? I'd be even more wary the next time I encountered her.

The Quality Committee meeting had ended relatively early, but after Samantha's treatment, I wasn't ready to go home and face more conflict with Josh. Besides, I was starved. I called Andrea and we agreed to meet at our favorite Italian restaurant for dinner and a glass or two of chianti.

After finishing our meal, I summarized my experience with Samantha, which elicited an outpouring of sympathy from Andrea. Eventually, the topic shifted, of course, to the murder.

"So you see, it's a real conundrum." I leaned back in the booth and looked glumly across the table at my friend.

"Hmmm. So you still don't know who the victim is—was?"

I took a long, last sip of wine, then nodded. "That's right. Pierce is about to explode. Rip off his traction contraption and go to the county lab and run the fingerprints himself. In his hospital gown if he has to."

Andrea chuckled at my description of Pierce's aggravation, and I had to smile. We were talking about a man who prided himself on maintaining a professional image at all times. I still felt guilty, but this had been a personal learning experience for Pierce, one that he was not going to forget for a long time. He would never survive the confinement of a desk job, and when he was finally forced to retire, he'd need a plan to keep busy.

"Would you ladies like some dessert?" Our charming waiter had appeared out of nowhere.

"Tempt us," Andrea said. She'd long ago accepted the fact that she'd always have a Rubenesque figure.

While he rattled off the selections, complete with mouth-watering descriptions, I sat quietly. I hadn't told Andrea about Josh's plans to go to Africa. She was like an aunt to Josh, and if she knew, she'd come at him with both barrels blazing. Not having children of her own, she sometimes didn't understand that strategy was an important part of a parent's bag of tricks for getting kids to do something, or to not do something. Especially when said kid was six inches taller than you were, and old enough to vote, be sent to war, or get married without parental permission.

Not that my strategies had worked on Monday night. No, I'd shown all the subtlety of a stampeding elephant. Before this morning, I'd only caught glimpses of him coming and going. Today, we passed each other briefly in the kitchen. He hadn't said a word, hadn't acknowledged my presence. And there hadn't been time for me to reopen the discussion.

Home would feel like an armed camp until we resolved this, an empty armed camp. At this point, all I had was an arsenal of a mother's love and emotion. At least I'd left a note on Josh's bedroom door about my Internet research on "the guy's" organization. But the deadline for Josh signing up was tomorrow.

Regardless of what happened, though, we had to resolve the tension between us.

Andrea ordered the cheesecake, and I ordered the tiramisu, both to go. Mine was a peace-offering to Josh. Hopefully, it would sweeten his mood to talk. While she made a quick run to the restroom, I toyed with my wine glass and looked around the restaurant. It was busy tonight, and most of the booths and tables were full, which wasn't surprising. The food was wonderful, the prices reasonable, and the staff was friendly without being smothering or ingratiating.

How nice to be in a place where no one was mad at me, yelling at me, telling me what to do and not to do, or threatening me. I could get used to that. But would I like it after more than a few days? Except for the veiled threats of being arrested or fired, I loved the drama. Every day was a new experience. Every patient was different. I never knew what to expect when someone walked in the door or called on the phone.

If Da was healthy, and I resolved this problem with Josh and identified the murderer before William was arrested, then life would be so much simpler.

Until the next round of disasters.

The next morning, I was staring at my dining room ceiling when Nathan stopped by to give me a progress report.

"When we did the tear-out, I checked the trusses, and they're in good shape."

"So that means the new roof won't cost as much." In my head, I put pennies back in the piggy bank.

"Not only that, but we'll get the job done quicker than I first thought. My roofer had a job cancellation, so he's picking up the new shingles and'll be here with his crew in the next half hour. If the weather holds, you should have a new roof by tonight."

"That's terrific, Nathan." I peered through the dark hole in the dining room ceiling. "What about inside?"

"We'll fix that next week. It'll be cold this weekend with the insulation gone, but I should have everything done by the end of next week."

Thankful that at least *something* was moving in the right direction, I left for work. When I reached the hospital, I didn't go straight to my office. Instead, on the slim chance Howard was free, I stopped by the Admin office suite to report on the Quality Committee to him. Still skeptical that an emergency had really called him away from the meeting, I thought I'd check to be sure. And if his story was true, then I had another plan.

"Good morning, Arlene. Is Howard in?"

His secretary looked at me with surprise. "Why no, Robyn. He was called away yesterday afternoon on an emergency." She frowned. "Didn't he tell you?"

I shrugged. "He did, but he didn't say if it was just for last night."

"Oh, yes, I don't expect him back until Monday at the earliest."

"That's too bad. I hope it's nothing too serious."

Arlene frowned. "He was a little vague, something about his brother being in an accident, but then I suppose he was upset and wanted to get out of here as fast as possible. Did you need to see him right away?"

"No, it can wait. I just wanted to report back on last night's Quality Committee meeting."

"Oh, I see. And how did it go?" Close to retirement age, she had a mother hen attitude toward all the managers.

"Pretty well," I said as cheerfully as possible.

Her raised eyebrow said she didn't believe me.

"Really. I survived, but now I think Samantha's more angry with me than she was before. There's no winning with that woman."

"But you're still alive and no bruises or cuts? How does she look?"

"The same, Arlene. She wasn't pleased when I side-stepped an ambush she set for me."

"Oh, dear, that doesn't sound good at all." Arlene shook her head in sympathy.

I gave her a thumbnail summary of what had gone on, then said, "Well, I'd best be off." I left the Admin suite.

Captain Roberts never showed up at the hospital until the afternoon. Howard was gone until Monday. That meant the coast was clear. Neither one would know that I'd been sleuthing.

I made a beeline for the Business Office.

Fortunately, Becky was at her desk. She looked up over a stack of papers, her half-glasses threatening to slide off her nose.

"Hi, Becky." I slid into the chair next to her desk. "Are you busy?"

She looked at me cross-eyed. "What do you think?"

I grinned. "Of course you are."

"Weren't computers supposed to make our lives easier? Paper-free?"

"I know. That didn't work. So, do you have a minute for me to ask you a couple of questions?"

She leaned back in her chair, stretched her arms high over her head, then let them fall into her lap. "Sure. Why not? Whatever you have has to be more interesting than what I'm doing."

I glanced around to be sure no one was close enough to hear. "Uh-oh," Becky said in a low voice. "This is about that bag again, isn't it?"

"It is. Please don't tell anyone I was asking, okay?"

"Sure." She frowned. "Say, you didn't get in trouble about before, did you?"

"Well, kind of. Captain Roberts complained to Howard that I was interfering in his investigation, but it wasn't about our conversations. He didn't know about those."

"That's good, because he hasn't even been to see me. You'd think he would. No one from the police has asked about the patient, or his bag, or his previous hospital stays. Doesn't that seem odd to you?"

"It sure does, and Detective Pierce would have a coronary if he heard about it." I shook my head. "I'm not the one who's going to tell him. Still, I think these questions are important. Who—"

"Rob, are you investigating for Detective Pierce?"

"No, no. Nothing like that," I said to reassure her. "It's just that he's still confined to bed and naturally he's curious about what's going on. It's a mental puzzle for him to work on while he's laid up." Would Becky buy that excuse?

"Well, if you say so." She sounded skeptical. "Go on."

"Okay. Who has access to the safe?"

"Everyone in the Business Office who processes patients for hospital stays and discharges."

"How many would that be?"

Becky scrunched her face in concentration. "About fifteen people who cover our twenty-four/seven office hours."

"Hmmm. Does the safe use a key or a combination?"

"It's a combination lock. I worked at a place with a key, and believe me, it was an absolute nightmare keeping track of it. For the safe here, we change the numbers every two months or whenever a staff person leaves, whichever comes first."

That seemed reasonable to me. Would it to Pierce? "This may take you some time to look up. Did the same person admit and discharge Jason Hilliard for all his hospital stays?"

"That's a good question, Rob. I don't know. I'll have to look it up." Becky scribbled a sticky note to herself and slapped it onto her computer monitor.

"It would be helpful to know if any of the employees have a connection with Jason Hilliard, except—"

"—he's not really Jason Hilliard," Becky finished for me. "Not much I can do on that one until we learn his true identity."

"Everyone involved in the investigation hopes we find out soon."

"I can't believe it's taking so long."

"This has been extremely slow."

"Why would that be?"

I hesitated.

"Ah, say no more. I tell you, Robyn, this whole safe thing is driving me crazy. You know, I followed up with my staff, as a group, and then with each one individually, and not a single person admitted they had removed Hilliard's bag from the safe and forgot to sign both the log book and the discharge sheet. I've drilled it into them that they'll be in a whole lot more trouble if they lie to me than if they admit they made a mistake. But it wasn't just that. They were absolutely, positively adamant that they hadn't forgotten those two tasks. In fact, they acted offended that I'd think they had."

"It has to be one of them, though, doesn't it? Someone who didn't work in this office would stand out like a sore thumb if they came into the area to open the safe."

"Well, you'd hope so," Becky grumbled.

"I better let you get back to this." I waved toward her pile. "Let me know when you've checked who admitted and discharged Hilliard."

"I will."

I left the Business Office, relieved to finally have some information to share with Pierce. Not that it would help us solve the murder, but it should help rule out possible suspects.

I made my usual morning stop to see William before doing anything else. Today he'd added framed photographs to his windowsill. Where had he found these? Did patients leave them behind, or, perish the thought, were they from someone's office? I'd have to touch base with Tom Geralding and Sarah

Fleming, manager of Human Resources, to see if anyone had complained.

In the meantime, the pictures added another homey touch. The space was unrecognizable as a hospital room anymore. And the transformation in William was amazing too. He was alert and greeted me by name as soon as I walked into his room. We chatted for a few minutes before I stood up to leave.

"I'll come by and see you later, William." I patted his hand and crossed the room.

When I reached the doorway, he said, "Miz Robyn?"

Turning back to him, I responded, "Yes, William?"

"You saved me from that bad man. I don't forget that."

I smiled broadly. "Thank you, William. I'm glad I could help." I left it at that.

There was no point in discussing it further because that would only agitate William. He didn't know he had only a few hours before Captain Roberts arrested him for murder. Why say something that would upset him?

He seemed very content where he was.

Which, in itself, was creating a problem for Katie in trying to find a safe discharge plan for him. William had been in the hospital for a week now. He was well fed, clean, happy to wear scrubs, and improving on medication. Letting him go to jail would destroy all his progress. Putting him back on the streets wasn't much better. But how long could we continue to let him live here?

Mulling over that problem, I went downstairs to see Pierce, pleased that Becky had given me answers to his questions. I knocked on his door and opened it when he called for me to come in.

"Rob!"

"Pierce!"

It was obvious we both had information to share. "You go

first," I offered.

"No, you go. I can wait." Pierce was bubbling over with excitement, but once he'd said he'd wait, arguing was fruitless. Then he glared at me. "Rob, have you been sleuthing?"

"It's okay. Howard was called away on an emergency until Monday, and Officer Tomlin told me your boss never shows up before noon. Besides, I told Becky not to mention to anyone that we talked."

"Well, as long as you aren't going to get in trouble, I suppose it was all right. Just this once though."

I grinned at his adamancy. "Just this once. And only because I knew I was totally safe doing it."

"So, what'd you find out from Becky?"

"I asked her those questions you had about the safe. It's a combination lock, changed every two months or when someone leaves the department, whichever comes first, and about fifteen people have the combination."

"That's a lot!"

"Not really." I shrugged. "You have to remember that patients are admitted twenty-four/seven, so most of the Business Office staff have to know the combination."

"From your perspective, that makes sense, but from a security—"

"Yeah, I know, this place is way too open. We've talked about it before."

"Fine." Pierce fluffed his pillow and straightened his sheets, clearly still annoyed with me. "What else?"

"She talked to everyone in the department about the log book, and they all claimed they wouldn't forget something as basic as that."

"Of course they did," Pierce scoffed.

"Well, Becky was convinced they were all telling the truth."

"So what else?"

"She's going to check Hilliard's admission and discharge records to see if the same person handled it every time."

"It'd be nice if that gave us a lead. But somehow, I doubt it."

"So, that's what I have. What's your news?"

Pierce grinned. "The fingerprints came back with an ID."

CHAPTER 18

"You know who Jason Hilliard really is?" After all this time, I was stunned to find out we might really and truly know the victim's identity.

"Yeah. His name is Jason Yancy. Last known address is in Yakima."

"So why would he come all the way over the Cascades for his healthcare? Yakima has hospitals."

Pierce shrugged. "Beats me. But now that we know who he is, we can start looking for connections."

I slumped into a chair. "Sure we can. You from your hospital bed, and me, who's been ordered to stay out of it."

"Rob, where's your spirit? You're the one who thrives under adversity."

Glaring at him, I knew he was right. "But what about you? You have your departmental laptop computer." I pointed at it to make my point.

"I do, but I can't log in to the department web site and start searching without leaving a trail."

"Fine. I'll do what I can, but it probably won't be until tomorrow."

Pierce pointed at his traction apparatus. "I'm not going anywhere. And besides, it's Friday. Captain Roberts always disappears around noon on Fridays, if he shows up at all, and he doesn't reappear until Monday morning. If he's not working the case this weekend, we have time."

"Are you sure? He's supposed to return at five o'clock to arrest William for murder and me for some trumped up charge." I scowled at Pierce. "From what I've seen and heard, it'd be right in character for him to do just that."

When I returned to my office, Margie and Connie were both there, talking and giggling.

"What's so funny?" I asked as I walked through to my office.

"It's one of the bride magazines Margie bought," Connie said. "Some of the ideas are insane unless you have an army of people to help and tons of money."

"Oh, I don't know," Margie said slowly. "I kinda like tatted picture frames with our picture as a present to each guest."

I stopped in my tracks. "Tatted? As in lace?"

"Uh-huh. I could make them in my wedding colors."

"Which are?" Connie asked.

"I haven't decided yet."

My turn. "And when is the wedding?"

"September," Margie said in that dreamy voice she had whenever she talked about the upcoming event.

"Margie. Do you even know how to tat?"

"No, but I can learn."

Connie and I looked at each other and rolled our eyes. "Sure you can," I said. "Along with the two hundred and fifty individually handmade and calligraphied invitations, and the renaissance-style wedding dress and bridesmaid dresses you're going to make, and the—"

"Okay, okay. Fine. I get your point." Margie scowled at us. "Geez. You two take all the romance out of it."

"No, Margie, we just don't want you to have a nervous breakdown."

"Humph." Margie picked up the magazine and headed for her office. "Might as well get back to work."

I grinned at Connie and went into my own office and shut the door.

I sat at my desk, paperwork flying as I plowed through the piles. The phones were quiet and no one had come to see us. Definitely not a full-moon, Friday the 13th. I knew Connie and Margie were both taking full advantage of the rare chance to catch up on their paperwork too.

For the first time all week, I was feeling pretty good about my job. The Quality Report was off my plate, as was the committee meeting. I'd resolved Sandra Jenkins's issue without a full-scale review of her complaint, saving my time and everyone else's.

It was time to leave for that tri-county task force meeting. I wasn't looking forward to it, but it did give me a reason to be in Seattle when Da and Lois needed a ride to the airport.

I picked up the sketch I'd made of the knot around Jason Hilliard—I mean Jason Yancy's—neck. I'd research that later this afternoon.

The meeting started on the dot at noon and finished exactly at one o'clock. We even accomplished something, leaving me hopeful that maybe this committee would be different.

I called Lois on her cell phone, and she and Da were waiting for me in the hotel lobby. After hugging them both and loading their bags into the car, I drove south on I-5.

Lois kept up a steady commentary of all they'd seen and done in the city, saying repeatedly that they really must come more often. Da just grunted noncommittally while he looked out the side window. His efforts to ignore me would be laughable if the issues weren't so serious.

Finally I broke into Lois' monologue. "Da, how'd it go with the doctor?"

Again the noncommittal grunt.

"Da!"

"You won't be letting this go, will you Robyn Anne?"

"No, Da, I won't." I softened my words with a warm smile. "How did the tests go?"

"They weren't too bad, but all that poking and prodding makes a man feel like a side of beef."

I laughed, and Lois joined me. "I know it seems that way sometimes. What did the doctor say?"

Lois chimed in. "He said your father'd had a T-I-A. Silly me, thinking it was a tia. Anyway, it's like a little stroke, and he said Patrick needs to take his medicine every day or he could have a real stroke and then where'd he be?"

So Da had relented and let Lois sit in on the doctor's discussion of the test results and treatment. That was interesting. I wondered if this meant they were becoming more than neighbors. But I suspected it was more the case that Lois had browbeaten Da into letting her be there.

"That man was just trying to scare us."

"He was not!" Lois swatted him from the back seat. "He said you have to take those medicines every day or else you'll die."

"We'll all be dying sometime."

"I'd prefer it wasn't next week," Lois snapped back.

Before they broke into an all-out argument, I asked, "What meds did he give you?"

"Oh, I don't know. Some pills."

"I have them right here in my purse." Lois handed them to me.

Traffic was amazingly light, so I cast a quick look at the vials. I recognized one as a statin and the other as an ace inhibitor. "I agree with Lois, Da. You better take these every day. And for heaven's sakes, get yourself a real doctor when you get home, not that old quack."

"Robyn Anne—"

241

"That man's incompetent, Da. A real menace. His license should've been revoked years ago."

He grumbled something, and then Lois patted my shoulder. "Don't worry, dear, I'll make sure he takes his pills. And the doctor here recommended a specialist in Denver."

"Waste of time. All that driving, and I'll be losing time from the ranch."

From the rearview mirror, I saw Lois roll her eyes. I smothered a laugh, but felt reassured that she'd keep Da on the right path.

We arrived at the airport in a few more minutes. I pulled up in front of check-in, and helped them get their luggage checked and their boarding passes from the skycap. Da gave me a hug, holding me tighter than he ever had before. Maybe the doctor had gotten through his thick skull, and he was more aware of his own mortality.

"I love you, Da," I whispered in his ear.

"I love you too, Robyn Anne."

In a flurry of waving hands and good wishes, Da and Lois disappeared into the terminal. I waited until they were out of sight to swipe at the tears welling up in my eyes. I'd use my vacation this year to go to the ranch. Spending time with him felt more important, more urgent, than ever.

When I hit the freeway, I decided to call it quits for the week and take the comp time I'd earned from last night's meeting. It was mid-afternoon by the time I reached home. I parked in the street because the roofers were hard at it, staple guns banging away, with stacks of new shingles and a dumpster full of old shingles and tar paper in the driveway. Nathan was right; I'd have a new roof by tonight. One problem down.

Josh's car was parked in front of the house too. How would he act today? Well, I was leaving right away, after changing my clothes, for the library to research the knot. Hopefully he'd at least acknowledge my presence. If he wasn't in his bedroom with the door closed.

Taffy greeted me at the front door, then bounded back to the kitchen. Josh appeared in the doorway, the tiramisu, or what was left of it, on the plate he held.

He swallowed the piece in his mouth and said, "Good dessert. Thanks, Mom."

Was this the same son who'd been so belligerent a few nights before? Who'd refused to acknowledge my existence for days? I hoped I could chalk it up to raging teen hormones, but "the guy" was still between us.

"How was your day?" I asked cautiously.

He bobbled his head from side to side. "Good, I guess." He stepped into the kitchen and returned without the plate.

"How's Chuck?"

"Fine."

Did I have to drag the information I wanted out of him? "Josh, about—"

"Mom, I'm—"

We both laughed, a nervous laugh, but still, it boded well. "You go ahead," I said before he urged me to start.

"I, ah, I found the note you left."

"About the tiramisu?" I smiled. "I can see that."

"No, Mom," he said in that long-suffering tone teenagers use only with their parents. "The note about Humanity for All."

"Oh. I see." Wary, I watched for signs of an explosion. But I saw none.

"I did what you suggested, and I looked them up on the web site you found."

Did this mean I could still give guidance on the big issues? That would be a major coup for a mom. "And?"

"You were right. It looked suspicious. For one thing, I looked at the pictures of the villages. The villagers were there, looking all happy and everything, but no volunteers. That was weird. You'd think they'd want to show the volunteers too."

My son had noticed something that subtle? Amazing. "So what are you going to do?" I held my breath for his answer.

"Oh, I've already done it. I went up to the guy in the HUB this morning and asked him those questions you raised."

"Really?" I was stunned that he'd taken that initiative.

"Yeah, and when he hemmed around, I started talking louder. Pretty soon, a lot of people were listening, so he grabbed up his brochures and signs and took off."

"So it was a scam?"

"Looked like it to me."

"Those poor students who already signed up. They lost all that money." I sighed.

"Oh, no," Josh said with a laugh. "They're getting their money back."

"But how?"

"I was so pissed that I called campus police and told them what was going on. They caught the guy in the parking lot. He was hard to miss carrying all that stuff with him. The checks were in his car and the cops confiscated them and took him to their office to investigate further."

"I'm so proud of you, Josh!" I gave him a high-five. That wasn't enough, so I hugged him. "Won't he just go to another campus?"

Josh's grin turned smug. "I think he's going to jail. But I sug-gested to the cops that they notify the other colleges around here to be on the lookout for this scam. There could be other guys doing it too, you know."

"You're kidding! You did that?" I was astounded that my son, the one who tried to escape the limelight at all costs, had spoken up like that.

"Yeah. Guess some of you is rubbing off on me."

I hugged him again, so relieved and happy to be on good terms with him again that I felt tears well up. When he stepped away, I swiped at my eyes, hoping he wouldn't notice.

"How come you're home so early?" he asked.

I told him about Da. "I think he's okay for now, but I'm going to visit him more often."

Josh looked thoughtful, but only nodded. He wandered back into the kitchen, and I followed him.

"What're your plans for tonight?"

He shrugged. "I'm going to a party later. I'm waiting for Chuck to call me when she gets home from her interview so I can pick her up."

"She had an interview?"

"Yeah, she's applied to work for an electronics firm this summer. It's just a grunt work job. I mean, she won't get to do any engineering, but she'll probably learn a lot by watching what's going on. She thought it'd look good on her resume."

I raised an eyebrow. "And that would keep her here this summer, instead of going home?"

"Hey, I guess it would." He grinned broadly as if the thought was new to him.

"But you don't know yet what you're going to be doing, right?"

His crestfallen expression told me he hadn't thought of that. I patted him on the shoulder. "Don't worry. It's only April. Something will come up, I'm sure."

"Yeah, well, I guess."

"I have to change clothes, then I'm going to the library. Do you want to come with me?"

"Why?" His grimace told me he thought he already spent enough time in the stacks.

"I need to identify that knot, the one tied around the murder victim's neck. No one recognizes it, so I thought the library would be a good place to go. I don't want my Internet search traceable back to me."

"Cool! You're sleuthing again?"

I couldn't lie. He was too old for that. Instead, I nodded. "Yes, I'm doing some *research,* but nothing dangerous."

"Can I come and watch?"

Laughing, I said, "Yes, I guess so."

"Can we have dinner first?"

I glanced at the clock. It was early, but I had missed lunch because of the meeting and taking Da and Lois to the airport. "How can you still be hungry after eating that dessert?"

He shrugged and gave me his winning grin.

"Okay, fine. I'll whip up some omelettes."

After we'd eaten, we climbed into my car and headed for the Madrona Bay branch of the King County Library before it closed. Fortunately, almost all the computers were available.

"I'll be right here." I set my purse on the floor and sat down. After logging on, I started a search for the knot. It was a tedious process, and soon Josh wandered off to roam the stacks.

Closing time was approaching, so I gave up and went to look for my librarian friend, Evelyn. I found her arranging books on the Northwest Authors display.

"Anything good?" I asked.

"Hi, Robyn," Evelyn greeted. In her early sixties, she'd worked in the library for years, but was the antithesis of the classic librarian. She was stylishly dressed, her curly hair short and loose, and I'd only heard her shush someone once. "Actually, they're all very good this month."

"Which one would you recommend?"

She shrugged. "Depends on if you want the truth about

politics according to the author, or romance, or murder and mayhem."

"Hmmm. I'll have to think about that. But right now, I need your help."

"Sure. What are you looking for?"

I held up my drawing. "I need to find out what kind of knot this is. It wasn't in Josh's *Boy Scout Handbook,* so I came here. I just spent some time on the Internet, but that overwhelmed me and I couldn't find a book in the catalog about knots."

Evelyn beamed. "Well, you've certainly made a valiant effort. From your drawing, I'd say it's a timber hitch."

I looked at her in awe. "How do you know these things?"

She laughed and said, "I grew up in this area, Robyn, when the timber industry was booming, and my dad was a logger. This was the knot loggers used to drag or hoist the logs. It's not very secure, but it was easy to tie and untie."

A logger's knot. That stumped me. Who did I know with logging experience? "Thank you, Evelyn. This's been a big help."

"Can I ask why you're interested in identifying a timber hitch?" Evelyn had an intrigued gleam in her eye. She didn't want just one piece, she wanted the whole story.

"I wish I could tell you, but I can't."

"Oh."

Another thought came to me, but I hesitated before asking the question. It would reveal too much, but I had to know. "Evelyn, could it be used as a noose?"

Her eyes widened. "A noose? What an odd question, Robyn. But yes, I suppose it could—oh, does this have something to do with that murder at your hospital last weekend?"

I nodded. "Please don't tell anyone I asked about it."

"My lips are sealed." She made a zipper motion across her mouth. "Can I help you with something else?"

I grinned. Evelyn loved a mystery as much as anyone. "Not right now, but you'll be the first person I call when I do."

"Okay. I'll see you at next week's Friends meeting," she said, referring to the Friends of the Library group.

"I almost forgot about that. I'll call Andrea and remind her too."

I left Evelyn and returned to the computer to search for Jason Yancy of Yakima. I didn't find much about him, but there was a fair amount about his father, Michael Yancy, from his obituary in last year's newspaper. He'd run a successful insurance business after returning from Vietnam.

Nothing was falling into place. Yet. Surely all the pieces were there, but I didn't know how they all fit together. Now was the time to work through the puzzle with Pierce.

After some searching through the stacks, I found Josh in the history section. The history section? That was interesting, but I didn't have time to pursue it now. "Come on, we need to go."

"Now?" Josh frowned. "Already?"

"Yes, already."

I waited impatiently for him to check out a book, then hurried him to the parking lot as Evelyn locked the door behind us.

As we climbed into the car, Josh glanced at his watch. "Are we going home?"

"Not yet. I have to stop by the hospital. I'll only be a few minutes, so you can wait in the car and read your book if you want."

Usually I'd ask about the book he'd checked out, or why he was in the history section, but not tonight. I felt an urgency to get to Pierce.

The hospital was quiet, with a few visitors, but without the daytime hubbub. I reached Pierce's room as he was finishing his dinner.

He looked expectantly at me. "Bring me anything good to eat?"

"No, sorry. But I do have information to share."

CHAPTER 19

He perked up, all business now, and listened while I told him about the knot and what I'd learned about Jason Yancy.

Leaning back in my chair, I said, "So, here's what we know. Jason came from Yakima to this hospital to be treated for recurring staph infections. Every time he came, he put a bag in the hospital safe that wasn't there when he was discharged."

"The last bag was full of money," Pierce added. "And he was murdered by someone who knew a logging knot." He eyed me skeptically. "That's not a lot to go on."

"No," I conceded. "But what about this? His father had a successful insurance business after he returned from Vietnam. He died a year ago. A few months after that, Jason started coming here to this hospital. Each time with a bag that was checked out of the safe without any of the standard procedures being followed."

Pierce cocked his head to one side. "And you think there's a connection?"

I shrugged, reluctant to share my theory in case it made me look stupid.

"Come on, Rob, tell me what you're thinking."

"Well, it just seems that the timing has to be more than a coincidence."

"Okay," Pierce said slowly. "I hate coincidences."

Since he was going along with my line of thinking, I was encouraged to continue and maybe make a logic leap or two.

"And since we've already decided that the money must be from some illegal activity, maybe it was something Michael Yancy started, and Jason picked up where his father left off. So it could have been drugs or fencing stolen goods or something like that, right?"

Pierce shook his head. "I don't know, Rob. I've heard of more than a few guys who went to 'Nam and set up drug trafficking when they returned. But that's a huge assumption. We have no proof whatsoever. And no connection to anyone here."

"But what if whoever murdered Jason was in on the scheme? Someone who went to Vietnam. And had worked as a logger," I said.

"Yeah, but whoever that was also had to have access to the safe in the Business Office," added Pierce. "That's going to be pretty hard to pull together to justify a warrant, even if we had a clue who met all that criteria."

I leaned back in my chair. Access to the safe meant it had to be someone from the hospital. But who could possibly fit all the criteria?

Slowly, all of my little niggling thoughts from that last few days coalesced. Open and closed doors. Trust. With a sinking feeling, I whispered, "I think I know who it was."

The door to Pierce's room opened, and Captain Roberts stepped into the room, leaving the door ajar. He looked at me and scowled. "You again. Don't you ever go home?"

Before I could answer, Pierce said, "What do you want, Captain?"

"I came to tell you that I'm arresting that homeless guy for the murder as soon as patrol gets here."

"But—" I began.

Pierce touched my arm to still me. "I assume you've run it by the prosecutor's office, and they think it's a strong case."

"I'll take care of that on Monday morning. You just get

yourself out of bed before the next detective case comes up. Nash is gone for another week, and I need you back at work."

Shaking off Pierce's grip, I stood up. "You can't arrest William for the murder. He didn't do it, and I can prove it."

"I told you she'd be trouble." Howard was standing in the doorway, a gun in his hand. He moved next to the captain, shutting the door as he did.

"Knowles, have you lost your mind?" Captain Roberts asked. "What're you doing with that gun?"

I froze. "You're in this together?" That I hadn't figured out. But now the murder investigation, or lack of one, made sense to me.

Howard ignored the question. "I'm sorry, Robyn. I really like you, and you're a good team player, but you just couldn't stay out of things that weren't your business, even when I piled on the work."

"That's what it was all about, wasn't it? The Quality Report. The committee meeting. The task force. To keep me too busy to discover who the murderer was?"

Howard shrugged. "Nothing you can prove."

"So you two were in Vietnam together?" Pierce asked.

"Yeah, along with Jason's father. Bill was a good man." Howard shook his head. "Things wouldn't have fallen apart if he was still alive."

"You were the one taking the money out of the safe, weren't you?"

"Howard, shut up," Captain Roberts ordered before Howard answered me.

"Oh, come on, Robby. They know. And since they know, they can't leave this room alive."

"You're out of control," Captain Roberts said. "No more killing."

"You killed Jason, didn't you, Howard?" I already knew, but

wanted to hear him say it.

"We were using the hospital to launder the money he collected. But the kid was making a spectacle of himself, flashing the nurses and all. I told him to stop it, and then, he had the gall to ask for a bigger cut in the profits. For the risk he was taking getting infected, he said." Howard shook his head. "I couldn't let him get away with that."

"So you strangled him with a logger's knot?"

A grin flashed across his face. "You figured that out too? I always knew you were a smart girl. Too smart, as it turns out."

I looked into his eyes and wondered how I could have missed the cold cunning behind his outgoing persona.

"I heard footsteps, so I hid in the family conference room across the hall before you rounded the corner. And when you hightailed it to the nurse's station, I ducked in and removed the knot from around Jason's neck before you returned." He sounded so smug.

I thought back to finding Jason's body and the aftermath. "You were in the parking lot, weren't you? Waiting for the AOC to call you. That's why you arrived on 3-West so quickly after the police showed up."

"Robyn, you're just too good at this." Howard turned to Captain Roberts. "You take care of your detective, and I'll take care of—"

The door flung open.

"Mom, I gotta go. Chuck called and—" Josh stopped just inside the room, quickly took in the scene, and started backing out. "Ah, maybe I'll just—"

Howard waved him in with the gun.

"Howard, let my son go. He doesn't know anything."

He laughed. "Good try, my dear, but he knows enough. Let's get this over with."

Then it all turned to chaos.

William rushed into the room carrying a floor lamp and shoved Josh to the floor. "The money man! It's the money man, Miz Robyn."

Josh scrambled out the door on all fours as Howard turned and fired the gun at William. I screamed and dropped to the floor.

But William kept coming. He swung the lamp and knocked the gun from Howard's hand.

I lunged for the gun at the same time Captain Roberts did. To my stunned surprise, Pierce catapulted from the bed onto his boss.

While they wrestled on the floor, I grabbed Howard's gun and stood up. "Stop!" Nobody listened to me.

William brandished the lamp again, hitting Howard in the jaw. He went down in a heap.

From outside the room, I could hear Josh hollering for help. Pierce and Captain Roberts were still scuffling. The captain was a bigger man, but Pierce was holding his own.

William turned from the unconscious Howard to wield the lamp one more time and hit Captain Roberts on the head. The captain slumped against Pierce, who pushed him off onto the floor, then gingerly rose to his feet.

"Are you okay?" I asked.

"Yeah, I'll be all right," he said, taking the gun from my shaking hands.

I turned to our rescuer to thank him, but my gratitude turned to dismay when I saw blood streaming from his shoulder. I gasped. "William, oh no, you're hurt!"

"I'm okay, Miz Robyn. Just a little dizzy. I couldn't let the money man hurt you." William slumped to the floor.

I started yelling for help, and in minutes William was on a gurney and headed to the OR.

During all his yelling in the hallway, Josh had also called 9-1-1. Officer Tomlin arrived with several other officers. They stopped at the door, stunned to find their boss on the floor with Pierce standing over him with a gun. They hesitated, unsure what to do.

"Arrest them both!" Pierce snapped. "Suspicion of murder and drug trafficking. To start, anyway."

It took him a few minutes to explain what had happened, but then Officer Tomlin cuffed Captain Roberts and Howard and walked them out while reciting their Miranda rights.

Josh stepped into the room, his eyes wide in amazement. "Gee, Mom, I didn't know you did stuff like this! Your job's more exciting than I thought!"

I grabbed him close, sobbing now that it was over, grateful that he wasn't hurt. He'd almost been killed because of me.

Then I let Josh go and turned to Pierce. "Is your back all right? And what was that leap out of bed? I thought you were still in traction."

Pierce laughed. "This probably didn't do my back any good, but it doesn't hurt. Your friend, Dr. Downing, came by this afternoon and said it was time for me to go home and follow up with the physical therapist next week."

"I see. And when were you going to tell me this?"

"You had so much information you were bursting to share, you didn't even notice I wasn't hooked up."

I shook my head. "I'm just glad you were free when we needed you."

"Me too." He put his arm around my shoulder and gave me a squeeze. "Me too."

Epilogue

The following week was insane. I packed up all my paperwork and took it home with instructions to Connie to tell anyone who called that I'd gone on vacation and couldn't be reached.

Now it was the weekend again, the first Saturday in May, and what a gorgeous spring day it was.

Instead of going to watch the opening day of boating season, we were having a barbecue in my backyard. Josh and Chuck played croquet while Pierce, Andrea, and I sat on the deck. We'd avoided all conversation about the murder while we were eating, but now Andrea couldn't hold back any longer.

"It was the police captain and hospital administrator behind the drugs?"

"Technically," Pierce said. "They'd been in Vietnam with Michael Yancy and got started dealing drugs. Before they came home, they set up a network over there for the drugs to be smuggled to Michael, who sold the drugs in eastern Washington, then the money was brought here to be laundered."

"Through the Spiffy Clean Laundry," I added. "When Howard was Chief Financial Officer, he set up dummy accounts. Michael dropped the money off to Howard, who then put it into the Business Office safe until he was ready to move it through Spiffy Clean's accounts. Since he was the CFO, and then the CEO, and kept legal documents in the safe, no one thought a thing about him going into it."

"I suppose not," Andrea said. "But why didn't his son follow the same plan?"

"Jason wasn't as reserved as his father was, so he figured out a way to be admitted to the hospital, which actually, when you think about it, made it easier to explain the presence of the bag in the hospital safe. Howard would take the money bag from the safe, then wash it through the hospital accounts as if we had a legitimate contract with the phony commercial laundry."

"From there," Pierce said, "it went to the Cayman Islands where it couldn't be traced."

I shook my head. "I still can't believe that Howard was the brains behind this whole scheme. I mean, everybody loved him because he was so great to work for."

"That was why no one ever got suspicious," Pierce said.

"Not until the Bloomingdale letter came out," I added. "Somehow, someone at the laundry screwed up and actually sent some ____ls and scrubs to our hospital, but they had the wrong name on them. The Bloomingdale writer had no idea this was more than a silly screw-up. If it hadn't been for that letter, I never would have figured it out."

"But you had the nerve to go there," Andrea said.

I shrugged. "It was right on my way to the airport to pick up Da, so it made sense to check it out."

"Face it, Rob," Pierce said with a laugh, "You're just a natural born snoop."

"Well, hear hear to our favorite snoop." Andrea hoisted her glass to me.

Pierce joined in. "Hear hear!"

"What are you cheering about?" Josh asked. He and Chuck crossed the lawn toward us.

I sighed. "They think my sleuthing—" I caught Pierce's raised eyebrows. "I mean, my snooping worked out well. But I swear, I'm never doing it again."

Pierce laughed. "Yeah, you say that now, but wait until the next time."

"Yeah, Mom can't resist a good mystery." Josh turned to me. "Did you tell them about William?"

"No, I haven't. Do you want to start?"

"It's really cool. All the publicity about him helping catch the bad guys made the national news with his picture and everything. His son in Indiana saw it, and he's coming to get him."

"That's right," I said. "We're invited to meet him at the hospital for the big reunion. It's going to be a media frenzy, I'm sure, but William did so much to help us that I'd like to be there." I hadn't come to terms yet with the fact that if he hadn't knocked Josh to the floor, my son would have taken Howard's bullet.

"I'll go too," Pierce said. "Interesting how he overheard Howard arguing with Jason and ended up calling Howard 'the money man.'"

"I know. I kept thinking he meant someone from the Business Office." I shook my head. "But even if I'd figured out he didn't mean that, I never would have put it together with Howard. Both doors to the family conference room were open, so William overheard Jason and Howard arguing about money. Later, he saw Howard leave the family conference room. William was afraid the 'money man' would come back and murder him. But when he was out scavenging more things for his room, he recognized Howard and followed him to see what was going on. Fortunately, his friendship with me overrode his fear."

We all sat quietly, then Andrea asked, "So what's William's story?"

Relieved to change the subject away from the murder, I said, "It turns out, he was in Vietnam too, but when he came back, he couldn't deal emotionally with what he'd seen there. He disappeared from his family about twenty years ago, and they've worried about what happened to him ever since. I don't think he'll be living in Central Park again."

"Did you tell Matt what we're doing?" Andrea asked.

"No," I said turning to face Pierce. "I don't think I did."

He looked at me expectantly. "Are you going to tell me now?"

"Andrea and I have volunteered to work at a soup kitchen in Fremont one evening a week."

If I'd said we were going to the moon, Pierce couldn't have looked more surprised. "You are?"

Andrea nodded. "Yep. We decided to get out and do something useful."

Feeling the need to explain, I said, "There are so many desperate people in the world. I realized that although I help people all the time, I only see the haves. I need to help the Williams too."

Pierce nodded. "I think I understand. I see the have-nots all the time, which is probably why I enjoy hearing your stories so much. They're a good counter balance for me."

"Well, here's to William," Pierce said, raising his glass.

I joined him. "May William have warm words on a cold evening, a full moon on a dark night, and the road downhill all the way to his door."

After we drank our toast, Andrea looked at me in amazement. "Gee, Rob, that was really nice."

"Oh, it's a little something I picked up from my grandmother," I said.

"Anyone for another game of croquet?" Josh asked.

"Sure, why not," Pierce said. He rose stiffly from his chair, then turned to me with a grin. "Have to keep moving, Dr. Downing says. Otherwise, I'll stiffen up again."

"I'll join you," Andrea said.

I watched them for a few minutes, grateful for all my many blessings. William had taught me a lot about seeing, really seeing, the invisible people. He'd led me to look inside myself and search for my own dirty laundry.

AUTHOR'S NOTE

This story is a work of fiction. The people Robyn works with and the murder and subsequent investigation are from the author's imagination and bear no resemblance to her actual experiences. The patients Robyn encounters in her role as a patient rep are composites based on real cases.

Many hospitals and medical centers have patient representatives who function much the way Robyn Kelly does. If you or a family member have a problem with medical care or service, do not hesitate to ask for their assistance.

ABOUT THE AUTHOR

For fifteen years, **Liz Osborne** managed the Patient Relations department for a large healthcare organization in western Washington. Her book, *Resolving Patient Complaints: A Step-by-Step Guide to Effective Service Recovery,* is considered a primer on the subject. She lives near Seattle with her husband and Brittany spaniel.